Love's Labors Tossed

LOVE'S LABORS TOSSED

Trust and the final fling

ROBERT FARRELL SMITH

DESERET
BOOK

SALT LAKE CITY, UTAH

Library of Congress Cataloging-in-Publication Data
  Smith, Robert F., 1970-
    Love's labors tossed : Trust and the final fling / Robert Farrell Smith.
      p.   cm. — (Trust Williams trilogy ; bk. 3)
    ISBN 1-57345-648-9
    1. Mormons—Fiction.   I. Title.
    PS3569.M537928 L6   2000
    813'.54—dc21   00-024711
Printed in the United States of America

10 9 8 7 6 5 4 3 2   18961-6640

*It may seem repetitive, but she's
just that amazing.
For Krista.*

The news thumped him like a wicker cannon ball, sending splinters of pain throughout every inch of his body. Toby quickly batted a fat cat off an overturned scrub bucket and shoved the tub behind his friend's weak knees.

President Heck sat.

"Does Trust know?" he managed to say.

"Yep," Toby answered.

"And?"

"He isn't thrilled," Leonard said, sounding as if he was talking about some child's reaction to a meal involving spinach. "How would you feel if your fiancée was taken?"

"I can't speak for Trust," Toby said soberly. "But I know I'd feel sicker than Mavis after our squirrel day buffet. Remember how Lupert accidentally hit her in the stomach with that bat?"

President Heck nodded.

"I still feel bad about him doing that," Toby said.

"Accidents happen," Leonard comforted.

"We've got to find her," Ricky Heck whispered. "If *he* has her, then she could be in real harm."

"Don't worry," Leonard said. "We've got the whole place searching. There's not a single good eye looking anywhere but for her."

No one was comforted.

1

ONE HEART, ONE BIND

Lightning tore across the sky, connecting with the tree-tops and setting their crowns afire. I smelled and heard the thick air wheeze as it gagged on ozone.

This was a bad idea.

I searched the darkness for human forms, knowing all the while that my eyes couldn't differentiate between a sumo wrestler and a toothpick in the mucklike night before me. Light flashed and the sky boomed, sounding like an ill-tempered Father Nature barking at his children for losing the remote.

This was the last ward campout I would ever attend.

"Leonard!" I screamed into the wet night.

Lightning snapped again, the sky acting like a horde of tourists with the need to photograph something. I didn't smile.

"Leonard!" I hollered.

It had started out as such a nice outing. Grace and I had come up together and pitched our tents by each other. I had impressed her by cooking dinner over a small intimate gas stove, and she impressed me by flashing back a smile, the image of which still burned on the inside of my eyelids. After dinner we had watched the ward's kids run around the Tom Cove campground while the members talked about how life would be so much more fulfilling if we still lived simply like the pioneers. Sister Barns went on and on about how she longed for a quainter life and then threw a fit when one of the young men accidentally unplugged her generator, thus causing her to have to go to the trouble of resetting the clock on the portable microwave oven she had brought up.

Tom Cove was a campground rooted in misrepresentation. It was not a cove, and it had no real connection with anyone named Tom. Apparently an early, uneducated explorer named Harold Locks had wanted to name the place after his buddy Jacques. Well, Harold had grown up traversing rivers and hiking hills instead of studying his spelling words. Consequently he had a really difficult time spelling Jacques's name. So he went with Tom since it was so much easier to pen. He added Cove because there was a woman across the ocean that he pined for by the name of Camille.

Most of the wards in Southdale held their outdoor get-togethers up at Tom Cove. It was a nice place that Tom—I mean Jacques—could feel proud about having named after him. There were pavilions and grills and a bathroom that smelled like my grandmother's cellar in summer.

There were two horseshoe pits and a big tree house with a wooden ladder that was missing every other rung and covered with thatch like patches of breeding splinters. The Thicktwig Ward had reserved the entire area for the weekend. It was all ours, and we probably would have had a perfectly fine outing if it had not been for Leonard.

Leonard Vastly was, at present, our ward's activities director. He had the enthusiasm of a medicated high school mascot and the common sense equivalent to that of most legumes—the lima bean not included. How a grown man could think that a ward tire roll was a good idea was beyond me. But he had, and for some reason the entire congregation in attendance had blindly gone along with it.

Leonard had pulled a few strings and gotten one of his brothers-in-law to deliver five giant construction tractor tires up to Tom Cove. They were huge tires. When stood up on their ends they were taller than I was by a torso or so and as wide as a small compact car. After families had eaten and all the campsites were set up, Leonard coaxed everyone into the five tires. Then with the help of his assistant activities director and two subcommittee heads, he prepared to push all five tires across what looked to be a thin, mild slope in back of the tin pavilions.

People laughed and chatted as they climbed into the huge rubber rings. I even heard Sister O'Shawn comment on what a clever activity this was and how Leonard was the best activities director our ward had ever had. Brother Max Evans, our previous ward activities director, then asked if it would be possible for him to ride in a different

3

tire than Sister O'Shawn. Despite Max's dented pride, everyone seemed to be excited about rolling around together.

Without really giving it the kind of thought I should have, I climbed into tire number three with Grace, the Relief Society presidency, and a solid one-fourth of the ward's Primary children. The moment Scott Gneiting kneed me in the nose I knew that this was not going to turn out well. I started to wiggle and fuss in hopes of getting out, but Sister Barns interpreted it as my being fresh and began lecturing me.

It was not my finest moment.

The second the tires started to turn, everyone collectively realized what I had caught on to a mere moment ago.

This was a completely disastrous idea.

Leonard and his assistants pushed the big tires for a few feet as we all began to spin within. Twenty feet into it, however, the tires began to get away from their pushers. Those doing the shoving began to jog in an attempt to keep up with their responsibilities. Unfortunately, jogging just didn't cut it.

The tires were loose.

Because I was spinning I couldn't clearly see what was happening, but even above the screams of the Relief Society presidency and the Primary children, I could hear Leonard yelling.

"Sweet mother of polished pearl!"

The tires gained some pretty impressive speed as they bounced down what had looked to be a harmless grade. I felt someone's foot kick my stomach as a stray elbow jabbed me in the kidney. I tried to grab for the inner edge of the tire in hopes of keeping myself from crushing Grace and some of the smaller children. It was impossible. We were out of control. The landscape flew by, spinning like a newspaper headline in an old movie. Our tire hit a tree and bounced backwards with great force.

Everyone flew out into the air, falling to the ground like scarecrows of putty, dust bouncing up in curtains and folding over us. I would just have stayed there and complained a while, but tire number five was heading right for me. I hopped up, spotted Grace, grabbed her hand, and ran out of the way. Sister Barns wasn't quite so lucky. Tire number five tagged her on the side, spinning her until she collapsed. Tire number one caught a bush and then twisted in place like a settling coin. When it finally stopped, everyone climbed out, stumbling about like inebriated marionettes. I watched tire number five end its journey by getting pinched in a large gully. Wedged tight, it jiggled about until it had shaken everyone up and out.

Leonard came barreling across the meadow waving his arms and screaming louder than any of those injured. He stopped and bent over, putting his hands on his knees and struggling to catch his breath. For a moment the worst appeared to be over. Unfortunately, as our ward had a tendency of doing, we grew too complacent too quickly.

Tire number two was still moving.

No one panicked at first since it looked as if it would simply roll itself out, heading for an open meadow that sloped upward in the opposite direction. We all watched as it rolled up the hill. We all watched as it reached the top of the hill. We all watched as it paused and then started coming back our way.

Everyone took off running down the narrow meadow and back towards the pavilions. Initially there was no more than a mild panic in the air. Of course that changed the moment Sister Barns pointed towards the tire and screamed.

"The bishopric's in that one!"

Well, taken on an individual basis, each member of the bishopric could not be categorized as more than just "a big guy." As a cluster, however, they deserved to be named and charted. And they were not alone in that tire.

"Run!"

It was every member for himself. The mild panic became a run-with-your-arms-above-your-head-and-mouth-wide-open sprint for your life. I saw Leonard step in a rabbit hole and go down. I stopped and reached to help him.

"Leave me," he commanded. "Save yourself!"

I have always been a fairly obedient person.

Grace and I would have left him for dead if the tire hadn't flown past us about four feet to the left.

Leonard stood up. "Whew, that was close," he said, as if all danger were done with. I guess he didn't realize that there were still women and children out in front of the now-flying tire.

The screams of the participants inside the tire grew even louder than the screams of those in its path. I saw the big tire bounce and watched as someone's leg from inside flew out and whacked Brother McLaughlin's large head as the tire tore past him. Scott McLaughlin went down like a fleshy folding chair, impeding those who were running directly behind him. Clyde Knuckles couldn't stop in time. He tripped over the McLaughlin mound and sailed through the air, eventually using Sister O'Shawn as his personal runway on which to land.

Brother Victor, the ward employment specialist, was in front of the speeding tire now. He looked back as he ran, sweat pouring from his tiny forehead and making him look plastic and even less lifelike than usual. He was never going to make it. Moments before the tire smeared him, he fell to the ground and curled up into a tiny ball. The tire hit him and jumped up into the air, soaring through one of the tin pavilions and taking out two of the wooden support beams. Pinched, the pavilion toppled over, squealing like a stuck pig as it fell to the ground.

Tire number two had come to a stop.

Everyone just stood there speechless. There was some coughing and weeping, but no understandable words were being uttered. Fair skinned, and fairly skinned, Bishop Leen crawled out from the downed tire. With his palms and knees against the ground, he tried to catch his breath.

"He doesn't look happy," Grace whispered.

"I can't imagine why," I whispered back.

Bishop Leen got to his feet and scanned the crowd, looking for Leonard. He finally spotted him ducked down behind the nursery-aged children, pretending to tie his Velcro-fastened shoes.

"Brother Vastly!"

It's important to realize that Leonard Vastly had not always been a Saint. He had been a petty thief early in his life, joining the Church after he mistakenly stole someone's scripture tote from an unlocked car. After his initial disappointment, he read the scriptures, gained a testimony, and got baptized. So I suppose it was an old reflex of his to jump up and bolt when the bishop started to yell at him. I had never seen a middle-aged man run so fast.

"Leonard!" the bishop called again, hoping to stop him.

It was no use. He was out of there.

The ward turned their attention to the wounded at hand. We helped pick up one another and clean any scrapes or wounds the tire travel had caused. Bishop Leen pulled me aside just as we got everything and everyone back in the right places.

"Trust, I've been in the lawn business for a long while," he informed me.

I didn't know how I was supposed to respond, so I patted him on the back and congratulated him for a job well done. He stared at me and continued talking.

"I mention it because I'm rarely wrong when it comes to predicting rain."

I looked up at the clear sky, wondering why he was bringing all this up.

"It's going to rain," he clarified.

I pointed up. "But it's . . ."

"Going to rain," he insisted. "Listen, I was all right with Leonard being stuck out in the woods when it's dry, but I can't leave him out there alone while it's raining."

"I'll let your wife know where you've gone," I offered.

"Actually, I should probably stay here since I'm the bishop."

"How about Brother Johnson?" I asked, referring to his first counselor.

"He needs to look after the young men."

"Brother Tugg."

"He's keeping an eye on the outhouses. I'm sure you remember what happened on the ward outing five years ago."

"The Sister Hood incident?" I asked.

Bishop Leen somberly nodded.

"So you want me to go find Leonard?"

"I figured since you're his home teacher, it would be appropriate. Besides, you would just be hanging around here making eyes at Grace."

He made it sound so cheap.

I left Bishop Leen, made a couple more eyes at Grace, threw in a longer than usual kiss, and then set off in the direction Leonard had fled. After I'd been walking for about ten minutes, clouds rolled in and it began to rain. Fifteen minutes later the sky grew completely dark. Ten minutes after that I began hollering Leonard's name in hopes of his hearing me.

"Leonard!"

Five minutes later I figured it was time to head back, with or without him. In another two minutes I realized I was lost. And a mere thirty seconds ago, lightning had struck the ground directly in front of me. I jumped back from the trail and rolled under a huge pine tree. Once again the sky screeched. Rain dumped as if the heavens were clearing their pipes. I scrambled back under the tree and up against the side of the hill looking for shelter. I pulled myself along the side of the mountain, feeling for someplace to plant myself. In the dark I felt something sticking out from the side of the hill. Whatever it was wiggled as I touched it. Lightning struck again, giving definition to what were two feet sticking out of a good-sized animal hole. Thanks to the fact that no other person in the Thicktwig Ward would be caught dead wearing camouflage dress socks, it was easy to identify the ankles and feet of Leonard Vastly. His toes were pointed downward as if he had been crawling on his stomach up into the hole.

"Leonard!" I yelled at the mountain, the rain making me almost mute.

There was no response, just some heavy wiggling from his feet. I wasn't sure about what to do, but I figured that getting Leonard out of the hole was probably a good place to start. I crouched and grabbed his ankles. He seemed to resist a bit and then went limp. I pulled as hard as I could, my efforts getting him about four more inches out into the open. Before I could yank again, my feet slipped in the mud and I fell face first into dirt and ankles. Leonard kicked like mad. I stood back up and pulled.

He was loosening.

Two more tugs, and he seemed to flop out like the mountain giving birth to a clod. The rain began to taper off. Leonard spit and shook for a good three minutes before saying anything.

"Face . . . hurts," he finally moaned.

Since it was too dark to see his face clearly, I was forced to ask for an explanation.

"What happened to it?" I hollered louder than necessary. "And why were you in that hole?"

"I was trying to get away from the ward," he said as if we were some ravenous bear with an appetite for destruction. "I didn't know those tires would take off like that. My side started hurting from running, so I tried to find someplace to escape to. I thought maybe I could crawl through this hole and out to the other side of this hill." Leonard breathed deep and then spit again. "I saw on the Discovery Channel that ants often dig tunnels with holes at each end so they can escape if a predator comes down one of them."

"That's not an ant hole," I laughed.

"I know that," Leonard defended. "I just thought that maybe it was something all digging animals did."

"Ants aren't actually an animal."

"That Discovery Channel sure leaves out a lot of important stuff."

Lightning struck, and I got my first good glimpse of Leonard's face. I jumped at least a good two feet backwards.

"Holy . . ."

His head and face were completely covered in blood. Long scratches marked every inch of his mug. His hair was missing in places, and his bushy eyebrows looked as if big bites had been taken out of them. His right eye was wide open, and his left eye looked bruised closed.

"What happened?" I asked in amazement.

"Let's just say I wasn't alone in that hole," Leonard blew out.

"Are you going to be all right?"

"The funny thing about badgers . . ."

I suppose Leonard would have gone on if we had not been interrupted by the sound of voices hollering out our names. We hollered back, and moments later a cluster of flashlights swarmed our way. It was Bishop Leen, Brothers Barns and O'Shawn, and two of the ward's young men, Norm Chavez and Benjamin Johnson. Benjamin was the first person to catch Leonard's face in his beam.

"Ahhh!"

"Good night!" Bishop Leen exclaimed. "What the heck happened to you?"

"He got stuck in a hole," I explained.

"That must have been one ugly pit," Hyrum Barns whispered.

"Are you all right?" the bishop asked.

"If it's an emergency, you're welcome to use my cell phone," Brother O'Shawn said with excitement, unclipping it from his belt and happy for the possible chance to dial anyone up.

"I'm fine," Leonard said, looking anything but.

Lightning struck, and the rain that had begun to die down picked up again. As a group we hiked back to the campsite together.

"You didn't need to run," Bishop Leen said apologetically to Leonard.

"Old habits die hard."

Back at camp Leonard accidentally stuck his head into

a tent full of young women. He'd thought it was his. His timing could not have been worse, seeing how one of the older Laurels had just finished telling a particularly haunting ghost story. The tent was literally ripped in half as young women frantically tried to make an escape. The badger Leonard had met earlier had nothing on these girls.

After everything had settled down, Grace and I retired to our separate tents that we had pitched side by side. We lay down in our sleeping bags and whispered through the thin walls. The rain had stopped, and the night smelled like something a soap manufacturer would kill to be able to duplicate.

"Quite a night," I whispered out to Grace.

"Umm," she softly sounded back.

"August isn't that far away," I said, referring to our wedding date of August eleventh.

"Trust?" Grace asked, obviously wishing to whisper about something else.

"Yes."

"Can we go home?"

"Now?" I asked, thinking that she was talking about leaving the campgrounds and going back to Southdale.

"Not now, but soon."

"The campout ends tomorrow," I explained. "Is that soon enough?"

Grace laughed. "Not Southdale," she whispered. "Thelma's Way."

"You want to go back home?"

"Can we?"

It was a pointless question. For the last five months I

had been begging Grace to let us go back to Thelma's Way for a while. I missed her hometown immensely, but more than that, I felt as if it was where we should be. Grace, on the other hand, had been reluctant to return. In fact, she had enjoyed her time in Southdale so much that I worried about her ever wanting to go home again. Now here she was speaking to me from beyond the nylon and admonishing me to take her back. I shifted onto my left elbow and faced her tent. Through the small gap at the bottom of the zipper I could see the outside of her tent. The clouds above crumbled, and thick moonlight pressed through the dark and lit up the landscape. Grace's tent seemed to glow as nature x-rayed the insides. I suppose if this had been some risqué movie I would have now been faced with the seductive outline of Grace as she lay within. But seeing how this was a ward campout and all, the most the skies could do was silhouette her bulky sleeping bag.

"You're serious about Thelma's Way?" I whispered with excitement.

"We could just go stay until we get married."

"When should we leave?"

"Whenever you're ready."

Two days later we were standing in the Dallas airport waiting for our connecting flight into Tennessee. I was very happy and excited to finally be going back. Yep, life looked just about as smooth as it could be.

I needed to get my eyes checked.

2

THE HOMELY ONE

He caught his breath and stared out at the small home through the dense trees. The burlap sack at his feet wiggled and squealed. He kicked it and yanked on the rope that was cinching it closed. His dark eyes looked once again towards the house. A big man with a hairy chin stepped out and glanced around.

It was time to leave.

He had played it too close this time. Normally he had taken care of things during the night. Lately, however, his circumstances had made him much more bold and careless. Everything that he had known was gone, and in his mind Thelma's Way was partly to blame. So he took a pig here, a pie there. He shopped for clothes off strangers' lines and collected blankets from open windows and unlocked doors. He had to live, didn't he?

He wasn't completely unaware that his presence was causing the residents of Thelma's Way to grow worried. But he was even more aware of how much he needed to survive. He threw the small pig over his shoulder and slipped deep into the woods.

3

ANOTHER LOG ON THE FIRE

To say that Cindy Finders was a piece of work was like labeling a forty-car pileup, with casualties, a simple fender bender. Cindy was the trickiest piece of work that the heavens had thrown down in quite some time. She was five foot seven with brown eyes, long dark hair, and nice hands. She was absolutely out of this world, unbelievably drop-dead gorgeous. She made perfect sunsets and priceless masterpieces look shoddy and worn. Her smile was a weapon; her walk, a doomsday device.

Yes, physically Cindy was really something. Unfortunately, emotionally Cindy was something else. Once you got past her outer shell, Cindy wasn't so easily defined or pleasant to look at. You could never say that with her it was the insides that count, because if you did, you would be running at a constant deficit. She was blunt, tacky, conceited, opinionated, and bossy, alternating with obtuse,

16

stubborn, and malicious, depending on the day, mood, and slant of the moon. She administered criticism like some sort of poisoned Pez dispenser, dropping her jaw down, her full lips pushing out sour negatives. She was constantly finding fault in nearly all she saw.

She alienated herself from most folks by acting better-than-thou and distanced herself from all the rest by being harsher-than-all. She didn't even care for her family. Her father had tried to be what she wanted, but what she wanted was for him to exhaust himself into an early retire-ment, from which point he could then spend all his time doing exactly as she demanded. Her younger brother Floyd confessed to love her like a sister but not like the sister she presently was. And her poor mother had worn out her knees praying that she would someday find a man, marry, and move far away, or at least two states over. She loved her daughter, but Cindy truly was the kind of child that even a mother could shove.

The genesis of Cindy's behavior was said to stem from a bad summer camp experience that she had been through many years ago as a youth. It had been her first and last summer camp. She and her friend Brittany Wence made all sorts of extraordinary best-friend-before-camp plans. There would be days filled with crafts and games and nights filled with pranks and sharing secrets. Well, the plans fell by the wayside due to Brittany's falling in love with a camp hand named Coop. Coop was a son of one of the older instructors and in charge of such charm-inducing tasks as spraying for ants and cleaning the stables. So, where once Cindy had been Brittany's best friend, now she was love's third wheel. Thanks to her, Coop and Brittany couldn't seem to find a moment alone. They tried to lose her by playing complicated games of tag, but Cindy was too quick. They attempted to ditch her with hide-and-seek, but Cindy's keen sense of smell and Coop's cheap cologne made it impossible. So, frustration being the mother of dementia, on the last day of camp, Brittany and Coop took matters into their own hands and locked Cindy in one of the far bathrooms out by the old drained pool and adjacent to the craft shack.

Well, two things happened as a result of that. One, Coop and Brittany discovered that they didn't really care for each other when they were alone. And two, Cindy was forgotten about until camp was over and Brittany was back home. The bathrooms that Cindy had been locked up in were far enough away from everything to prevent her banging and screaming from being heard. And since it had been the last day of camp, nobody had returned to that area until Brittany went home and Cindy's parents had become curious about why their daughter had not returned too. It took Brittany all of an hour to tell the truth, and after unsuccessfully trying to get ahold of someone up at the now-deserted camp, Cindy's parents drove five hours to rescue their child. When they finally located her and opened up the door, what walked out of that bathroom was a completely different person from what had been pushed in.

Cindy had seen the dark.

She now knew that she could not and would not trust another human being for as long as she lived. If her best

18

friend could turn on her, then how could she ever believe or tolerate another human being?

As a result of that conviction, Cindy was now all of twenty-five, all of rotten, and all of unmarried. She had served a mission in Spain because her parents had promised her a car if she did. They had hoped that she would return a new and nicer woman.

Nope.

The only difference was that she could now pick them apart in Spanish as well as English. Cindy simply couldn't find her place in this world. In fact, she had been unsuccessful at locating a single spot that she could tolerate for longer than ten minutes. Everything seemed to be against her.

She knew of only one relief.

Yes, early in life she had discovered the magic of romance novels and their ability to take her away. She consumed them. If a book had a woman and a man on the front, she read it. If the man was shirtless, she read it even faster. The books were her world. Within their pages was an existence far less painful and disappointing than the elements around her. The men were men, and the women were women.

Cindy was a woman.

And Cindy felt that her bitter life could be made better if she could just find that fictional Mr. Right. A man with the ability to recognize the world as she did. And not to mention, a washboard stomach.

Was that too much to ask?

Cindy thought not.

Well, her prospects in Georgia had dwindled. All the single men her age had either moved away or were currently looking for job transfers that would help them do so. No, her hometown of Homerville, Georgia, and the small communities surrounding it were obviously not going to be able to fill her needs. She had tried ads in the paper and on the Internet, but even in type Cindy was offensive.

```
SWF What's it to you?
Looking for someone non-
pathetic enough to not
need to be looking here.
```

She had even considered becoming a nun. The idea had merit, seeing how she could then spend her days complaining about the great sacrifice she was making. But the local nunnery smelled funny, and they refused to let her wear her hair loose and full.

Well, just like in her books, it took complete darkness to usher in hope. So, while clinging to the end of her romantic rope, she discovered an unopened letter that had fallen back behind the desk in her room. It was quite by accident, seeing how Cindy never did any cleaning herself. But she had accidentally dropped her favorite crushed rose petal bookmark, and while retrieving it, happened upon the letter.

The letter was from her aunt, Daisy Cravitz, who lived many states over in the town of Southdale. According to the postmark, it was more than five months old. Cindy could only figure that her mother had done an incomplete job of making her aware of it when it had originally arrived. Cindy considered throwing it away. She had no time for outdated news. But Aunt Cravitz was one of the few people that Cindy almost respected. She was blunt and levelheaded to the point that anything sensible rolled right off her. She was widowed and wise to the world and its often lacking participants. And, like Cindy, she was blessed with the gift of not giving a hoot about what others thought of her.

So Cindy opened the letter and read.

"Interesting." Cindy smiled.

It seemed that Aunt Cravitz had found a man for her niece. Cindy pulled out the picture that had accompanied the letter.

"Very interesting," she shuddered.

Cindy looked at the picture again. He wasn't half bad. He was standing in front of a chalkboard looking away, but his hair and shoulders made up for his not being attentive to the camera. According to Aunt Cravitz, he was dating a girl that was all wrong for him.

"How unsurprising," Cindy sniffed. "Looks like he needs a little direction in his life." Cindy touched the photograph affectionately. "Well, Trust, set your dial for Cindy."

She set the picture down and smiled. Well, to her it was a smile. To anybody else, it was more of a cold, wicked wince.

4

ONE ETERNAL NOW

From Dallas we flew directly to Knoxville, Tennessee. Somewhere over Mississippi we hit an extremely rough patch of air. Grace and I worried for a moment, but we kept a brave face. The turbulence, however, caused the older gentleman sitting next to us to react a little more strongly. He panicked and screamed, "We're all going to die!"

He buried his face in a couple of tiny airplane pillows and sobbed. A few minutes later, when the air smoothed out, he looked as if he might have been more comfortable if he had plummeted to earth in a fiery ball of flame instead of having to face all of us who had witnessed his behavior. He removed himself to one of the plane's bathrooms for the remainder of the flight.

With him gone I pointed out the window at landmarks I didn't know anything about and made up stories for Grace.

"That's the valley where Abraham Lincoln and Pocahontas built their summer home."

I thought I was being clever and charming but when I turned to spot the admiration in Grace's face, I realized that she was too busy reading the instructions on the sick bag to listen to me.

I knew where I ranked.

We landed in Knoxville and wandered around until we found the car rental booth. They were out of anything small and economical, so we got a car that must have been a boat in its previous life. It was huge. When we set our suitcases in the trunk they seemed to disappear into the vast unknown—there were houses in Thelma's Way with less square footage. The front leather bench was so long that Grace, while sitting on the passenger's side, was more than two arm's lengths away. She tried to scoot closer, but the bulky seat belt heads stuck up like metal fists, making the in-between very uncomfortable.

"Maybe it's better this way." She smiled from across the leathery meadow.

People view things differently. I could see no advantage to her being so far away from me. But she sat by her door and I sat by mine while we drove through Tennessee in a car that even my grandparents would have been embarrassed to be seen in.

One advantage of a huge car is that you get to stop and gas up a lot. We could actually watch the gas gauge drop each mile we drove. We stopped in Collin's Blight to fill up again and then made it to Virgil's Find with nothing but fumes keeping us moving. We turned the car in and walked with our bags to the edge of town where the trail to Thelma's Way began.

"This is it," I said to Grace as if she didn't already know that.

Grace set her small bag down and looked at the weathered wood sign that said "Thelma's Way" with an arrow beneath it.

"You know, a lot's changed since we left all those months ago," Grace observed.

I knew perfectly well that the change she was speaking of had to do with herself and not with Thelma's Way.

"They're going to be blown away," I smiled.

She smiled back, picking up her bag and slinging it over her shoulder. "My father used to talk about how nothing ever changes in Thelma's Way. He would go on and on about how nice it was that everything remained just as it was. I thought he was crazy. But now I can think of nothing nicer than walking back into exactly what I left."

I leaned in as if to kiss her. She had other plans, stepping off towards Thelma's Way at a pace that made me have to jog a few steps to catch up with her.

Before we reached the meadow we could hear that something was going on. We walked faster, our curiosity making us even more excited than we had already been. When we got to the meadow, there was a rally of sorts taking place. A big table had been set up, and Sister Watson was standing on top of it while everyone else was gathered around listening to her. She had on a big feathery cap and was waving her arms while she talked. She was so excited about whatever it was she was saying that I instantly grew concerned about her keeping her balance up on the table. We slipped up behind everyone, unnoticed and mid-sentence.

" . . . I for one am not going to just stand by and let this . . . this . . . thing terrorize us. We have got to make a decision."

Paul Leeper yelled out, "What about me?"

"What about you?" she shot back.

"If you haven't noticed, I'm . . ." Paul looked around, realizing that his words would be better heard if he too were up on the table. "Do you mind if I step up?" he asked.

"Suit yourself," Sister Watson frowned.

Paul climbed up, looking like a toddler struggling to climb into a big bed. He stood and spoke. "I know that I did this town wrong once, but I'm wanting to make up for that. That's why my project is so important. Certainly you all want me to feel truly repentant. And a road would destroy my dream."

"No one wants your shelter," Sister Watson insisted.

"Well now, wait a minute," Toby Carver spoke up. Then, without permission, he too climbed up onto the table and started speaking his mind. "Paul's idea has some possibilities. I mean, it might be kind of nice to have a dry meadow year round."

"What are they talking about?" I whispered out the side of my mouth.

"I have no idea," Grace whispered back.

"I wouldn't mind keeping my shoes clean in winter," Toby continued. "God put us out here to improve our state."

25

"It ain't natural," Teddy Yetch booed. "I think that . . ."

"Put her on the table!" Frank Porter yelled from the side of the crowd, unable to understand her from the height at which she was speaking.

Paul and Toby reached down from the table and hefted her up. Teddy smiled, delighted to be the center of attention.

"I'm just saying that it ain't right to stop the rain and snow," she pointed out. "Besides, if we had a road, I could finally get me a car before I die."

Sister Watson put her arm around Teddy, creating the perfect photo op—her cause, whatever it was, finally had a face. Teddy wanted a car before she died.

"I think we should take a vote," Sister Watson shouted. "As long as we're isolated we could be in danger. We must be more progressive. So, all in favor of a road, which brings safety, say aye."

"Aye!" the crowd hollered unanimously.

"All opposed, say nay."

"Nay," everyone yelled.

"You can't have both," she fumed.

"Hold on a minute," Roswell shouted from the audience. He too must have felt a need to stand on the table, because he hoisted his old body up there and stood. After rubbing his knees for a few moments he said, "This town has done just fine without no road. I don't see why we need one now. You slap down some asphalt, and we'll get all sorts of lowlifes drifting into our blessed meadow." Roswell paused, drew in air, and then spat forcefully over the heads of everyone there. He wiped his lips and continued. "I've seen some of them kids in Virgil's Find. Colored hair, big shoes, pretty teeth. Who needs 'em. I'd hate to wake up and see some city person sitting on the banks of the Girth poking 'round for my fish."

"They want to pave the trail?" I asked Grace in amazement.

"I can't believe it."

"Can I say something?" Pete hollered out.

Sister Watson rolled her eyes, and Pete climbed up and took a place on the extremely unstable table. Pete turned and faced the crowd.

"I just want to say, Has anyone seen my good knife?" he asked. "I seem to have misplaced it."

"This is not the place or time for that," Sister Watson scolded.

"Wait a second," Ed Washington said. He climbed up onto the table and fished through his pockets. "This it?" he asked, handing Pete a knife.

"Thanks, Ed." Pete slapped Ed on the back, and the entire table swayed.

"We've strayed from the subject," Sister Watson complained. "We have got a criminal running around our town. A road would give us a chance to chase him out. So, do we make a nice pretty road into our town, or do we remain unsafe? Not to mention stagnant and moldy?"

I saw Wad sniff himself as if she had been talking about him personally.

"A road into here would change everything," Grace whispered.

"And what's this about a criminal?"

Lupert Carver heard us whispering and turned around. He smiled and then pushed through the crowd and up to the table. He tugged on his father Toby's pant leg. Toby leaned over, and Lupert whispered something into his left ear. Toby then stood and put his hand above his eyes, scanning the crowd. He spotted Grace and me. The exact moment our eyes met, the table gave out, dropping everyone on it straight to the ground. None of them fell over. The table legs had just folded up underneath and lowered them quickly down. They were now standing level with everyone else. The crowd all stared at them, wondering if that was supposed to have happened. As soon as Toby got his bearings, he pointed through the crowd to Grace and me.

To enhance the mood, the misty sky sucked itself in as if tightening its corset. Not to imply that anything as windy and vast as the sky need always be equated to the female gender. I could just as easily have said that the sky sucked itself in as if it were a construction worker's gut in the presence of a beautiful passerby. But honestly, although nothing wonderful, the first comparison was more fitting.

Toby couldn't believe we were back. He kept turning around and then quickly turning back. Each time he looked more surprised than the last.

"It's you!"

"What are you two doing here?"

"I can't believe it."

The crowd quickly encircled Grace and me, everyone commenting about how much we had been missed. The attention was good for me, but it was great for Grace. She had left Thelma's Way a different person. Now here she was standing before the people that she had grown up with and looking like something wonderful the heavens had held back until this very moment. Digby Heck spotted his sister and ran to fetch the folks. Pete Kennedy pulled the guns from his hip and shot off at least fifteen rounds into the nongendered air. The bell had been sounded. In moments the entire meadow was completely filled with the faces I had longed to see just moments ago. As people patted me on the back and commented on how fancy my Target-bought clothes looked, I spotted Patty Heck at the tree line with Narlette by the hand.

The emotion was so great that the clouds began to drip. As a single body we all pushed into the boardinghouse and out of the wet. The boardinghouse was still the biggest and most fitting center of town. It had belonged to Roswell and Feeble, the Ford twins, but Feeble had passed away a few years back, so now old Roswell was the only one at the helm. It was a two-story building with a pitched roof and a sagging rock chimney. The bottom floor was used as a community center and store. There was also a large first-floor bedroom that Roswell lived in. The top had a couple of junk-filled rooms that were cleaned out every so often to house whomever might be in need of a lumpy bed and a leaky roof.

Sister Watson jumped up on top of the store counter and whistled. Her wig shifted as she acknowledged the crowd with a nod. It was obvious that since we had left Sister Watson had grown accustomed to talking while on top of tables and counters.

"Who here knew that Grace and Trust would be back?" she asked, wanting to get a feel for how deep the surprise was.

Narlette raised her hand but was ignored.

"Well," she went on, "it looks like we were caught completely off guard."

Everyone blinked and nodded in agreement, totally comfortable with the off-guard position.

"I'm glad I'm wearing clean underwear," Frank Porter whispered to Paul Leeper, happy that he hadn't been caught at this impromptu reunion with dirty shorts. His comment caught a few listening ears and painted a couple of faces with worry, as if they themselves weren't as well prepared as Frank.

Sister Watson held up her hands to calm the slightly restless crowd. I could see that she had written herself a reminder on her left palm. From where I stood it looked as if it said, *"tape Dateline."* The crowd silenced as she continued to pat the air in front of her.

"As a lot of you know, I didn't really care for Trust here when he first came around all those years ago. He had that sort of look."

Sister Watson pulled a face that I prayed I had never actually had.

"The kinda look that a lot of young cocky boys get."

"Like Philip?" Toby questioned, pointing at eighteen-year-old Philip Green.

Despite the extra finger he had, Philip was looking incredibly self-assured.

"Exactly," Sister Watson said, jabbing the air. "Minus the overbite."

I was going to respond to that, but someone came crashing across the porch and into the boardinghouse. He pushed through the crowd and up to us.

President Heck was by far my favorite person in this hidden valley, if not in the world. He was the most run-amuck, discombobulated, mentally askew individual I had ever had the pleasure of knowing. He was brilliant and childlike all in one sentence. He could enlighten and confuse simultaneously. He saw nothing wrong with the world aside from his own spiritual deficiency.

His hair had given up all hope of holding onto anything darker than dapple gray. In fact, there were spots where white strands were letting their presence be known. He had put on a couple of pounds since I had last seen him, and those pounds were resting upon the few he had put on a little earlier than that. He was closing in on fifty but wore the smile of a kid who had just won a six-foot stuffed animal at the state fair.

"Elder Williams." He hugged me, still not able to forget what I once was.

He then looked around as if searching for his daughter. If it had not been for Grace's red hair, I don't think he would even have recognized her as she stood there holding my hand.

"Grace?" he asked in amazement.

"Dad," she smiled.

"Well, I'll be a corn-fed pig."

It wasn't Hallmark, but it was touching.

Ricky Heck looked around at everyone, wondering if they too had noticed the difference in his daughter.

"Toby, you seen her?" he asked in awe.

"She looks right pretty, President," Toby answered, as if Grace weren't directly in front of both of them.

Ricky Heck smiled. If the buttons on the front of his shirt hadn't popped off weeks ago from his new weight, they surely would have shot across the room at that moment.

Let me just make it perfectly clear. Grace was always the most beautiful girl my eyes had ever rested upon. Her red hair, pink lips, and green eyes were like mesmerizing ornaments on a perfectly shaped tree. I think, however, that until I had taken her away from Thelma's Way, I was the only one who really understood this. In Southdale, she had come around, realizing for herself what a remarkable person she was—her confidence had changed her countenance. You would have had to be a blind man with no sense of wonder not to recognize the differences.

Leo Tip, who was rumored to have liked Grace at one point in the past, looked down at his pregnant wife, CleeDee, and then back at Grace. He looked at CleeDee again.

"What?" CleeDee asked impatiently.

"Nothing," Leo sighed.

CleeDee caught on and dragged her man out of the boardinghouse to tell him a few things she felt he needed to know right then.

Sister Watson called for a cheer to celebrate our arrival, but no one could agree on which cheer to do. So we all just hollered into the air, happy to be back together. And for the second time in a couple of days I realized that I couldn't be happier. It seemed as if my entire life had been building simply to usher in this moment. I couldn't foresee a single black cloud on the horizon.

5

A LITTLE BLACK CLOUD IN A DRESS

Cindy was upset. The e-mail she had just received from Aunt Cravitz indicated that this Trust fellow was getting along better with this Grace person than had once been the case. It said that Grace had really turned out to be a lovely girl and that Cindy shouldn't get her hopes up because the two of them were planning to marry in August. Aunt Cravitz then electronically lectured her niece about opening mail when it arrived, telling her that five months ago Trust and Grace might have been unsteady enough to topple. Now, however, it was too late.

Cindy pulled Trust's picture out of the book she was reading. She had been using it as her bookmark and felt that it greatly enhanced her reading time.

"Grace," she sneered. "I suppose people in Tennessee have a hard time finding clever names to name their children."

Cindy put the picture back in her book and set them

34

both down. She looked in the mirror. Her head was covered with thick spongy rods and coated with perm solution. She imagined how vixenlike she would look once it was done. She held up the shirt she had just bought at the outlet store in Bourbonville. It was exactly like the one the heroine on the cover of her book was wearing. She puckered up for the mirror. Some perm solution dripped down her forehead, and she pushed it back up above her hairline.

Normally Cindy would have let the notion of Trust go, giving it no more thought than a nonfiction book—perfectly content to simply bad-mouth him until she had forgotten every intriguing thing his picture did to her. But there was something about his face and his build that made her want to fight. Something inside her told her that it was Trust or eternal misery. Something inside of her told her that this was her one shot at fulfilling romance and that she shouldn't give up. If she had learned anything from her books, it was the importance of fighting for your man. Certainly Grace's hold on Trust would be nothing once he got a look at her. Cindy was no stranger to mirrors. She knew perfectly well that she was the most fetching woman Trust would ever set eyes on.

"It's been a while since I visited Aunt Cravitz," Cindy rumbled, pulling open the drawer beneath her bed and extracting a huge pile of cash. "I could catch a plane out this afternoon."

She counted the money carefully, very familiar with every bill there. It was, after all, her nest egg, set aside for a rainy day.

A storm was brewing.

6

A FLY IN THE OINTMENT

It took me no time to feel right at home in Thelma's Way. Tuesday morning when I woke up and looked out the window it was as if I had never left. From the top floor of the boardinghouse I could see kids playing on the rotted pioneer wagons in the meadow—collecting splinters and exhausting themselves so that, come evening, their folks could count on their dropping off sometime before the sun did. I watched Wad supervise Digby Heck as he nervously cut Miss Flitrey's hair. Up until a couple of weeks ago, Digby had been unsure of just what he wanted to do with his life. He had prayed and prayed that the heavens might reveal just how he should go about making a living. He began looking for a sign, a marker pointing the way to his would-be livelihood. He thought that Toby's dog unexpectedly giving birth in the boardinghouse pantry might be a sign for him to go into commerce, but then he

36

remembered that he wasn't good with money. He still wasn't sure just how four quarters made a dollar.

"They turn into paper?" he would ask in confusion.

When Jeff Titter got wedged in a small passage down in Martin's Cavern while exploring, Digby was momentarily swept up in the romantic idea of becoming an explorer. But then he remembered that unknown things made him uneasy.

Digby was in a laborer's funk. Luckily, Tindy Mac-Dermont caught a nasty cold from one of the Porter boys. Digby was in the meadow thinking and thinking about what he should do when Tindy came walking by. She didn't talk, but her *achoo*s spoke louder than words. To Digby it sounded like heaven whispering over and over again, "Hair school. Hair school. Hair school."

Could it be any clearer? The heavens wanted Digby to cut hair.

Well, Thelma's Way had no hair school, but it had Wad, and Wad was willing to take on an apprentice. So for the last little while, Digby had been honing his hair skills under the wrinkled tutelage of Wad. Reports were that Digby was actually quite good at it. The only problem he had with it was that he was supposed to wear an apron— Digby felt they looked silly. So once again, he found a new purpose for Saran Wrap. He would roll plastic wrap around his torso and over his shoulder. It worked rather well. Sure, the first day he had put it on a little too tight, binding his lungs and causing him to pass out halfway through Sister Bickerstaff's tint job. But after Wad unwrapped him and then shook him for a while, Digby came back breathing strong.

I watched Digby nick Miss Flitrey's neck. She yelled at Wad, and Wad tried to yell at Digby, but due to Wad's lack of assertiveness, I'm not sure that Digby got the point. I saw Pete Kennedy taking potshots at a line of rusted soup cans he had propped atop a charred rail on the burnt and unusable Girth Bridge. He hit four in a row, and then, spotting a bird flying directly over the meadow, he pointed his gun and pulled the trigger. With the kind of precision he demonstrated in no other aspect of his life, he hit the bird. It bucked in the air and then fell like a rock, straight down. It hit an unsuspecting Toby Carver on the head and bounced onto the pile of old shirts he was carrying. I watched Toby look at the bird and then at the sky. He smiled and walked off, happy about the blessing that had just magically dropped into his lap.

I was glad to be back.

I spotted the older missionary couple that was currently living in the small cabin that I had lived in while serving here. Their names were Elder and Sister Knapworth. They were from Montana and had been out on their mission a little over two months. I had met them yesterday and spent a short while talking to them. They were the first full-time missionaries to serve here since I was dragged out after my spill down the falls. Elder Knapworth was a funny, short man with thick arms and bowlegs. His teeth were small and his lips big. He had a hollow voice that seemed to travel in clips—like a poor radio transmission. The only hair he sported was a small patch on the point of his forehead. The rest of his free-spirited noggin had allowed itself to go completely naked. He smiled a lot and wore glasses that looked as if they were better suited for a woman. Sister Knapworth was a fireball. She was the kind of woman who would have made an outstanding barmaid had she been inclined to slide in that direction. She talked loudly and happily as if every word she said were an announcement of something spectacular or the punch line of a really funny joke. She had high gray hair that was laced with red strands, showing that at one time she had been a real redhead. That made her instantly fond of Grace. Of course, I think Sister Knapworth was instantly fond of everyone. She hugged and slapped and pinched people as if they were lonely balls of touch-activated dough. The two of them had only been out on their mission a short time and were definitely more in love with each other than I ever had been with any of my companions. They hugged and kissed as if their mission were to give people a chance to witness public displays of affection.

I watched Elder and Sister Knapworth hold hands and talk to Jerry Scotch about something. She laughed and Elder Knapworth kissed her. Jerry just smiled. I turned from the window when I heard a knock at my door. Roswell entered before I could even answer.

"Sleep okay?" he asked, his gray head looking particularly pale today.

"Fine," I answered, realizing that I wasn't even fully dressed yet. I quickly put on a shirt.

"Don't worry 'bout me," Roswell waved. "I've seen a mess load of half-dressed men in my lifetime."

If I wasn't worried before, I was now.

"Listen," he went on, taking a seat on the edge of the bed. "I'm glad you're back and all, but I'm wondering whose side you're gonna be taking?"

"I don't know what . . ."

"Hold on," he said, showing me his palms. "'Fore you go sidin' with Mavis Watson, you need to know that I can't stand foreigners."

"Foreigners?"

"Anyone from anywhere besides exactly where I'm from."

"That means me," I pointed out.

"In a broad sense, yes," Roswell agreed, sounding as if he had wanted to use the phrase, "in a broad sense," forever and was now thrilled that he had finally found a place to put it.

"I see," I said.

"Listen, Trust, you're okay. I can make exceptions. One or two strangers is fine, but people just weren't meant to get too mixed up."

I sat down on the edge of the bed, hoping he wouldn't mind my doing so. He stood up, obviously having minded. He rubbed at an age spot on his right hand and then leaned up against the large bureau that was at present housing the few items of clothing I had brought with me.

"Mavis Watson thinks she knows everything," Roswell complained. "Her ideas ain't no more special than anyone else's. Wearing a wig don't make you a dignitary."

"I don't even know what Sister Watson wants to do," I

informed him, hoping to put this part of the conversation well behind us.

"I'll tell you what that woman wants to do," he frothed. "She wants to lay down a road from here to Virgil's Find. She wants the state to build us a highway. A highway," he hawed. "More like a low way." Roswell smiled to himself at his brilliant and unexpected wordplay. "A low way," he repeated. "She thinks it will make our town progressive and safer. Everyone's been seeing goblins ever since Toby's pig turned up missing."

"I don't know about goblins," I reasoned. "But it might be kind of nice to be able to drive in and out of here."

"It might be kind of nice," he mocked. "It might be kind of nice to have a third arm, or tail, but you don't see me begging God to change things."

"A tail?" I asked, smiling.

"Not a real long one," he said, as if that made the notion any less ludicrous.

"You know, there's probably nothing to worry about," I said, trying to be comforting. "I can't imagine the state's paying to put in a road here."

"So we can count on you to support Paul?" Roswell brightened.

"I didn't say that, I . . . support Paul in what?"

"His weather shelter," Roswell said firmly. "Paul wants to build a covering over the entire meadow. It'll keep the rain and snow out of our town twenty-four seven."

"You're kidding."

"Nope," Roswell beamed.

"Twenty-four seven?" I asked.

"I don't know what that means," he admitted. "But I heard Paul guarantee it. I for one wouldn't mind being able to make my schedule according to my own need, instead of having to wonder, Is it gonna rain today? Is it gonna snow this week? I'd like to walk out into the meadow on January twenty-fifth shoeless and without a hat. Is that too much to ask?"

I shrugged my shoulders as I tied my own shoe.

"Paul's got himself a good idea this time," Roswell insisted. "It ain't like the other times."

"It just seems a little extreme," I said.

"Bah," Roswell blew.

"And crazy," I added.

"Crazy? That's what folks said when Noah began building that boat."

"Ark," I corrected.

"No, they said crazy."

"Why can't Paul just build his thing over the road?"

"Because his idea calls for exactness," Roswell spit. "He wants his cover to run the whole length of the trail. How can he build it if the state's smearing our ground with tar and paint?"

I simply shrugged. I finished getting my shoes on and stood up next to Roswell. He looked me up and down. He was every bit as old as I had remembered him, but he didn't look half bad, considering that a couple years back he was thought to be dead. Actually, to the folks in Thelma's Way he had never died, just simply been translated and lifted up to heaven on a golden chariot. Now here he stood before me, his limbs as thin as angel hair

42

pasta and his skin as wrinkled as the brow of a simpleton at a science fair. His pitch-black pupils stared at me.

"So you're gonna wear those pants?" he commented.

I patted him on the back and then tried to kindly push him out of my room.

Roswell halted. "All right, Trust," he said in hushed tones. "Do you want me to be honest?"

"It depends on what you're divulging."

"I got a business venture on the line."

"Really?"

"No, I ain't selling houses." He looked at me like I was dumb. "You remember my cousin from Virgil's Find?"

"Sure."

"He's got a wagon and horse that he's willing to sell me for cheap." Roswell looked guilty. "All right, truth be told, I won it in a card game."

"I thought you gave up gambling."

"Sort of," he hedged. "The important thing is that I'm going to use my spoils to make me a little spending money. You're looking at Thelma's Way's first official ice cream man."

"And you were against progress."

"That's the point," he pointed out. "We put a road down, and there'll be competition from Virgil's Find."

"Oh."

"See my dilemma?" he asked.

I saw his problem.

"You really don't need to worry. Probably none of this will ever come to pass," I said as we both started down the stairs to the first floor.

"None of what?"

"This road. Or the meadow cover thing."

"Weather shelter."

"Or the weather shelter," I restated. "Building a roof over the meadow would be a costly endeavor."

"I have no idea what that means," Roswell said honestly. "But if you're talking 'bout money, Paul's gonna find that old Book of Mormon and sell it for funds."

"So it's never turned up?" I asked, having forgotten all about it.

"Never."

"And Paul knows where it is?"

"No, but he's got an idea."

"He's probably had it all along," I thought aloud.

"The idea?"

"No, the Book of Mormon."

"Doubt it," Roswell snipped. "He would have turned it over to Roger when he was here if he had known."

"Roger?"

"That's not important," Roswell brushed it off. "You know what's important, Trust?" he asked as we shuffled down, his thin knees popping with each step.

"What?"

"I'm old."

I felt it best not to say anything.

"Chances are, even if Mavis or Paul wins, I won't never see any of this stuff before I die anyhow."

I think he was waiting for me to say, "Sure you will," or "Don't say that," but I thought since he was being honest, I should be too.

"Everyone dies," I tried.

He just looked up at me and scrunched his old face into an even more wrinkled mug. "I guess Grace is just looking for a pretty face," he insulted me. "You know what though?" he asked.

"What?"

"I don't think I could settle down good and dead if I knew a road was coming in here."

"I wouldn't worry about it," I tried to comfort him.

We stepped down from the stairs and onto the main floor of the boardinghouse. Roswell shuffled away from me. I was planning on simply walking out the front door and heading over to the Heck residence to check up on Grace, but my vision was impaired by the sight of a certain someone's backside as he leaned over the counter talking to Briant Wilpst. I just stood there, dumbfounded and listening. I felt as if I had just spotted a butterfly in a fish bowl— both things fine in their own right but entirely wrong when combined.

Leonard Vastly had found Thelma's Way.

Leonard was leaning on the counter talking to Briant as if he were a piano salesman about to close a key deal. He wore white pants and a faded orange dress shirt. As usual, his wardrobe was too tight. He wasn't overweight; in fact, he fit nicely into the "skinny" category. But Leonard hadn't bought a new article of clothing for years, deciding instead to force fabric that was as old as I was to clasp and close more times than it had been intended to. He had bushy eyebrows and a long head that looked like the result of a fun house mirror. He was a completely unique individual with a completely unique way of looking at life. An added bonus to his unusual personality was the fact that he usually reeked of garlic due to the pills he took.

"You know, you could give up that cane entirely if you rubbed your ankles with a couple of magnets every evening for say, ten, fifteen minutes," Leonard said to Briant.

"Magnets?" old Briant said with enthusiasm.

"Sure."

Briant Wilpst looked around, his eyes stopping at the big clock hanging on the wall. He reached up, grabbed the clock, and smashed it up against the counter. Glass fell across the floor, sliding up against the far wall. Briant then sifted through the pieces and pulled out a tiny magnet.

"Like so?" he asked, showing Leonard the magnet.

"Well, for best results, I prefer something in the four-pound range."

"Leonard," I said in amazement.

He turned and faced me. "Trust."

"What are you doing here?" was my reply.

"Well, it's a long story," he said, nodding towards Briant, indicating that it was for our ears only. I don't know why it mattered. Briant was so busy rubbing the magnet on his elbows and ankles he didn't even look up.

"How long of a story?" I asked.

"I guess we won't know that until it's over."

Leonard motioned for me to follow him out onto the porch.

I've always been a glutton for punishment.

7

SHOVING A CAMEL THROUGH THE EYE

I had no one to blame but myself. Well, maybe Grace. You see, a few months back while having Sunday dinner at my house in Southdale, Grace had mentioned to Leonard that her family owned a lot of land in Thelma's Way and that they were the kind of people who would give anyone an acre if they really wanted it.

Well, Leonard wanted one.

After the flood in Southdale all those months ago, Leonard had bought himself a brand-new double-wide mobile home and placed it on the land where he had once had his single-wide Bio-Doom.

The neighbors complained.

They had put up with his single-wide home because they had been forced to. After all, it had been there before most of them had ever moved in. But they saw no reason, now that it was gone, why Leonard couldn't simply build a house that fit within the covenants of the neighborhood. Leonard was livid. He couldn't imagine ever living in something so confining as a glued-to-the-ground home. He liked the idea that if prompted by prophet or peril, he could simply hook up his house and haul it with him. He talked often about how surprised he was that the Church leaders didn't command everyone to get mobile homes, seeing how we could all then drag them to Missouri when the time came.

Well, Leonard took his complaints about his intolerant neighbors to city hall. He spent weeks on the steps of the courthouse with a sign that read, "I have a pre-fab dream."

Remarkably, city hall finally listened to him. In fact, the judge overseeing his case grew sympathetic until Leonard made the mistake of commenting on how lucky the judge was to be able to wear a robe to work, seeing how he, the judge, was probably a good forty pounds overweight and the cut of the robe really did a nice job of disguising it.

If I haven't mentioned it before, Leonard Vastly is a man of little tact.

The judge ruled Leonard's house as being in violation of zoning and then went on and on about how according to European high school textbooks he was at his ideal weight. Leonard was ordered to move his home and build something less portable.

Well, that was months ago.

Leonard had stalled as long as he possibly could. But it had finally gotten to the point that he had to get out or get arrested. So when he heard Grace and I were coming back here, he talked one of his buddies into pulling his home across the country to Thelma's Way, where, according to Leonard, the promise of free land beckoned like a lost love ringing the dinner bell.

"You brought your home here?" I asked in amazement.

"Yep," Leonard answered.

"Where is it?"

"That's the problem," Leonard answered sadly. "I've got it set up on blocks at the beginning of the trail. There's no way to get it back in here. What kind of place doesn't have a street leading in?"

As fate would have it, Sister Watson was walking by just as Leonard asked his question.

"A believer," she whispered, stepping up onto the porch and sticking her hand out to Leonard.

He looked at it and then told her that he had read that most germs were transmitted by people shaking hands.

I thought Sister Watson would be offended. But she simply said, "A sensible man. You're a rarity 'round these parts."

"He's a rarity around any part," I added.

"Thank you, Trust," Leonard said, not catching the sarcasm.

"Do you mind if I sit?" Sister Watson asked, pulling up an empty porch chair.

"I've never known a woman to do anything other than exactly as she pleases," Leonard replied.

Sister Watson blushed and tittered as if she had just been supremely complimented. I didn't understand, or perhaps I refused to believe, what was going on right in front of me. But if I had been forced to answer honestly, I would have to say that what I saw seemed to be an enamored Sister Watson.

"I don't believe I caught your name," she said.

"Leonard. Leonard Vastly."

"How regal."

Whereas I was initially intrigued, now I was nauseous. I stood up, stepping away to leave them alone. I had to tell Grace that Leonard was in town. I went back up to my room and changed my pants—Roswell's approval obviously meaning more to me than I cared to admit. When I got back down, Leonard and Sister Watson were gone. A mere three paces into my jaunt through the meadow, my plans were thwarted. Paul Leeper slipped up next to me, matching my stride with his slightly shorter legs.

"Have a moment?" he asked.

We stopped at the rotting pioneer wagons and leaned. If Thelma's Way was a rose, which it wasn't, then Paul Leeper would be the biggest and most obnoxious thorn on its stem. He was constantly causing and creating trouble for a town that had plenty of its own to begin with. He was fairly mean-spirited and as dishonest as a used-car salesman with a late mortgage payment. I know he was trying hard to rebuild his reputation, but it seemed like an impossible task. I just couldn't see how anyone claiming to have dug out a large portion of the Grand Canyon by hand could ever be taken seriously again.

I looked into Paul's scrunched and poorly arranged face. His thick, helmet-like hair was as dark and plastered as ever. He had an apple in his shirt pocket, causing his upper-wear to hang at an angle on him and making me feel as if we were leaning.

"We got a situation here," he said. "Seems as if you wandered back into town at a rather interesting time."

"Really?"

"Trust, I'm looking to better this place," he said seriously. "My project will completely cover the meadow and the path into Virgil's Find. And all I ask in return is for a small gold plaque hung somewhere obvious with my name on it and thanking me for my sacrifice. Not a bad trade for a year-round wonderland."

"Actually," I informed him, "it won't be much of a wonderland. If you cover the entire meadow everything beneath it will die."

"There'll be skylights," Paul barked. "Do you think I haven't thought this through?"

"Well, the whole idea does seem rather ridiculous."

"I see," he sniffed. "I suppose it would be to you, seeing how you're an outsider and all. You have no real roots here."

"Maybe so, but I'm marrying one of its residents."

"A blue blazer don't make a lamppost any more important."

Oddly enough, I understood his insult.

"Paul, I didn't come here to side with anyone," I insisted.

"Do you think the state should put down a road?"

"It's not an awful idea."

"Why? Because you're scared there's someone lurking in the woods like everyone else?"

"I know nothing about any lurking."

"It's all spit," Paul spat. "So Leo's misplaced his portable stove and Sister Lando can't locate her cooking sherry. Big deal. It don't mean we got some loony running 'round our town. And what's a road gonna do, huh?"

"I don't know."

"Some fancy police car will drive in here and declare that there's nothing for us to worry about. Real comforting. Well, Trust, do you know who will be right behind that police car?"

"Who?"

"A band of soft-from-convenience freaks. That's who. Ready and willing to overrun our meadow."

"You don't know that," I reasoned. "A road might help this town."

I don't know what it was about Paul and me. We had really never gotten along. He had pestered me my entire mission here. And even though we were now civil with each other, I still seemed to bring out the worst in him.

"That's it," he said, throwing his hands up into the air. "Trash my idea, but I'll find that Book of Mormon and finance my project before Sister Watson can even get the state to come out and look at her road. Once I've got my shelter built over the path and meadow, no one will want to build a road."

"You have a point."

"I do?" he asked with surprise.

"If you cover the meadow, no one, not even the locals, will want to spend time here."

"I see," Paul said blindly. "Well, your nay-saying won't

put a dent in my desire. I'll find that book, and I'll build my masterpiece."

"And just how are you going to find that book? The entire town's been looking forever."

"I got some ideas."

"I'm sure you do."

"What's that supposed to mean?" Paul snapped.

"I just think it would be awful convenient if that book turned up someplace that only you knew of."

"I didn't take it," he insisted. "If I'd had it, I would have handed it over to Roger when he was here."

"Roger?" I asked for the second time that day.

"Don't Roger me," Paul misinterpreted. "You smart-alecky city people make me sick. I know you came to foul me up," he insisted. "I can read your mind, Trust."

"Well then, I'd like to apologize for what I'm thinking."

Paul fumed for a moment and then walked off towards the Girth River.

I shrugged and stepped lively toward Grace's place.

8

THIS LITTLE PIGGY

Cindy sat on the outdated couch, fuming over her misfortune. She had caught the first flight to Southdale only to discover that her promptness was not going to pay off. She stared at the porcelain pig that sat as a centerpiece on the overpolished coffee table. Grief clouded her thoughts. Trust had slipped away from her. Her levelheaded aunt's e-mail had failed to mention that Trust and Grace were leaving Southdale and returning to Tennessee. Light reflected off Cindy's painted nails as she opened and closed her angry hands.

"Tennessee," she hummffed. "That state produces nothing but uninspired noise." Cindy couldn't remember a single good character from any of her romance novels who had hailed from Tennessee. Okay, there was Virginia, the buxom physical therapist with a gift for kneading secrets out of people. But in Cindy's eyes, Virginia was a dolt, turning down tall Darien to be with stocky Chad.

Aunt Cravitz emerged from the laundry room. She

wiped her hands on her skirt and then squeezed the gray bun wound tightly on her head.

"Still upset?" she asked Cindy.

"I have a right to be, don't I?" Cindy snipped. "I put a lot into this venture."

Aunt Cravitz sat down close to her niece on the couch. Their weight shifted, and the two of them leaned into each other, knocking heads lightly.

"Do you mind?" Cindy snapped.

Daisy Cravitz had not remembered her niece's being so stubborn.

"Cindy, you know there's a nice man in our ward who would make a wonderful . . . well, decent catch. He's a little older than you and sports an enormous head. I suppose finding a nice-fitting hat isn't easy for him, but he's kind. Besides, you wouldn't have been happy with Trust. He has baggage."

Cindy stared at her aunt as if she had gone crazy. She didn't want anybody besides Trust. His name was the omen her foolish imaginations had subliminally sought after. He was handsome, good-looking, and attractive—three attributes Cindy demanded in a mate. Yet here was her aunt offering up another while tearing apart the man she loved.

"It's not like he's dead," Cindy pointed out.

"He's engaged, dear," Aunt Cravitz tried to say calmly.

"Certainly I'm prettier."

"Grace is a lovely girl. Besides, he's in love."

"That can be changed."

"I don't think so."

"I didn't ask what you think," Cindy growled.

"Watch your temper," Aunt Cravitz warned sternly.

"I'll do as I please," Cindy insisted. "I always have and always will. I don't need you telling me what to do."

"Remember who's your elder."

"How can I forget with you sitting there all wrinkled and withered and wearing what must certainly be hand-me-downs from Eve herself?"

Daisy Cravitz's face turned pale. "Just where did you learn to speak like that?" she demanded.

"Never mind." Cindy brushed it off, standing and smoothing down her hair. "So where is this Thelma's Choice anyway?"

"You will sit down and forget about Trust."

"Where is he?" Cindy ranted. "Tell me."

"When pigs fly," Aunt Cravitz said smugly.

Cindy eyed the porcelain pig upon the table and smiled.

"You wouldn't," her aunt gasped. "I made that in Homemaking!"

Cindy picked it up, shifted it from her left to right hand, and then threw it across the room and through the small window by the square bookshelf. The pig sailed through the glass and out onto the front walk, slamming against the ground with a sound that resembled no part of "oink." Glass from the window fell to the floor and crinkled against the plush carpet below it. Cindy looked satisfied. Aunt Cravitz sat there dumbfounded. For a woman of so many words, she was amazingly speechless.

Cindy brushed her hands together and stomped out of the room but not before saying, "I'll find him myself."

Daisy Cravitz caught her breath. Her sister's child had turned out to be a real tornado. She picked up the phone and nervously dialed the one man she knew could calm her.

Three rings later, Brother Victor was on the line trying to soothe his woman. Three hours later, Cindy was on a plane complaining about the small peanut portions and heading towards Tennessee.

9

ROLLING ALONG
◇

The Heck home was one of the nicest abodes in the Thelma's Way area. They kept it up and kept it painted. In fact, it seemed as if President Heck recoated the place every couple of months or so. Not holding down a job left him with a lot of free time and unused energy. Their house was currently brown with dark blue trim—soon to be something else of a similar nature.

I stepped up to the porch and onto the handmade welcome mat that said, "Bless this Mess." Their two-legged dog lay beside it, chewing on something round and orange. He looked at me, tilted his head, and then went back to gnawing. I knocked on the door, not yet feeling enough like family to just walk in.

No one answered.

I looked through the front window, thinking that I could hear something inside. No one was visible. I stepped back off the porch and gazed up at the second floor. I couldn't see anything moving around through the black shingled dormers.

"Grace," I hollered.

There was no reply. I was going to walk away, but I needed to be confident enough to simply walk inside and see if anyone was home. After all, I was going to be family soon. So, I knocked again and then turned the doorknob. It was unlocked, of course. I stepped in and yelled out.

Again no answer. I was about to turn around and walk out, when I spotted a man with a towel wrapped around his waist and a shower cap on his long head step out from the bathroom and walk over to the icebox. He opened it up and began looking through it for food.

"Leonard?" I asked in amazement.

He jumped at my voice. "Trust," he said, putting a hand to his heart. "It's extremely bad manners to go sneaking up on people like that."

"I didn't sneak. I was just standing here."

"Still, it smacks of poor upbringing." Leonard pulled out a plate of cold chicken, set it down on the counter, and scratched his bare stomach.

"How'd you get here so fast?" I questioned.

"I was talking to that Watson woman, and I realized I hadn't had a shower in days. Thought I'd run up and take care of business."

"Why'd you come here?" I asked.

"I ran into President Heck down in the meadow," he said without looking at me. He peeled back the plastic wrap on the plate of food.

"And?" I queried.

"And he said to stop by sometime."

"Stop by and shower, or just stop by?"

"It's hard to say for sure." He picked up a piece of cold chicken and licked it for taste. "Ugh, this tastes awful."

"Seriously, Leonard," I tried again. "Do they know you're using their shower?"

"I thought you said these mountain folks were laid back and open?" he defended his actions.

"To a point."

"And what's that?"

"Some point you crossed miles ago."

"Listen, Trust," Leonard said, pushing the chicken into the kitchen trash can and opening the cupboards to find something else to eat. "It's not easy having your home sitting four miles away from town. I'm sure the Hecks would be honored to know I'm using their facilities."

"Honored?"

"Exactly."

I rubbed my forehead.

"Are you not feeling well?" he asked.

"I'm okay."

"I've got a whole suitcase full of herbs back at my place."

"So is your home just sitting there at the trailhead?" I asked, reminded of his mobile house that didn't fit down our trail.

"I got a couple of locals watching it. Leo and CleeDee. Pretty name—I wonder where his folks came up with it."

"Leo and CleeDee are watching your home?"

"Didn't I say that?"

"Yes, but . . ."

"They said they wanted to try living away from town for a while, so I lent them my place *gratssi*."

"*Gratis*," I corrected.

"Thank you."

I decided to wander into a different swamp of conversation. "Do you know where the Hecks are?"

"President Heck was down by the school talking about a chair he just found at the dump," Leonard explained. "I don't know where the wife is. Paulette, Penelope . . ."

"Patty."

"I suppose."

"And Grace?"

"Haven't seen her. You know, Trust, you really have been holding out on me."

I thought he was talking about the strong opinions of him I wasn't voicing at the moment. When he saw I wasn't going to comment, he went on.

"This town is a gold mine," he said with sudden excitement, simultaneously spotting a box of sugared cold cereal. I couldn't discern what he was happier about, the cereal or the town.

"I haven't seen this stuff since I was a kid."

It was the cereal.

"I wouldn't mind having a couple cases of this in my storage," Leonard said.

"So you like this town because they have easy access to Fudgy Nuggets?"

"No, no, although it's an added benefit," he conceded.

"I love this place because they have a need, and I can fill it."

"A need for what?"

"Oh, Trust," Leonard grinned wistfully. "There's still so much you have to learn."

I couldn't believe Leonard was in Thelma's Way. It was like tossing a rusted bolt into a vat of clean caramel. This place was socially sticky as it was, but now it was about to be tainted with rust and metal shavings.

"Yummm," Leonard said, biting into a spoonful of cereal.

"So about the town," I prompted.

"Do you think I should grow a beard?" he said, traversing down a completely different conversational trail.

"I don't . . . ," I began to say.

"It just seems like folks would take me more seriously with a nice face of hair. I used to have one, but between you and me, it was nothing spectacular. Us Vastlys were never very good about growing facial hair. Now, back hair, well . . ."

"Leonard," I pleaded, not needing the obvious pointed out to me.

"I just want the town to know I'm one of them."

"You are?"

"Sure. If they'll have me," he added humbly. "Like the sun, life moves in phases. And I have entered the Thelma's Way phase of my life. It's very appropriate, actually, considering that a couple of weeks from now it's my anniversary. I hate the term *birthday*. Man has one birthday," he said firmly. "And that's the day when the heavens drop

62

him into the arms of some unsuspecting couple all helpless and bawling. So I use *anniversary*. I suppose the exact term would be the 'anniversary of my birthday.' Forty-eight years. I wonder what the anniversary gift for forty-eight is."

"Moon," I said, having tuned him out sentences ago.

"Wow!" Leonard said in awe. "That could be pricey. But I suppose if people pooled their money . . ."

"No. The moon has phases. The sun just shifts."

"Huh?"

I wasn't sure why Leonard was bothering me so much at the moment. It wasn't as if he were acting any different than he usually did. Besides, he and I were actually pretty good friends, despite the fact that he was considerably older and odder than I. We had been through a lot together over the last six or seven months. He looked at life as if he were like a ten-year-old gazing out of a plane window, seeing everything as objects small enough for him to pick up and play with if only the glass of normal behavior weren't holding him back. He had no steady job but seemed never to be out of funds. He did sell and peddle almost every pyramid scheme ever constructed, but he seemed to make more people mad than he made money with those ventures. He was Leonard, and I liked him. I suppose the incident that brought us closest was when he took me with him to visit a cousin of his that lived just across the Nevada border in a town called Twelve Laughs. It was named so because when it was first settled by a Mormon pioneer named Lawrence Telly, twelve laughs were precisely what his wife let out before saying, "You have got to be kidding."

Twelve Laughs was not a particularly beautiful town. In fact, it was dirt ugly—emphasis on dirt, accent on ugly. It was founded by Mormons, but they all left after a particularly warm summer fermented all their canned goods and caused the entire town to go a bit loopy during the following winter. Afterwards, making eye contact with their neighbors was virtually impossible. So, the good folks of Twelve Laughs figured it was an omen and packed up and left before the wicked heat returned in the spring. Most moved to Seven Snickers, two states over in Colorado. Only one family stayed.

The Jeffery Vastly family.

Jeffery Vastly was Leonard's third great cousin, twice removed and thrice confused. He ran the whole town by himself until he died, leaving the legacy and family grocery store to his son Horace. Horace passed away unexpectedly while playing with dynamite, leaving his responsibilities to his only boy, Robby. Robby Vastly did all right with the grocery store, but a huge corporation announced plans to build a gigantic store in Twelve Laughs, the result of which would most likely be the end of the Vastly family business.

Well, with things a little tighter than Robby liked and not having the money to afford a good lawyer, Robby wrote to Leonard and asked if he would help him out, seeing how he sold Pre-law and had seen so many legal movies.

Leonard was all too happy to help. He coaxed me into going along with him as co-counsel. I wouldn't have gone, but Grace was busy that particular weekend and I had some sort of sick fascination with watching tragedy unfold before my eyes. When we arrived in Twelve Laughs, Robby was holed up in his basement, refusing to come out until his wife, Dinny, agreed not to shop at the new store that was threatening to come in. Dinny said that was a promise she couldn't keep, seeing how Robby was such a pathetic grocery store owner and he never stocked the items she needed. That actually was the problem at its simplest point. Amazingly, things found a way to go downhill from there. Robby, realizing that his demands were not going to be met, decided to change his request. He now refused to come out unless the fabled pirate ghost Hookums, that he had been told stories of as a child, appeared and told him he was forgiven of all his sins.

Robby was not the sharpest tack in the box.

I would have laughed off the request, but Dinny kept talking about how much I resembled what Hookums was rumored to look like. The rest of the incident is rather foggy. All I know is that at night's end, I found myself dressed as a pirate and holding Robby on my lap. Leonard talked his relative into closing the store and moving someplace where he could live in twenty-four-hour monitored bliss. Last I heard he was in Florida someplace, and Dinny was selling vinyl siding in Oklahoma with a new husband named Tim. Despite the results, the trip brought Leonard and me even closer together. Now, however, he was here in my personal place, eating cold cereal out of my future in-laws' house and talking about settling down.

It wasn't right.

"Anyhow," Leonard interrupted my thoughts. "About

this town being a gold mine. Did you know that there is not a single independent distributor in this entire valley?"

"You can't sell tea tree oil and legal aid in this place," I laughed. "These people have no money."

"I'll teach them how to make a little."

"Leonard," I said for lack of anything else.

"Trust," he replied with equal cleverness.

I was going to say something a little more complicated but was stopped by President Heck's walking through the front door, dragging what looked to be a well-weathered kitchen chair.

"What a day," he said happily, acting as if it were perfectly normal to see me and a towel-clad man standing in his house. "Look what I found."

I looked at the chair again, wondering if I had missed something. He explained himself with no prompting from us.

"The garden's been killing me this summer," he said, as if the mere thought of it made him tired. "All that bending. And the chickens are taking longer and longer to feed. That rooster's right good at making new mouths to stuff. Anyhow, I think my back's aging faster than any other part of me. Not anymore," he said, holding up his chair as if he were standing on the center podium at the cerebral Olympics and hoisting his trophy.

He looked back and forth between Leonard and me. I tried to act as if he were making perfect sense to me.

"Wheels!" he exclaimed, tipping the chair upside down and showing me the swivel wheels on the bottom of his treasure. "I'll sit on this and scoot around."

"You're going to have a hard time maneuvering that

thing across the ground," Leonard said, puncturing Ricky Heck's dream.

"Toby gave me a shed full of cement."

"Oh," Leonard said, as if that settled that.

"He got it from a lady in Virgil's Find who just passed away." President Heck bowed his head for a moment of respect. Leonard crunched his cereal loudly. Ricky Heck looked up and continued, "Toby would read to her in the afternoons at the hospital. Her husband used to sell concrete and left her with a garage full of the stuff. She willed it to Toby. Some folks are so lucky."

"Right place, right time," Leonard agreed.

"I'll say," Ricky said. "Anyhow, Toby said I could have my share if I help him clear out the trees back behind his saturated leech field. Shoot, I would have done that for free."

"And you were calling him lucky," I contributed.

"Trust, you've got a real nice way of looking at life," Ricky smiled.

"Don't give him a big head," Leonard warned.

Tired of just standing there, I walked over to the couch that was facing the kitchen and sat down. As usual the entire sofa rocked back just a bit. Ever since I had known President Heck, he had been trying to find the right piece of wood to balance his couch. He wasn't there yet.

"Anyhow," Ricky continued. "I'm going to put in a cement path around our house, with a few shoots going out to the chickens and around the garden. I can scoot myself around just like them kings."

I was unfamiliar with any rolling kitchen-chair dynasties.

"I'd be happy to help you with your path," Leonard offered nicely.

"I'd be happy to let you," Ricky replied.

"It'll give me a chance to talk to you about a couple business opportunities."

"I'm all for that."

The two of them walked out of the room together, President Heck blissfully unaware that Leonard was wearing nothing but a towel or that he had ulterior motives.

I helped myself to a bowl of cereal and then set out to find Grace.

10

THERE IS BEAUTY ALL AROUND

I was almost to the meadow when I spotted Grace coming my way. I stepped behind some trees in an effort to surprise her. I watched her get closer, amazed at what I saw. She was a completely different girl from the one I had once met in these very woods. She walked with confidence and ease, passing through the forest like nature's inner child. Her green eyes looked ahead, full of wonder and finding new interest in the same surroundings that she had wandered a million or more times before. She stopped and tied her hair loosely behind her head. Strands broke free as soon as she began walking again, brushing in front of her face and making the stunning forest look simple and passé.

She walked closer, passing me by without noticing. I stepped out directly behind her.

"Hey," I whispered.

She stopped but didn't turn.

"It's not safe to be out in the woods alone," I informed her.

"Really?" she said, still not turning to look at me.

"Really," I confirmed. "Just a couple of years ago a girl in these exact woods fell in love with an average guy and was eventually tricked into getting engaged to him."

"How awful."

"For the girl," I agreed. "The boy, however, really made out."

"Did he?" Grace said, turning to face me.

"I mean he got a good deal," I clarified.

"A good deal of what?" she asked.

"Not of what," I corrected, realizing that I was choosing my words poorly. "He just got lucky."

"Oh really." Grace's soul backlit her green eyes as she smiled.

"You know what I mean," I tried.

Grace put out her right hand and took mine. She pulled me back behind a thick trio of trees and began thanking me for bringing her home. Nothing even close to inappropriate took place, but I feel safe saying that I had never received a thank-you like that from anyone else during my lifetime. When we stepped back out, Toby Carver was standing there staring at us.

"I heard some rustling," he said with concern. "I thought it might be that stranger who stole my pig."

"It was us," I explained.

"Oh."

"We were just looking for Grace's shoe," I said, throwing

out the first thing that came to mind. "It flew off while she was walking."

Grace laughed, offering no help whatsoever.

Toby looked down at her shod feet. "I see you found it."

I nodded and whewed.

"Well, I was wondering if either of you had seen Winton."

"Winton?" I asked.

"Jerry's uncle," Toby answered. "He came to stay with Jerry a couple months ago after he accidentally burned down the apartment complex he was living in back in Georgia."

"Never seen him," I said.

"Neither have I," Grace added.

"Well, I suppose I best keep on looking," Toby said cordially. "I'm glad you found your shoe. I know how hard it can be to go around with just one." Toby walked off towards Lush Point.

"Looking for my shoe," Grace laughed after Toby was out of earshot.

"What? It worked, didn't it?"

Grace stuck out her hand again.

"Really?" I said happily, thinking she wanted to hide behind the trees again.

"No," she smiled. "I have something I want to show you."

Now she was choosing her words poorly. She took my hand and dragged me down the hill, into the meadow, and towards a discovery I had not been expecting to make.

II

PLANE AS DAY

Cindy hated planes. Not because she was scared of crashing or because turbulence made her nauseous. Nope, the problem was that thanks to new FAA laws, she could be arrested for acting up and causing a commotion on a moving flight. So she sat in her aisle seat thinking up ways to subtly annoy people. She kept retrieving things from the overhead bins and moving other people's stuff around. She stuck her long legs into the aisle and pretended to be asleep so the stewardess couldn't pass out the drinks on schedule. She shifted a lot in her seat, elbowing the woman next to her and kneeing the seat of the passenger in front of her. Eventually both of those in harm's way picked themselves up and found other places to sit. She buzzed the stewardess every few minutes to ask where they were and insisted on the pilot's coming out and introducing himself to the passengers, seeing how it was only fair for all of them to be able to see the face of the man holding their fate in his hands.

After the woman sitting right next to her left to find another place, Cindy began to pester the bald gentleman sitting one seat away by the window. She would lean all the way over, sticking her head in his space and pretending to look out the window. After a couple of minutes the man spoke up.

"I must say I don't think I've ever met anyone more desperate for attention than you," he said with a British accent.

"Think again," Cindy snipped. "We've never actually met."

"Pathetic," he said with polish.

"Excuse me?"

"I wish that I could."

"And what's that supposed to mean?"

"It means you're a woman of little goodness."

Cindy was silent while she thought of something mean to say.

"Nice hair," was all she could come up with.

"Extraordinary," he tisked.

"Thanks," Cindy said, brushing her curly mane back.

"Amazing," he said in disgusted astonishment.

"It's about time you noticed."

"You are the most unbelievable creature I have ever encountered."

"There's a line I've never heard before," Cindy said sarcastically.

"You're not fooling anyone," he said solemnly. "Your insecurity and ugliness are as plain as the nose on your face." With that he got up and relocated.

Cindy sat alone, bothered and thinking about her nice nose.

12

CAUGHT ON AN EYE

He looked closer. Yep, it was red. His heart whirled like a one-winged bird tossed from a high tree. Never had he seen anything more fixating. His simple mind focused in on her as he huddled back behind the thick brush. He willed his large frame to be more compact and unnoticeable.

If he were spotted, it could ruin everything.

This was the closest he had ever been to anyone in town, and he liked it. She was pretty. Her white skin and green eyes reminded him of something nice—a warm meal or new boots. He liked her. He had never desired anything from Thelma's Way besides the bare necessities. His wish list, however, was changing.

One redhead, hold the boyfriend.

13

FAMILY SECRETS

Grace pulled me across the meadow, up the porch steps of the boardinghouse, and into Roswell's room. I thought of Feeble, Roswell's unidentical twin brother who had died a couple of years ago. His sagging twin-sized bed still sat there, rumpled and worn from all the nights of rest it had provided his big body for all those years.

"You wanted to show me Roswell's room?" I asked Grace.

She kept silent, dragging me over to the cluttered desk in the corner. She picked up a picture frame and handed it to me.

"Roswell showed this to me earlier," she explained. "I couldn't believe it."

"What's so . . ."

"Just look," she said with excitement.

It was a group picture taken at one of the annual Thelma's Way Thanksgiving get-togethers. Roswell was front and center, smiling and letting the world know that he had little understanding of dental hygiene. Sister Watson was wearing a rust-colored dress, and the Hecks were standing on the right. Paul, Ed, and Toby were standing on the left. It was obvious that whoever had taken the picture had asked those being photographed to say "cheese" because slower-than-the-rest Ed Washington was still forming the word as the picture was captured.

It was a perfect likeness of Ed.

I handed the picture back to Grace. "That's nice," I said, wondering why she had wanted me to see it.

"Did you see my family?"

"They looked great."

"Look again."

I picked it back up and stared at the Hecks. They were all smiling, having properly finished saying "cheese" before the flash. Narlette was holding her mother's hand, and Digby was kneeling so that everyone could clearly see the upper half of his father. President Heck had one arm around his wife and the other over a person I couldn't quite identify. It was a he, and this he was wearing a hat that covered a good portion of his face.

"Who's that?" I pointed.

"Can't you tell?"

I looked again and shook my head.

"I think it's your father," Grace said.

"Why would my dad be in this picture?" I replied, instantly realizing as the words came out that Thelma's Way was where he had gone all those months ago when he was missing. "I don't believe it."

"He must have wanted to see where you served," Grace said happily.

"Then why didn't he tell me?"

She shrugged.

"And how come your folks have never said anything?" I questioned.

"I have no idea," Grace answered honestly. "But we could find out."

We walked out of Roswell's room with me carrying the picture and feeling incredibly confused. Six months ago, right after I took Grace to Southdale, my father suddenly disappeared. He would call occasionally, but he never let on where he had gone. After a few weeks, he stopped calling. My mother went nuts wondering what had happened to him. Just before we all gave up hope, Dad had phoned my mother and told her that he had been in some sort of accident and that he would be home soon. When he did return, he was a different man than he had been when he left us. No longer was he all business and distant—he was now the father we had longed to have. But even at his return, he refused to tell us where he had been or why he had gone. We had tried to guess it out of him but gave up when we realized that it was a secret he would share only when ready. Now here I had stumbled upon the truth, and I couldn't understand it.

"Why would my dad come to Thelma's Way?" I asked as we walked through the boardinghouse. I was very anxious to get to the Hecks' and question them about my father's stay here. I suppose we would have gone straight there if it had not been for the pair of people who were in our way, standing on the boardinghouse porch kissing.

It was Elder and Sister Knapworth poised amongst a bunch of bags and clutter. Grace and I tried not to interrupt them. Sister Knapworth noticed us and pulled away from her husband.

"You'll have to forgive us," she said. "We're not acting much like missionaries, are we?"

"You're fine," I said.

"Well, aren't you a flirt." Sister Knapworth batted her eyes at me. "Grace, dear, where did you find him?"

"Right here," Grace answered.

"Not a bad place to meet," Sister Knapworth laughed. "You know we're having a hard time not feeling like we're on a honeymoon instead of a mission. So, Elder Knapworth," she said to her husband, "what do we have on the agenda today?"

He saluted her with his free hand. "President Heck wanted us to go through those records, ma'am," he answered.

"Let's get to it, then," she laughed.

"Give me a second to take our bag back to our place first," he smiled. "We just went into town," he informed us.

"Can I help you carry something?" I asked, nodding towards the bags on the porch.

"We're all right," he said happily. "These aren't all ours. We just have this duffel bag full of love," Elder Knapworth cooed, kissing his companion on the lips. Sister Knapworth hugged him, brushing a wisp of his hair patch down.

I squeezed Grace's hand, executing the international

symbol for "if we were alone I would be laughing so hard about that 'duffel bag of love' remark." She squeezed back twice, indicating that she agreed, while at the same time she thought it was sort of sweet.

Men and women are different.

They walked off to take their bag home and work on the records. We watched them try to stroll and kiss at the same time. They just about had a semiawkward rhythm going, but then they tripped over Lupert Carver and decided that holding hands would have to be sufficient for the moment.

"Do you think we'll be like that?" Grace asked.

"I think I hope so," I answered, putting my arms around Grace and trying not to feel as goofy as they had just looked.

Sister Watson came stomping up the porch steps. She had a sign under her right arm, a hammer in her left, and two nails pinched tightly in her lips. She pulled the sign out from under her arm and nailed it up to the front of the boardinghouse. She read it a couple of times to make sure it still said what she had written, and then she walked inside. The poster said:

> *We have a problem. Gather in the meadow this afternoon for details.*

I wondered which particular problem they would be discussing.

"Remember how you used to say that Southdale was

just as different and odd as Thelma's Way?" Grace asked me while looking at the sign.

"Yeah," I answered.

Grace looked up at me, her green eyes hitting my blue. "Never mind," she waved.

Some things were best left unsaid.

14

WHAT YOU SEE IS MOST DEFINITELY, WITHOUT A DOUBT, POSITIVELY, UNDENIABLY NOT WHAT YOU GET

Cindy paid the taxi driver and then told him that he would never be a successful cabman, or human for that matter, with such a putrid-smelling vehicle. He sped off, leaving her alone in Virgil's Find and standing in front of the trail that led to Thelma's Way.

It had not been simple getting this far. Thelma's Way, Cindy had discovered, wasn't on any map, and most people in Tennessee had no idea it even existed. So Cindy had been forced to use her wits. Drawing upon a plot point from the book *Desire's Handmaiden*, Cindy called the Knoxville mission home and pretended to be an investigator looking for directions on how to get to her Mormon friend who lived in Thelma's Way. True, the plot to *Desire's Handmaiden* really had nothing to do with her idea, but there had been a phone involved, so she went with it. The mission home gave her directions and informed her that the Church had a set of older missionaries serving there. Cindy would have thanked them, but the woman on the phone had a funny accent. Besides, the directions she gave did not exactly make Cindy happy. It had been a major upset when Cindy discovered that in order to get to Thelma's Way she would have to hike four miles on foot. It was so much an upset that she thought about giving up her quest. But then she remembered that she had her father's credit card and warmed up to the idea of buying some new, suitably feminine hiking clothes. So after a quick stop at a mall, she was driven by taxi to the start of her hike.

"How awful," she complained aloud as she looked around.

Cindy was in a particularly foul mood. Although she would have adamantly denied it, her current disposition didn't stem from her long plane ride or from the fact that she was now going to have to hike. It stemmed from the conversation that she had been forced to have with that awful bald man.

"You're not fooling anyone," he had said. "Your insecurity is as plain as the perfect Roman sculptured nose on your fabulous face."

Or something to that effect.

"'Not fooling anyone.' Ha!" Cindy laughed. "Just because I'm honest, people get all bunched up and hurt. 'Not fooling anyone.'"

Cindy picked up her bags and walked down the road to where a sign stood pointing the direction to Thelma's Way. On the left of the road sat a double-wide mobile home. It was sort of angling into a ditch and hooked together rather poorly.

"Beautiful place," she snipped.

This was not going to be easy. Maybe the man on the plane had been partly right. Maybe Cindy had been going about this all wrong. If she was going to get Trust, she needed to be something different from what she had always been. That's how it usually worked in her books. Most of the really believable heroines acted like something they weren't to win the man they needed. Then they simply slipped back to who they really were once Mr. Right had pledged his heart and soul to the perpetuation of their eternal happiness. Cindy knew she could be honest to a fault. And at times she even sensed that being so open about her amazing beauty was a turnoff to others. So maybe if she acted the part, she could lure Trust away long enough for him to become eternally bound to her.

Cindy giggled, although to anyone looking on, it could easily have been mistaken for an evil cackle. She picked up her bags and walked past the mobile home. Just as she cleared the kitchen window, Leo Tip stuck his head out.

"Who goes there?" he said, having taken up the responsibility of monitoring who walked in and out of his hometown.

Cindy bit her lip, stopping herself from telling him off. If this were going to work, she would need to be someone other than who she actually was.

"What's your name?" Leo asked impatiently.

Cindy looked at him and winced, although to anyone looking on, it could easily have been mistaken for an innocent smile on a lovely girl's face.

"Hope," Cindy threw out pleasantly. "Hope Hayhurst."

Let the games begin.

15

JERRY RIGGED

We hiked back to Grace's house to have a talk with President Heck about my father's being in Thelma's Way. He wasn't there—President Heck, or my father, for that matter. According to Narlette, her dad was off collecting the beginnings of his shed full of cement. I thought about questioning Narlette, but I felt that it would be best to bring it up with President Heck first. So Grace and I sat on the unstable couch in the front room and waited—her on one end, me on the other. I thought we were being good.

"It's nice to be back," I said, trying to start some light, nonintimate conversation.

"It is," she stopped it.

"Things seem just like before," I began again.

"Weird, isn't it?"

"The town?"

"No . . . well, yes," she changed her mind. "I wanted to come back so badly, but now that I'm here, I don't have any idea what to do."

"We could hike into Virgil's Find," I suggested.

"I don't mean this afternoon," she laughed. "I mean this week, this month."

"We could hike into Virgil's Find then too."

"I'm serious, Trust."

"Why do you need to do anything?" I asked. "Isn't being here enough?"

"No."

"It used to be," I pointed out.

"It really never was."

"So you want to go back to Southdale?"

"Not yet."

"Me neither."

Grace shifted one of the books on her parents' coffee table. Then she shifted it back. I noticed a small photo lying on the table.

"What's that?" I asked, trying to pick it up.

"Nothing," she said, grabbing it before I could touch it. "It's just a really bad picture of me."

"Is there such a thing?" I asked.

Grace crumpled it up and threw it away. "Not anymore. What were we talking about?"

"About enjoying being here," I said, thinking that I needed to remember to dig that picture out of the trash later. "This is probably the last time in our lives when we'll have nothing to do. After the wedding, it's back to Southdale for school."

"I know," Grace said. "So where should we live when school's over?"

"In a golden castle in a magical land."

"Trust."

"In a crummy apartment near a bus stop so that I can easily commute to my slightly-better-than-minimum-wage job."

"That'll be great," Grace joked.

"Yeah," I answered honestly, thinking only about the fact that Grace would be my wife.

Grace changed the subject. "So do you think there really is some stranger hiding in the woods up here?"

"Besides Pete and Ed?"

Grace smiled.

"I don't think so," I answered.

"Sister Watson swears she saw him."

"Sister Watson sees a lot of things others don't."

"I suppose so."

There was a moment of silence.

"So, do you want to hike into Virgil's Find?" I asked again.

We cut through the woods and connected with the path near its center. Once in Virgil's Find, we saw a movie and ate at a restaurant that charged seven dollars for a hamburger. After that we went to the mall and visited Jerry Scotch at the Corndog Tent. He was very happy to have visitors.

Jerry was one of the few residents of Thelma's Way with outside employment. He had worked at the Corndog Tent for as long as I had known him. He was still just a regular employee, but he hadn't stopped dreaming of becoming an assistant manager someday. He was happy to report to us that the sportswear manager at Sears had recently told him that if he ever got tired of selling corn dogs there was a place for him folding sweaters or straightening hangers at Sears.

"I got options," Jerry bragged.

Jerry was in his forties and by far the most average-looking person I had ever seen. Whenever people met him they always felt that they had known him before. He constantly wore his corn dog outfit. In fact, he had sort of become the law in Thelma's Way, seeing how he was the only person with any sort of uniform. I had seen him settle many disputes by the authority of his outfit alone.

"Met my uncle yet?" Jerry asked us while staring at Grace.

"Winton?" I recalled.

"Yeah," Jerry said, as if he were recalling a pleasant memory.

"Not yet."

"You sure got pretty." Jerry blushed at Grace.

"Thanks, Jerry," she smiled.

"I asked out a woman from the Gadget Shack yesterday." Jerry was letting us know that he had options of a different sort.

"That's great," I congratulated him.

"Not really," he said sadly. "She was busy for a really long time. And after that she said she might get married."

"At least you asked," I said supportively.

"I suppose."

Jerry was constantly seeking female companionship. I would say it was because he enjoyed the company of the opposite sex, but truth be known, I don't know that he had ever really been alone with someone of the female persuasion long enough to find out for sure. But he tried hard and had an amazing collection of rejection stories. One of my personal favorites was the time he knew he was in love with a girl named Jenny who worked two shops down from him at Happy Feet: dress shoes for men. Well, Jerry was a man. So, for two solid weeks he spent every lunch break buying a new pair of dress shoes from her. She would help him find his size and fit him personally. By the end of two weeks, Jerry knew it had to be her or no one else. Doped up on love, he was moved to buy her something to express his feelings. Unfortunately, the twenty pairs of shoes he had invested in had put a real dent in his spending power. So using information that only he as a mall employee was privy to and figuring that Jenny, like most human beings, liked to eat, he hid out behind the Rotisserie Chicken's dumpster late one night and waited for them to pitch the birds they had not sold that day. Jerry picked the best castaway, washed it off, and then wrapped it in one of the outdated Corndog Tent aprons.

Well, nothing says loving like a day-old chicken wrapped in a faded apron.

Jenny was not impressed. In fact, she was repulsed to the point of calling mall security. As they dragged Jerry away, he begged her to reconsider. She then pointed out that she was happily married, had three kids, and was expecting her fourth sometime in the coming month. And as if that were not barrier enough, she had vowed early in life never to get involved with a grown man who doesn't wear socks.

Jenny quit her job a couple of days later, and Jerry

never saw her again. One nice thing had come out of the relationship, however, and that was that Jerry had a pretty good supply of gifts to give people for the next little while. I had actually been there when he gave Sister Watson a nice pair of men's dress shoes for her last birthday.

Jerry currently had his eye on one of the mall security women who had dragged him away all those months ago.

"Hope it works out," I said.

"Love's tricky," he admitted. "I been up at nights just thinking about it."

Grace looked at her watch and reminded me that Sister Watson would soon be disclosing one of the town's problems. We said good-bye to Jerry and then headed back to Thelma's Way. I was only slightly curious about what Sister Watson was going to say. I figured it had something to do with the road that she wanted. If I had known who awaited me in Thelma's Way, however, I might have picked out a nice spot in Virgil's Find and sat it out.

16

COMPLICATIONS

As we passed Leonard's displaced mobile home, Leo stuck his head out and demanded that we stand and be noticed. Since we were already standing, the procedure didn't take long. CleeDee hollered out a hello through the window.

"She'd show her face," Leo explained, "but this warm weather's chapped things up something awful."

CleeDee Tip had the most sensitive face of any person I knew. A gentle breeze could suck every bit of moisture from her mug. She was pale, with dirty brown hair and a clean, tight smile. She had married Leo in the Atlanta Temple a year after he was baptized. She was protective and overly jealous about her man. In her eyes it didn't seem possible that any woman could go through life without falling for Leo. Leo, after all, was quite the catch. Not only was he handsome in a gangly, backwoods kind of way, but he also received monthly royalties from an invention his grandfather had patented years ago. Thanks to those checks, Leo and CleeDee were quite possibly the most financially secure couple in all of Thelma's Way.

"So, how's this working out?" I asked Leo, referring to living in Leonard's house.

"There are drawbacks," he admitted. "For one, this home ain't hooked up to any electricity or water. But shucks, them things seem mighty trivial when I look at the fancy gas stove and gigantic tub we have."

"Of course neither of those things actually work," I pointed out.

"We weren't sent to this life to be comfortable," an eavesdropping CleeDee screamed out.

If anybody knew about that, it was CleeDee. Not only did she have the skin thing going on, but she was also six months pregnant and living in a nonfunctioning mobile home.

Grace and I left the Tips to themselves and hurried down the trail and into Thelma's Way. We made it to the meadow right on time. Sister Watson and Leonard were draping yarn along the ground to section off an area where whatever was going to be talked about might be talked about with plenty of space. I watched a few people pat Leonard on the back and act as if he belonged here. I was amazed at how quickly he had worked his way into my turf.

I had heard rumors that Pete Kennedy had taken up the trombone. Those rumors were rock-solid truth. Pete was on the edge of the crowd puffing and playing, making this get-together feel more important than it would have without him. Teddy Yetch and Sister Watson had selfishly talked him into learning. They had hoped to get him interested in something besides guns—it had always made the entire town nervous to have Pete spontaneously shooting off. Well, their plan was marginally successful. The only hitch was that now, whenever Pete perfectly executed a song, he would fire off a couple of rounds into the air. Of course, hearing him now slaughter "Twinkle, Twinkle, Little Star," I couldn't imagine him ever making it flawlessly through a single piece.

I saw President Heck talking to Sister Lando. His arms were covered with cement up to his elbows. It was obvious that he had torn himself away from his path-building to be here. Sister Watson clapped and then stood patiently waiting. Realizing that no one was going to settle down, she walked over to Pete and whispered in his ear. He set down his trombone, pulled a gun from one of his holsters, and fired up. Only a few people seemed to notice. He shrugged and went back to playing his trombone. Sister Watson was extremely put out. This was her event, and folks weren't even paying attention. Roswell, showing uncommon sensitivity towards Sister Watson and wanting to help, whistled loudly. The whistle gathered little attention, but the act of whistling caused him to have a coughing spasm.

It was the perfect attention grabber.

After a few minutes of awful hacking, Toby walked up to Roswell and patted him on the back. It was a nice display of Toby's medical expertise. Amazingly, it seemed to help. Roswell stopped and wiped his thin lips on the end of his untucked shirt.

"Thank you, Roswell," Sister Watson said gratefully, as

she stood in the middle of the yarn ring. "We're gathered here because we've got a problem."

Everyone nodded and agreed.

"I know that some of you think that Paul's weather shelter is not a bad idea, even though it's for vanity purposes that he seeks to build it. And I know that a lot of you more sensible people want a road that will offer us growth and security in this insecure time. Well, even a pony with mange would know that we couldn't have both. So, with Paul's consent, I've hired an independent counsel to investigate and decide what's best."

This seemed to please most everyone.

"Let me introduce to you Brother Leonard Vastly. He hails from out west, and according to him, he has vast experience in a number of things."

Leonard stepped into the ring and took a bow. "Thank you," he said. "I want you all to know that I desire nothing but justice. If it be the security of a road you seek, you shall have a road. If it be shelter, then by goodness you shall have it. My goal is your good."

There was some spotty, halfhearted clapping.

"I'd like to open up the ring for questions," Leonard announced, as if presenting us with some fabulous privilege.

Frank Porter raised his hand. Leonard scanned the crowd for a while, pretending that he had more than one hand to choose from.

"You in the plaid shirt and overalls," Leonard finally nodded towards Frank.

Seven men all began speaking at once, thinking he had been addressing them.

"With the single eyebrow," Leonard clarified.

That eliminated two.

"And a pen behind your ear."

Frank had the floor. "So what side are you on?" he asked Leonard. "You want a road or a covering?"

"Originally I was for the road," Leonard admitted. "But in talking to Paul, I now see some real potential in this weather shelter."

Miss Flitrey raised her hand. Technically she wasn't a Miss anymore, seeing how she had wed Wad a while back. It had been a long time, however, since anyone had actually referred to Wad as anything other than just Wad—so long, in fact, that he couldn't remember his last name. He had a feeling it was something like Stevenson, but he just couldn't be sure. So Miss Flitrey kept her own name and title. She still taught school, and he still cut hair. But now at the end of the day, the two met at the far end of the meadow, held hands, and would not separate until morning or meals.

Leonard pointed at her upheld hand. "Yes?"

"I'm for the road," she announced. "It makes sense to have a better way in and out of town. I feel half-dressed with that crazy person running around. With a road we could better run him out of town. So like I said, I'm for the road. And so is Wad. Also, Digby will find his work conditions uncomfortable unless he sides with us. That makes three."

"Good to know," Leonard thanked her. "As your independent counsel I will make it my duty to investigate all of you and your opinions."

"I've never been investigated," I heard Janet Bickerstaff say. She then shivered as if she sort of liked the idea.

"I could help," Pete Kennedy said.

"No helping," Toby argued. "If this is going to be fair, then you gotta only use yourself on this."

"I promise I won't listen to another outside influence," Leonard vowed. "The conclusion I make will be completely untainted by anything else."

I couldn't believe how quickly Leonard had come and conquered. In the space of a day, he had made himself an important part of this town. And whereas most of the folks here didn't care for outsiders, Leonard seemed to be instantly accepted. I suppose they saw him as a kindred spirit or a philosophical equal.

I would have gone on thinking about Leonard and his quick assimilation into Thelma's Way but my right eye caught sight of something most unusual. A girl about my age stood still against the landscape gazing at me. I had never seen her before. In fact, I had never seen anything like her before. She was built perfectly. Her deep eyes and curly hair made my imagination wander like strong weeds through a wet garden. Briant Wilpst momentarily shuffled through my line of vision. By the time he moved out of the way, she was gone.

"That's weird," I said quietly to myself.

"I agree," Grace said back, having been the only one to hear me and thinking that I had been talking about Leonard.

I looked around as nonchalantly as I could, wondering where this unknown *she* had gone.

"I'll set up my headquarters at the boardinghouse," Leonard was saying. "You'll probably all be called upon to testify. There won't be a single person that I won't know intimately. If the issue goes to court, then I have a black rain poncho that will work nicely as a robe."

"That's settled then," Sister Watson clapped.

Leonard marched off toward the boardinghouse to set up his operation. Everyone parted to let him by, treating him like something special. I wanted to have a talk with him about his position, but I was distracted by President Heck standing at my side.

"An independent counsel here in our town," he said proudly.

"It's just Leonard," I said.

"Judge Leonard," President Heck corrected.

I was just about to ask President Heck about my father when *she* appeared again, standing near the cemetery and watching me like a stalking spirit. I tried not to look too hard, seeing how I had Grace on my arm and didn't think it would be that appropriate to gaze longingly at another woman. Grace followed my line of sight.

"Who's that?" she asked.

"I have no idea."

"Me neither," President Heck threw in.

"She's pretty," Grace observed.

"I hadn't noticed," I said, fog in my voice.

Grace shook me out of it. I looked down at her and smiled. When I looked up, our visitor was gone.

The meadow was getting crowded.

17

EXPANDING GIRTH

I hadn't remembered Thelma's Way feeling so busy. When I had served my mission here, life seemed slow, and folks seemed to have nothing to do but mind their neighbors' business. Now, however, it looked as if everyone had something they had to get done. Sister Watson was campaigning for her safety road, Paul was gathering material for his weather shelter, President Heck was building his chair path, Leo and CleeDee were keeping watch and keeping away, and Toby Carver and Frank Porter were working on genealogy together. It hadn't started out as a team effort, but they quickly realized that their family tree had very few branches and that they were both heading up the same trunk. Roswell was painting and fixing up his wagon in preparation for selling ice cream. One of the biggest difficulties he had discovered was getting the ice cream from Virgil's Find to Thelma's Way before it melted. He had been trying out a number of different solutions. The one that seemed to work best so far was to have Pete pick it up for him and then run it really quickly back to Roswell's freezer. Narlette had joined a Girl Scout troop in Virgil's Find and was selling cookies like mad. She was getting large orders from everyone due to the fact that payment wasn't required until the cookies came in. People were happy to sign up for something they didn't have to shell out cash for now. When I tried to explain to Sister Washington that she would eventually have to pay for the sixty boxes of cookies that she had committed to, she called me silly and naive. Ed Washington was going to summer school part-time, and Jeff Titter had organized a Thelma's Way softball team that practiced every day in the meadow. Sure, they didn't have anyone to play against, but no one seemed to care. Digby was cutting hair with Wad, and Leonard was busy with his investigation/sales. He would call people into the boardinghouse, ask them if they wanted a road or weather shelter, and then flip off the lights and give them a ten-minute video presentation on selling prepaid phone cards. Teddy bought two, even though she had never actually used a phone in her life.

The town was busy.

It took some creative listening, but I found out that the girl I had spotted the day before was named Hope. Everyone who had met her seemed to think she was extraordinary. Sister Watson was so impressed with her that she offered her a room at her house to stay in while here.

I was very bothered by her. I had no reason to think about anyone besides Grace, but this Hope seemed to have a passkey to my mind. So it was with the intention of telling her to stay out of my head that I watched her walk over to the Girth River and decided to follow. Grace was in Virgil's Find helping her mother, and I felt that I should say a few words to this girl in an effort to confirm how much less she was than Grace.

I approached slowly, watching her throw rocks into the water. The great Girth pushed across the ground, sounding like a mushy train and keeping my presence a secret. I stepped closer to her.

"Pretty," I commented about the river.

"Breathtaking," she said with feeling.

"I'm Trust."

"Hi, Trust."

She walked a little farther down the banks. Amazingly, I followed.

"So why are you in Thelma's Way?" I asked.

"I'm doing some painting."

Awkward silence.

"So you paint?" I tried, desperately wanting this visitor to feel welcome.

"I do."

"That's neat." I was so smooth.

Hope turned to look closely at me. Her dark eyes were like portholes of poetic possibility.

"Do you paint?" she asked.

"Me?" I acted surprised. "No. I've never been any good at that sort of thing."

"Have you tried?"

"Oh, I've tried."

"Well, maybe you've just had the wrong teacher."

"That's possible," I agreed. "My art teacher in high

school didn't like me because I sat on one of her finches that she let fly around in class. How was I to know that it had perched itself on my seat?"

Hope just smiled.

"So how long do you think you'll stay here?" I asked.

"As long as it takes," she smiled.

"Are you painting something in particular?"

"Let's just say I'm working on a certain project," she replied.

"That's great."

"I'm glad you think so, Trust."

I felt so completely guilty over how much I enjoyed hearing her say my name that I almost ran to the meadow to find President Heck and confess.

"My middle name's Andrew," I offered lamely.

"Trust Andrew," she said.

I felt awful. I needed to tell her where I stood and how happy I was to be engaged to Grace. But, "If you ever need any help with anything, let me know" was what came out.

"You're all right, Trust," she smiled. She then walked off down the shore like a fading dream.

I stood there for a few minutes, wondering if it was possible to measure how amazingly pathetic I was. I would have been content to keep doing that for a while, but Toby Carver approached me and said, "Incredible, isn't she?"

I looked around nervously. "Sure, I guess."

"Worries me a little," he admitted. "How about you?"

"I have nothing to worry about," I said defensively.

"You're not nervous?"

"About Hope?" I asked in confusion.

"What about hope?" Toby stared.

"What were you talking about?"

"I was talking about the Girth River."

"What about it?" I said, looking at it.

"It's growing."

I had been so concerned about valiantly telling Hope where I stood that I had not even noticed that the Girth was almost twice its size. I was standing up on the meadow and the edge of the river was running right by me. When I had last been in Thelma's Way, the river was down below the meadow and outlined by sand and limestone-covered banks. There were no banks to be seen. Even in heavy summer runoff I had never seen it like this.

"Why is it growing?"

"Don't know," Toby answered. "More water, I guess. It's been rising for a while. It's almost impossible to paddle across anymore. I haven't been to the other side since Roger's accident."

"Roger Williams?" I asked.

"Yeah," Toby said with excitement. "Do you know him?"

"I think so," I said with confusion. "Why was he here? And what accident?"

"He worked for a paper or something," Toby tried to remember. "He came out here to write a book."

"He did?"

"I was going to be on the front cover," Toby bragged.

"You were?"

"Well, if I found the Book of Mormon. He really wanted us to find it so he could write about it."

"Really?" I said, beginning to get a glimpse of my father's real motive.

"He made us all kinds of deals," Toby went on. "He wanted that book. I guess it was real important to his research."

I was sick. I felt like I had just had my stomach removed, stomped on, and shoddily put back. My dad didn't come here to see where I had served. He came to make a buck. I couldn't believe it. He had tricked the people I loved into searching for it. I should have known. He hadn't changed. He had simply been trying to cover his tracks.

"He was a great guy," Toby added. "How do you know him?"

"I don't," I said sadly. "I thought he was someone else."

"Happens to me all the time."

I walked over to the boardinghouse and tried to call home. No one answered. My smooth life was beginning to ripple.

18

BITING HER TONGUE

Cindy could get the hang of this. She was blown away at how much power her good looks and pretend smiles could achieve. Fake could move mountains. People were much easier to manipulate when she acted as if she were a kind and caring human being. Yes, Operation Trust was running smoothly. Sure, he had not shown signs of great intelligence yet, but Cindy felt that in time he would be a worthy devotee and eternal companion.

Despite her successes, however, Cindy was suffering. Living with Sister Watson was as great a trial as any person had ever been faced with. The woman was a fossil, a busybody, and a moral vigilante all rolled into one. She was the kind of person that Cindy would gladly take apart if given the chance. But Cindy couldn't—not now. She had a role to play and a woman to ruin.

Grace.

How her man could be interested in such a person Cindy just couldn't comprehend. But then again, all good stories needed some bland tart that the man could eventually lose interest in without anyone's caring or mourning her loss. Cindy would make this entire dumb town not only forget, but also run out, Grace. She was in the way, simple as that.

Cindy pulled out her sleeveless dress and perfect sandals. Tomorrow she would turn up the heat. After all, even she had her limits. It's not like she could wait around forever in this sour pit of society. She needed to get Trust, get out, and then parade him in front of everyone who had ever done her wrong.

It was going to be one long parade.

19

IDLE HANDS

I don't know what it was. Hope came to town, and suddenly Grace had reason to be busy and away from me, leaving me with idle hands and a one-track mind. Thursday, Grace went with her mother to Collin's Blight for an overnight craft show that Patty Heck was participating in. I asked to go, but Grace insisted that I stay here and enjoy myself.

She could be so cruel.

I walked up to the Heck home and tried to have a conversation with President Heck concerning my father, but he was so preoccupied with his chair path that he couldn't seem to focus on anything else.

"Do you remember Roger Williams?"

"Trust, will you hand me that board?"

"I was just wondering if you could tell me a few things about him," I said, handing him his wood.

"I didn't realize how quickly this stuff sets up." He

ignored me. "I had to chisel out the dog's tail after he let it lay too long."

Realizing this wasn't the best time to be asking him questions, I went to the boardinghouse and tried to keep myself busy. While I was hanging out on the porch with Roswell, Hope walked up and kindly offered to teach me how to paint. I declined, lying about having promised Ed Washington to help him out with something.

"With what?" Hope smiled.

As if fate wasn't messing with me enough already, Ed passed by at that exact moment. Poor Ed couldn't even look at Hope without hyperventilating.

"Hello, Ed," she cooed. "Are you going to take Trust from me?"

That really threw him for a loop. Hope tried to explain.

"Trust said he was going to help you out today."

"Remember how I said that?" I begged.

"Not really," Ed shrugged. "But I have been wanting to get to work on my idea."

"Yes," I exclaimed. "That's what you said. You needed help with your idea."

"What idea is that, Ed?" Hope asked, brushing his arm with her finger.

It took Ed a couple of minutes to catch his breath.

"I wanted to build a catapult so that we can fling things to the other side of the Girth. The river's getting too wide to cross."

Hope smiled. "Sounds important."

"Yeah," I sighed, wishing I wasn't so valiant.

As soon as she was gone, Ed took a couple of deep

breaths and then promised to meet me near the Girth in thirty minutes. We worked late into the afternoon building a catapult. The idea was ridiculous, and I kept trying to explain to Ed how you could fling certain things across the river but you could never, ever, fling people. Every time I tried to drive this point home, he looked disappointed and crushed.

Despite its impracticality, it was actually kind of nice to have something constructive to work on. We fastened a long telephone pole that Ed had found in Virgil's Find to some wheels and a wood base with a catch and hook to pull the beam down. The catapult would have been worthless if it had not been for the gigantic spring that Roswell had won in a bet. It had come from some huge piece of equipment somewhere. It was powerful, and when that pole was cranked down and set into place, the tension was so great I was certain that Ed's catapult could fling anything anywhere. It was early evening before we were done.

"Let's test it," Ed said happily.

"All right, but not with a person."

Once again Ed seemed bummed. People began to gather, offering suggestions of what should be our guinea pig—guinea pig being an actual suggestion from Lupert. Bags of trash and porch chairs were considered, but we went with an old plastic ice chest of Roswell's that he was planning to take to the dump soon anyway. Pete thought we should load the ice chest with something that would explode, but we passed on that. We put the empty ice chest on the pole's mitt and Ed took hold of the release rope. We had a good-sized audience, so I called on Digby Heck to give us a drum roll.

He did.

Let me just say that we had dramatically under-estimated the spring. Ed pulled the rope and the giant pole flipped forward so fast that it pulled up the entire base and flung itself into the ground, smashing the ice chest into a million bits with a noise not unlike that of a planet giving birth. Dust exploded everywhere as the ground wobbled like a disturbed water bed. Pieces of rubber shrapnel from the cooler flew through the air, stinging and wounding almost everyone in attendance, and dirt rained down and covered us all. Luckily, there were no serious injuries, but Roswell sure threw a fit over the destroyed ice chest that he was going to take to the dump anyway.

"I'm glad no one was standing in front of it," Ed said in awe.

"It's got a few kinks." I tried to brush myself off.

"It's got potential," Leonard Vastly said. I hadn't noticed that he had been there or that he was standing right behind me. I would have jumped, but I was so used to Leonard's popping up in my life that it hardly fazed me anymore.

We worked long into the night fixing our creation. Pete and Leonard stayed around to help, and Frank Porter lent us a hand until he got a really bad splinter and went home. Pete and I tightened down the spring adjuster and took out some screws that were keeping the give of the spring too loose.

"Save these," I said to Pete, while lying on the ground

and unscrewing them. "We might need to put them back later."

"Where should I put them?" he asked as if confused.

"Put them in your pockets."

"I don't have any front pockets," he informed me. "I cut out the bottom of them so that I could stick my arms down in and scratch my legs in private."

I shook my head. "Put them in the back ones then."

"The front of my legs ain't the only things that get itchy."

We secured the base and made corrections where we thought they were necessary. By the time we were done, it was too dark out to test it properly. Ed whined, however, until we agreed to give it just one fling.

"We need something to use," I said.

"I've got just the thing," Leonard volunteered.

A few minutes later he came back with a thirty-pound medicine ball. The only time I had ever seen one before was at the gym back in Southdale.

"Where'd you get that?" I asked.

"It's a long story," Leonard said while setting it on the catapult.

"We might not be able to find it once it's flung," I warned him.

"That's okay," he waved. "I've got a couple more."

I turned to Ed. "Fire."

He pulled the rope, and the giant spring propelled that ball through the air at such a breakneck speed that I lost sight of it until it whizzed by the almost-full moon.

"Wow," Leonard whistled. "That thing could toss a mule to the Heck house."

There wasn't much else to say, except maybe that Grover Fairfield, a carpenter who lived across the river and deep in the woods, now had a new, though unexpected, entryway in the front of his house.

"This could come in handy," Leonard added.

"How?" I questioned with a smile.

"I can think of a thousand things that I would simply like to fling away."

"A thousand," Ed said in awe, as if contemplating such a high number made him dizzy.

"I don't know," I wondered. "It sort of makes me nervous to have something like this lying around."

"Want me to shoot it up?" Pete asked, pulling out one of his guns.

"No way," Ed hollered. "This is my creation. My creation," he repeated, having so liked the sound of it.

Pete put his gun away, and we called it a night.

All right. That's not completely true. Pete put his gun away, and they called it a night. Me? I walked across the meadow and stepped into a big old pile of complications.

20

THE DEAD MAKE LOUSY CHAPERONES

The night was vacant, the moon making the surroundings look two-dimensional and thin—I breathed with caution, afraid to blow the dark away. Everyone had turned in. Even the boardinghouse looked unusually dead. Before I made it there, however, I was stopped by the sound of someone's calling my name.

"Trust."

I really didn't want to look.

"Hope?"

She was standing a few feet away and wearing shorts and a billowy shirt. I tried not to notice her amazing knees.

"I guess Ed's idea was a success," she said soothingly, stepping up so close to me that if I were wearing a tie she could have been straightening it.

I tried to step back, but her aura held me like a net.

"Can we talk for a minute?" she asked, filling my personal space with her presence.

"It's kind of late," I tried, looking around for someone to save me from myself.

We were all alone.

"It won't take long," she pouted.

It was one powerful pout. I looked over at the cemetery and figured it was as good a place to converse as any. I prayed silently that the spirits of those who were dead might act as chaperones.

"Let's go to the cemetery," I suggested.

"Oh, you're bad, Trust," she cooed, lightly tapping my chest.

"I'm not really," I pleaded.

She ignored me, walking over to the small gate by the bronze statue of Thelma. I had to follow, seeing how the whole cemetery thing was my "bad" idea. I wanted us to sit down by the Watson mausoleum, seeing how dead Bishop Watson's corpse was lying in there. He had been my bishop when I first came out on my mission, and I needed him now. But as I tried to sit, Hope took my hand and pulled me to the back of the cemetery by the river. The Girth River was spilling up into the cemetery, its border practically touching the tombstones.

"It's so much prettier back here," she insisted.

I suppose if your definition of pretty is sitting by a large river under the moonlight, in a deserted—except for the dead—cemetery with a girl of unfathomable beauty, then it was all right. We sat down on the chairs that had been cemented at the head of Feeble and Roswell's graves. I had helped dig the graves. Feeble's was full, but Roswell's coffin was empty because he had been presumed translated at that point. We had used their favorite porch chairs as headstones. It was much less expensive and provided a nice place to sit while visiting their graves. At the moment I cursed our frugality and practicality.

The one nice thing was that since the chairs were permanently planted, Hope and I couldn't scoot too close to each other.

"I like it here," Hope began.

"Yeah," I said, trying to hold back my charm.

"So you served a mission here?" she asked.

"I did."

"Did you enjoy it?"

"Um, hum."

"You're quite the talker," she laughed.

"I'm engaged," I pleaded, as if she were some terrorist torturing me for details.

Hope laughed again.

"I know. I've seen her," she said nicely. "She's beautiful. I've always thought red hair was so pretty. Me, I'm stuck with this mop."

"It's not a mop," I said with way too much I'm-totally-in-awe-of-your-earth-shattering-beauty in my voice.

"Thanks, Trust."

"So how did you know about Thelma's Way?" I asked.

"My father was an explorer. He came through here many years ago. He would always talk about how beautiful the Girth River was and how perfectly secluded this place is. I wanted to see it for myself before he dies."

"Is he sick?" I asked.

"Yes," she said with emotion. "While scaling the Himalayas he broke his back. He was trying to save a child trapped under an avalanche. He broke his back falling off an ice shelf. Even with his injuries he dug the child out and brought him back to safety. He collapsed after the experience, his body was so weak from the rescue. He probably would have been okay, but he got pneumonia, and now the doctors are giving him no more than a couple of months to live. That's why I'm here painting, Trust. I want to bring the pictures home to him so that he can get one last look at this land that he loved."

We were silent for a few minutes while nature did everything it could to make this as uncomfortable for me as possible. The river shimmered, and a cool breeze brushed past us while the theater of the sky dropped shooting stars like it was the end of the world.

"What about you?" I asked, wanting to talk about something that would distract us from our environment. "Is there a someone in your life?"

"There was." She answered so sadly that I wanted to wrap my arms around her and make everything better. "I'm sorry," she tried to laugh. "It's just that I've never talked to anybody about it before. I don't know what it is about you, Trust. I just want to open up. I feel like I've known you before."

"Thanks, I guess."

"You guess?"

"Thanks." I still guessed.

"He was a Spaniard," she spilled. "His name was Rolio. We met at an art exhibit in Paris."

"You've been to Paris?"

"Sure," Hope waved it off. "We fell madly in love. One thing led to another, and he proposed to me at the pyramids in Egypt right after he bought me this necklace. I said yes, of course. I was in love, Trust."

She had such a nice way of throwing my name around. Hope leaned over and showed me her necklace. Her shoulder brushed my arm.

"It was made by an Egyptian woman with no arms. She actually makes these with her feet and mouth. It takes her a year to make just one. There are no more than fifteen in existence."

"With her feet?" I questioned.

"With her feet."

A group of six deer walked by us to the right. They stopped and stared at us, their eyes catching the light of the moon. An owl hooted, and they walked away.

"Those deer remind me of him," she went on. "He was the head of the international animal rights group. Sadly, I think he cared for creatures more than he cared for me."

"So it didn't work out?" I asked. "You and this guy."

"Rolio left me the day before our wedding for a woman he met on the subway in England."

"I'm sorry."

"It's all right," Hope said, brushing tears from her eyes. "I know something better will come along. I've just got to have faith."

She was so spiritual.

"Enough about me," she turned to face me. "Tell me about you and Grace."

"There's not much to say," I said lamely. "We met just over there by that tree stump. And I asked her to marry me under a bridge in Southdale."

"How wonderful," she said mercifully.

"Yeah," I said, suddenly embarrassed about Grace's and my relationship.

"I'm sure she's everything you've ever wanted in a girl."

"She is great," I confirmed.

"I hope you two are very happy together."

"We are," I said with less conviction than I needed.

"Trust, can I tell you something?"

"Sure," I answered cautiously, shifting on Feeble's head-stone.

"I really shouldn't," she hesitated. "But you're being so open with me. It's going to sound silly, but when I first saw you I wished so badly that you might be free. There was just something in the way you stood that made me like you right off. It must have been love at first sight," she joked. "Just my luck, I fall for the married guy."

"Engaged," I shouldn't have added.

Hope smiled. "Trust, you really are great. You make Rolio look like nothing."

The compliments didn't hurt.

"I just wish I had met you earlier," she said.

"Me too," I heard myself say.

I couldn't believe it. Grace was my everything. Sure, Hope was knock-your-socks-off, make-every-other-woman-in-the-world-feel-bad-about-her-self-image beautiful. But she honestly had nothing on Grace.

I looked over at the tree stump where Grace and I had met. I could still remember her face and how she looked when she woke me up. Our relationship had not always been easy, or even possible for that matter. But we had gone through a lot together, discovering in the process that we were made for each other. I had taken Grace back to Southdale, where she had seemed to change my entire town. Now here we were, waiting out the short while before our wedding. I started thinking about how smart short engagements were. A giggling couple that was walking through the cemetery interrupted my thoughts.

It was the Knapworths, and they weren't exactly tracting.

"Hello, Trust. Hello, Grace," Sister Knapworth said happily. "Whoa, that's not Grace," she suddenly noticed.

I stood up quickly, looking as guilty as an alcoholic surrounded by empties. "You two know Hope, don't you?"

"Haven't had the pleasure." Sister Knapworth eyed her.

"Nice to meet you." Hope stood, looking far too beautiful to be alone with.

"Where's Grace?" Elder Knapworth asked, obviously not happy about what he saw.

"She's in Collin's Blight with her mother."

"Oh," they both said.

"We were just talking," I defended. "Hope's new here and needed someone to talk to. Isn't that right?" I asked her.

"Trust was just keeping me company," she said, putting her arm through mine. I shook it off.

"I wasn't keeping anyone company," I insisted.

"We'd better go," they said.

"Don't go," I begged.

"I don't know what's going on, Trust," Brother Knapworth said righteously. "But it looks wrong."

"There's no wrong going on here."

"Good night, Hope," he said. "I hope the graves you're standing on didn't witness anything inappropriate."

"I really should go too," Hope said. "See you later, Trust."

Everyone left me. I was completely alone with myself. I have to say I could barely stand the company.

21

CANDY FROM A BABE

Cindy closed the door to the spare bedroom in Sister Watson's house and smiled. It was the first honest and genuine thing she had done since she had arrived here.

She was happy in a wicked way.

The cemetery had been the perfect place to unleash the beginning of her plan—how nice of Trust to have suggested it. She couldn't believe how closely the whole incident had mirrored that of the current book she was reading, *Digging for Love*, an account of Dusty Earth's obsession with a long-dead grave digger named Newly Tilled. It was obvious that fate was with Cindy.

This was going to be so much easier than she had anticipated. Trust was breakable. It was just a matter of time before he was completely fooled into falling for her. Sure, it would take a while, but he was a weak link in a short chain. The only thing Cindy need do was wait. She couldn't push this too fast. She hated the fact that this course of action required her having to hang around

Thelma's Way a little longer than she had originally thought, but the sacrifice would be worth it.

Trust would be hers.

She couldn't believe how willing these people were to accept her. She had been given a free room and unchecked kindness from everyone. She could manipulate these simple minds like clay—pushing and pounding them into flat doormats that she could walk over.

Her next move was to back off a bit to give Trust some time to think about her. Much like the brilliant sea stewardess Glinda from her book *Salted Passion*, she had set the bait and would now wait to throw the net.

Cindy could be patient this once. After all, once Trust was hers, she would never have to be patient again.

22

THE PAIN OF SEPARATION

Friday morning I was awakened by a loud knock on my door. I rolled out of bed and opened it to find an angered Teddy Yetch holding an empty metal dish.

"I was going to make you a pan of Tickberry bread, but after hearin' what you done in the cemetery I decided against it." Teddy threw the pan down and stomped off.

"Wait, Sister Yetch . . ." It was too late.

So the Knapworths had squealed. The word was probably all over town by now. I thought about writing a letter to the Knapworths' mission president and telling on them for all the kissing and hand-holding they had been doing. What kind of people tell on another person for something that wasn't even what the people thought it was? There was another knock on the door. I opened it up expecting to find Sister Watson wagging her finger at me. It was President Heck.

I half wished for the finger.

"President," I said nervously, forgetting that he was the same person who could get excited about finding a rolling kitchen chair.

"Can I come in?" he asked calmly.

"Sure."

He stepped in and closed the door behind him. He walked to the window and looked down on the meadow. "That catapult sure is impressive," he said, trying to make small talk.

"Ed did most of it," I explained.

President Heck turned and sat down on the desk chair next to the bed. He then sighed as if there were air at the bottom of his toes that needed to come out.

"You know, Trust, I have always thought of you as a son," he said. "If there is anything you would like to tell me, I'm always there for you."

"Thanks."

"Anything."

"Thanks, again."

"I mean it. Say you're having a problem with stealing or morality," he emphasized. "I'd be open to listen."

"I'd be happy to talk."

"So do you have something to say?"

"Actually, I'm glad you mentioned it," I said, trying to keep this conversation light. "I stole a pack of gum from the store in Virgil's Find."

"What flavor?" he asked solemnly.

"Strawberry."

"That's my favorite."

I think he was expecting me to give him a piece.

"I'm just kidding," I clarified.

He seemed disappointed.

"Listen, Trust, I heard some things," he said, making eye contact with me. "Seems folks are talking about you kissing Hope at the cemetery last night."

"I never kissed Hope," I guffawed.

"So it's not true?" he asked with relief.

"I went to the cemetery," I tried to explain. "But I certainly didn't kiss her."

"Trust."

"Honest," I insisted. "I'm in love with, and engaged to, your daughter."

"Going to the cemetery seems like a silly way to show that."

"Hope wanted to talk," I explained. "It's no different than me going there with Nippy Ward or Sister Watson."

"Have you seen Nippy lately?" he asked.

"No."

"It's different."

"You have to believe me. Nothing happened."

"Hope's a beautiful girl," he said as if he wasn't listening to me. "I'm not too sure why she's even here. But then again, I'm not too sure about a lot of things. But I know my daughter loves you. And I know that this isn't going to make her happy."

"I didn't do anything."

"I'll spread the word that you're innocent. But you'd better talk to Grace before someone else does."

"I will."

"It's too late. I've already told her," he confessed.

I wished the window were open so that I could throw myself out.

"She's anxious to talk to you."

"Where is she?"

"Downstairs."

I wanted to talk to President Heck about my father, but I felt that Grace took first priority. I tossed some more clothes on and ran downstairs to look for her. Everyone there threw me dirty looks.

"We were just talking," I shouted at a scowling Roswell.

"Talk is cheap," he threw back, misusing a common cliché.

I couldn't see Grace anywhere. I walked out into the meadow and over by the Girth River calling her name. The only response I got was when Frank Porter told me that it served me right that I couldn't find her. I felt awful, but I was also amazed at how wide the Girth River was. The burnt bridge was now covered with water at the ends. With no sign of Grace, I headed up to the Heck house. No one was there, but I was lucky enough to get a good glimpse of the work President Heck had put into his chair path. I ran back to the boardinghouse and waited around. I was hoping that Grace would simply appear and that I could explain this all away. She never showed up. I couldn't even find President Heck.

I leaned against the rail of the porch and sighed.

"Women," Leonard commented, suddenly by my side.

"I guess you heard?"

"I've always had good ears."

"Nothing happened," I insisted.

"Listen, Trust, you don't need to tell me," Leonard sniffed. "In the monkey world males never settle down with just one mate."

"This isn't the monkey world," I pointed out.

"Well, then I guess you were out of line."

"I didn't do anything."

"Keep telling yourself that," Leonard said, taking off one of his shoes and looking down in the toe as if searching for a bothersome pebble. "I know everyone's always blabbing about how people shouldn't lie to themselves, but I'm all for it. Heck, my life would be sorely lacking if I didn't have my fabricated reality."

Leonard's actual reality was so skewed and absurd that I couldn't fathom his fabricated one. I changed the subject.

"How's the investigation?" I asked.

"People got a lot of problems." He slipped his shoe back on.

"That's the truth."

"I could be serving a lot more effectively if my house wasn't four miles away."

"It's not like you're living there," I pointed out.

"It's the principle of the thing."

"Where are you staying?"

"I'm a private person, Trust."

I left it at that, going inside and drowning my miseries in a gallon of ice cream that Pete had not been quick enough to save. By seven that evening Grace still had not shown up. I had the distinct impression that she was mad at me.

23

WRITTEN BY THE FINGER OF . . .

I got up early Friday morning to look for Grace. With the directional help of Lupert Carver, I found my way to the small cabin that she used to hide out in. It was empty, with no sign of recent life. I couldn't believe that Grace was working so hard to avoid me. Desperate to get my mind off her being mad at me, I called my home from the boardinghouse to see if I could find out more about my father and his time here. My mom answered—I had forgotten that there was a time difference. I was a little concerned, seeing how my mother wasn't an easy person to talk to on the phone even when she was alert.

"I can call back later," I volunteered.

"This is fine," she said, sounding like a martyr. "I'm already awake."

"I'm so sorry."

"What's done is done."

"Is Dad awake?"

"I doubt it, but I have no way of knowing, seeing how he's not here," she informed me.

"Where is he?" I asked, wondering if something was wrong.

"He took Abel and Margaret fishing. They won't be home until Tuesday."

"Mom, did you know that when Dad was missing all those months ago he was here in Thelma's Way?"

"Now why would he go there?"

"I don't know," I answered. "But I think it's because he wanted their Book of Mormon."

"That makes sense," she said. "He has sure taken to the scriptures lately."

"No," I tried to explain. "He was after their first edition. It's worth quite a bit."

"Did he find it?"

"I don't think so. But I'd like to talk to him about it. Why do you think he wouldn't tell us that he was here?"

"He's a private man," she yawned.

"That's nothing to hide."

"Maybe he wanted it to be a surprise."

"I'm surprised all right. He came here to take something that didn't belong to him."

"I'm sure that's not true."

"I've got witnesses."

"Those mountain people are unreliable."

"Mom."

"Trust, your father is a wonderful man. Whatever happened in Thelma's Way was obviously good for him."

"Will you tell him I called?"

"I'll write it down when I get up. How's Grace?"

"She's fine," I lied.

"We picked up your wedding announcements," my mother informed me.

"How do they look?" I asked halfheartedly.

"I must say, I wish you had worn a different shirt. I sent them out to you to see what you think."

"You sent them all?"

"Some of the pictures could be different."

"Mom, it's the same pose."

"Just look them over and let me know."

"I really should go. Sorry about waking you up."

"These things happen," she said groggily. "Tell Grace hello."

"I will as soon as I see her."

"Oh, there was something I was supposed to tell you," my mother remembered. "It had something to do with Sister Cravitz."

"Sister Cravitz?"

"She was concerned about something."

"What is it?"

"I can't remember," she said. "Maybe it will come to me when I'm more awake."

"Good-bye, Mom."

"Good-bye, Trust."

I hung up and wondered why my life was suddenly so muddled. I saw Hope enter the boardinghouse. Roswell, still in his pajamas, asked her if he could help. I quickly

129

slipped out the back door before she noticed me. I wanted none of that.

Out back there was a man I didn't recognize washing up in the rain barrel. He had a square neck and a bean-shaped head. He was wearing a bow tie and white button-down shirt that looked far from freshly laundered. His round shoulders seemed to dip twice before they connected with his blocky neck. He peered up at me with eyes that looked big and spread—as if they were being viewed with a magnifying glass.

He said, "Whumpeethuuuuh."

"Hello," I said back.

"Leempeerdaaaaz. Hatheeeepattee."

I had no idea who this person was, or what he was saying.

"Leempeerdaaaaz. Hatheeeepattee!" he said again and with feeling.

"Nice to meet you too."

He shook his wet head at me. I looked up at the sky and pretended to know what he was saying.

"Could be. You never know about the weather."

"Nuuverdimple," he laughed. "Iradira dadddle."

I thought I had guessed right, and he was agreeing.

"And your name was?" I asked.

"Wooosdhdaay."

"Nice to meet you." I stepped away from him and around the boardinghouse. Jerry Scotch was there, filling his water bottle with water from the spigot.

"Did you meet my uncle?" he asked, pointing in the direction from where I had just come.

"That was Winton?"

"Didn't you say howdy?"

"I did, but to be honest I couldn't understand a word he was saying."

Jerry looked relieved. "I thought it was just me. He got spooked by a couple of the neighbor kids back in Georgia last Halloween. Now he can't seem to say anything clearly."

"What'd the kids do?"

"He told me, but I couldn't understand him."

"Have you seen Grace?" I asked.

"Nope, I just got up," he answered. "I was up all night wondering . . . what's all that noise?" he interrupted himself, nodding toward the meadow where the yelling was coming from. "Sounds a little like Wad screaming."

I walked around the boardinghouse and spotted Wad off in the distance standing on top of his haircut shack and waving his arms. He would scream for a moment and then point down at the meadow with great vigor. I jogged over to him to see what was the matter.

"Wad, what's . . ."

"Look," he pointed.

Toby joined us, holding his Ace bandage loose and ready. I looked at the meadow where Wad was pointing but saw nothing more significant than the rotted wagons and tall weeds.

"I can't see nothing," Toby said for me.

Wad crouched down on top of his shack, threw his knees out from under him, and then rolled down to the ground. He quickly laced his fingers together and motioned for me to step into his palms so that he could hoist me up. I saw no reason not to. From up on top of the shack I could see the entire meadow clearly. I still couldn't understand what he had been so excited about.

"Do you see it?" he yelled up.

"See what?"

"The writing," he gulped. "The letters?"

I looked again and instantly saw exactly what he was talking about. In the center of the meadow the weeds were trampled down perfectly to spell

MATS

"Wow." I tried to sound excited.

"Let me see," Toby pleaded.

I climbed down and helped Toby up.

"What's it mean?" he asked, his dark eyes trying to figure it out.

By now others had come, everyone wanting to see what was stamped into the meadow.

"How'd it happen?" Sister Watson asked.

"I don't know," Wad would answer to every question.

"I'm sure someone walked it out as a joke," I offered.

"Trust, you always were the last to believe," Teddy Yetch scoffed.

"No one could have walked that out," Paul said loudly while taking his turn up top. "There's no connecting trample points."

"Trample points?" I laughed.

Digby and Ed ran out to where the letters were and began to examine the ground.

"Paul's right," Ed yelled.

I felt this could all be settled simply by asking if anyone had done it. Aside from Paul, folks in Thelma's Way were honest to an additional fault. No one had any trouble speaking exactly what was on his or her mind or fessing up to any manner of deed.

"Does anyone know who did this?" I asked.

"It was him," Sister Watson gasped.

"Who?" I asked.

"Him," she repeated. "The same him that's been stealing our things and terrorizing our town."

Everyone became instantly afraid, looking around as if they were shoplifters checking for prying eyes. I spotted Hope, one Toby down and a full Pete over.

"Well, what's it mean?" Teddy asked.

"He's gonna stomp us like mats," Toby offered.

Everyone looked around and nodded their heads, impressed by Toby's interpretation.

"Maybe his name's Matt, and he's staking claim to our meadow," Tindy tried.

"Don't be silly," Sister Watson scolded. "This is clearly a sign of how much we need the road. There could be a whole squad team in here by now if we had more than just that dirt path to plod on."

"Maybe you did this, Mavis," Paul said bitterly. "This is just some sort of trick to win you your road."

"Well, I never," Sister Watson whined. "I'm trying to help the town progress."

"Don't get all high and flighty," Paul growled. "We all know what you would do to get that street."

President Heck joined our group and began to counsel Paul and Sister Watson. They were slow to heed. I was about to jump in and try to smooth things over when I noticed Leonard standing no more than two inches behind me and breathing his garlic breath up my neck.

"Looks like things are heating up," he observed. "I'll tell you one thing, this town sure knows how to make things more confusing than they already are."

"That's true."

"I could get used to it," he added.

"So what do you think did it?" I asked Leonard.

"Hard to say," he replied. "I read once where certain ducks will settle in long grass to lay their eggs."

"So you think some settled here?"

"Do you?" he asked.

"No."

"You may have a point."

"People," President Heck shouted, "we need to establish the time this mystery occurred. Who was the last person in the meadow yesterday?"

"I walked through it at about ten to get some water from the Girth," Tindy said.

"Anyone later than that?" President Heck asked.

"Elder Knapworth and I took a stroll around it at about ten thirty," Sister Knapworth admitted. "We were out working on our . . ."

"Discussions," Elder Knapworth said for her.

"All right," President Heck said. "I was in the meadow this morning at around six gathering bags of concrete. So

134

the deed must have happened sometime between ten thirty and six o'clock."

"I can help narrow it down even further," Jerry volunteered. "I spent a good three hours from about eleven to two, pacing back and forth in the center of the meadow and trying to work out a few women problems in my mind."

"Okay," Ricky nodded. "So it had to have happened between three and six."

I raised my hand.

"Trust?" President Heck acknowledged.

"Maybe we should ask Jerry where he was pacing," I suggested.

"In the middle," Jerry pointed. "About where the letters are."

"Shoot," Toby said. "If you had just stuck around a little while longer you could have seen who it was."

"Sorry," Jerry apologized.

"I think he did see who it was," I said.

"The glass is always half full to you, isn't it, Trust," President Heck said.

I was surprised I had to point so precisely to the truth for them. "Jerry must have stamped it out while he wandered around."

Everyone looked at each other, contemplating the significance of my words.

"Jerry can't spell," Roswell argued.

"He must have done it without knowing," I explained.

All eyes were on Jerry.

"I guess it could have been me," he shrugged.

Everyone booed and hollered, disappointed by the easily explainable answer. Toby tried to keep the mystery going.

"Maybe he was prompted to spell that out for us," he said, desperate to make his explanation still valid. "We could still be stomped like mats."

"No one's going to stomp us," President Heck said sadly, patting Toby on the back.

"Well, that's that," Leonard observed as everyone began to scatter.

"This place never ceases to amaze me," I replied.

Leonard tilted his long head at me. "I'd stay and chat, but I've got interviews to conduct."

The moment Leonard left, Hope approached me. She walked up so fast I didn't have time to turn and run.

"Hi, Trust."

"Hi," I said dispassionately, trying not to look right at her.

"I hope I didn't get you in trouble by talking with you last night."

"Don't worry about it."

"I guess Grace was mad."

"I don't know. I haven't had a chance to speak to her about it."

Hope ohhed.

"Well, if I can help, let me know," she added.

I wanted to let her know that she could help by leaving Thelma's Way so that I didn't become distracted again, but I didn't. I thanked her and wondered once again how one person could be so perfectly put together.

President Heck coughed behind me. I turned to face him.

"We were just talking," I explained.

"I know," he said. "I heard. How come you didn't talk to Grace yesterday?"

"When I went downstairs, she wasn't there."

"I wonder why she hung up." He scratched his head.

"She was on the phone?"

"Yeah. Didn't I say that?"

I put my head in my hands.

"She called to say she won't be back until tomorrow night," he went on. "Patty's craft show is going real well."

"Can I call her?"

"Sure, if they had a phone. They're staying at a campground with a bunch of other crafty women."

"I wish you hadn't told her about Hope and me."

"Me and Hope," he falsely corrected.

"Me and Hope, then."

"Trust, life is a series of choices."

I chose to spend the rest of the day watching TV in the boardinghouse and pretending like everything was going to work out just fine.

I'm not too terribly convincing.

24

HARD OF HERRING

Cindy had discovered one glitch and that was Winton
Scotch. Cindy had recognized him instantly. She had met
him at a singles function in Georgia, back before he
couldn't speak. He had had the nerve to ask Cindy out. It
was a disgusting thought, and Cindy had told him so. Then
she had keyed his truck out in the parking lot.

Cindy was certain that Winton knew just what kind
of person she really was. She took some comfort in his
current speech impediment, but she still felt it best to
avoid him altogether. Her plan could not be thwarted. If
anyone knew what she really was, she wouldn't stand
a chance. Not that she wasn't worlds better and more
beautiful than Grace. People just weren't smart enough to
always know it.

Cindy had put too much time and effort into all of this
to have some skeleton from her past ruin it. Winton would
need to be watched. If he proved to be a real problem,
Cindy would simply have to take care of it. There was

nothing she wouldn't do to make things work between her and Trust. If it meant getting rid of Winton or rubbing out Grace, Cindy would do it.

She was committed.

25

WORKED INTO A LATHER

He slipped up to the back of the large home and over behind the trash can with the large rock on its lid. He picked up the rock as if it were a pebble and set it down quietly on the ground. Once the lid was removed, he rummaged through the trash, looking for anything of value. There was no food or valuables, but there was a small crumpled picture of the redheaded girl he so admired. He smoothed it out under the moonlight and gazed affectionately at it. He would have considered it bounty enough if it had not been for the low growling coming from his stomach. He looked towards the chicken coop. They would be noisy gain, but well worth it.

He stepped over the odd cement path and squatted down by the latched door. The rusty hook whined as he lifted it up. The chickens began to murmur. He reached his hand into the shed and grabbed at anything that might be there. His big hands felt feathers and he squeezed.

A dog barked.

Momentarily startled, he dropped the chicken and looked towards the dark home. No lights came on. He pushed open the coop door and stomped in, feeling around for the chicken he had already silenced. The fowl went wild, screaming and clawing like toddlers on a tilt-a-whirl. He reached out and grabbed the first chicken he could catch. He shoved the bird into his bag and pushed out the door and into the open. A light blinked on in the large house, the window looking like a single eye searching for him.

He ran.

By the time two more windows were lit up and Ricky Heck was on the porch, he was long gone.

26

TRIAL AND ERROR

Saturday morning Leonard made an announcement on the steps of the boardinghouse. The gist of it was that he was tired of interviewing people, so it was time for a trial. He was also really disappointed in the poor sales he had experienced.

"I offered you folks a chance to get in on the ground floor," he chastised. "But that's neither here nor over there. Trial's set for this afternoon at three."

Justice moved swiftly in Thelma's Way.

I went up to the Heck home and helped President Heck with his path. We had to break up and redo a large section where he had gotten overanxious to try out his chair and had not waited until it was fully dry. The path really was taking shape. He had completed a ring around his house and the beginnings of two offshoots, one heading towards his garden and another towards the chickens.

"You know," he said as if deep in thought, "I bet I've got enough concrete to make a path all the way into town."

"You want to scoot yourself all that way?" I smiled.

"My knees might get a little sore, but my back would be great."

"So what happened to your head?" I asked, noticing a large bruise on the right side of his neck.

"Someone killed a few of my chickens last night," he explained. "By the time I got up and out here to see who it was, he was gone. Since I was up I helped myself to some leftover pie. I guess I didn't realize how tired I was," he said. "I fell asleep while eating my third piece and knocked my neck against one of Patty's good bar stools."

"Who was it?"

"I couldn't tell you," he admitted.

"Do you think it was you-know-who?"

"Could have been."

"Have you told Sister Watson?" I asked.

"No. She'd only get all fired up about it. She thinks that road would cure everything. She's got more drive for that project than I've ever seen her have. She seems a little sad, though," he said, as if he had given the idea a lot of thought.

"About what?" I asked.

"I guess I'd have to spend a night in her head to figure that out." He went back to mixing the cement.

The time seemed perfect to bring up my father.

"You know, there's something I've wanted to ask you," I said seriously.

"I've put on about thirty pounds," he answered. "But I've decided to go on that meat diet Jerry's been talking about."

143

"Actually, that wasn't what I wanted to know," I smiled.

"I have a problem with speaking before I really think about it," he smiled back. "What's on your mind?"

"Do you remember Roger Williams?" I asked.

"Of course."

"Well, he's my father," I said, expecting him to gasp.

"I know," he said, not missing a beat as he mixed.

"You knew?"

"I figured it out after he had his accident," he explained. "He was unconscious for a while, and I would sit by his bed and just stare at him. Well, it finally dawned on me that he looked too much like you not to be related. When he came to I was dying to ask him about it, but I figured he would tell me when he wanted to. I tested my idea by saying a bunch of real nice things about you and seeing how he'd react. He's mighty proud of you, Trust."

"Does anyone else know?" I asked, not wanting to become emotionally sidetracked.

"I don't believe so."

"Why didn't you tell me—or Grace?"

"I figured if you didn't know, it was something he needed to tell you."

"I can't believe it."

President Heck took a couple big handfuls of cement and threw them down in the wood frame he had constructed. "Your dad was hurt pretty bad," he commented.

"I heard the accident was pretty hairy."

"Sure it was, but he was hurt long before that motorcycle dragged him down river. He was confused, had a lot of dazedness in his eyes. Sort of like Mavis Watson," he said as if the comparison had just come to him. "Sort of like Mavis."

"I worry about his intentions for coming here," I confessed.

"Let it be, Trust," President Heck said. "He did a lot of good here. You saw what kind of attendance we get at church. That's because of him."

"I know, but . . ."

"No 'I knows.' Sometimes we gotta just drop what we know and go with what we don't."

We left it at that.

At two-thirty we cleaned up and headed out to the trial.

The boardinghouse was brimming with spectators and participants. A few folks were inside sitting on the windowsills, their posteriors hanging out.

I recognized Toby.

President Heck and I pushed our way inside. I found an empty foot of floor space up by the counter and next to Leonard. Leonard was wearing his black rain poncho and one of Sister Watson's light-colored wigs. Jerry Scotch was standing in front of the counter with his work uniform on. He had his arms crossed in front of him, keeping the peace. Due to their missionary tags, the Knapworths had been enlisted as additional security. I watched Jerry nod at them as if they all shared some sort of secret security brotherhood. Both Paul and Sister Watson were sitting on a long bench pushed up against the far wall. Next to them were six empty chairs.

The room was incredibly hot. Not only was it summer but the nonair-conditioned building was packed tight enough to make any fire inspector panic. I was envious of Toby and the fact that his backside was open to the outdoors as he sat perched in the window. At three o'clock on the dot Leonard stood up and began the proceedings.

"Residents of Thelma's Way," he addressed the crowd. "It is the very fabric of life that has woven us to this moment. I want you to know that I do not take my position lightly. I have been with you but a few days, and already I feel a part of you and this mess."

Narlette raised her hand.

"Yes?" Leonard asked.

"You've got something on your lip," she pointed out.

Leonard wiped at his mouth and continued. "A little background, if I may. I've sold Pre-law for a number of months and have seen every episode of Perry Mason ever made. I visited a real courthouse not long ago while fighting for my freedom to have a movable home. There I learned the hard lesson that real justice is a farce and we have no one to count on but ourselves. I promise you, however, that I won't let that experience taint my performance here. This problem is dear to my heart," he went on. "If you approve the road, I'll be able to bring my home into your town and live on free land. Again, don't think for a moment that this personal angle will affect my decisions here today. Any questions?"

"You've seen every Perry Mason?" Ed Washington asked in awe.

"Every one." Leonard looked around. "If there are no

146

other questions, we will continue. Sister Watson and Paul have already promised that they will abide nicely by whatever our decision here today is. So when we walk out of that door in a little while, I want this issue to be resolved."

"That means finished," Ed whispered to Frank.

"I know what *issue* means," Frank whispered back defensively.

"I have decided that this situation could best be served if we use a jury," Leonard went on. "Toby?"

Toby jumped down from the window and picked up a can sitting on the floor.

"I've put each of your names in that can," Leonard said. "At least those that I could remember." He pointed at Janet Bickerstaff. "Jolene?"

"Janet," she corrected.

"If Toby pulls out Jolene, that's you."

Wanna-be actress Janet reveled at the possibility of being someone else for a while.

"Toby, draw," Leonard commanded.

Toby stuck his hand in the jar and mixed it around. Then with a very dramatic flare he pulled a slip of paper out.

"Wad," he announced.

Wad stood, curtsied, and then held his arm up and waved.

"In the seat," Leonard pointed.

Wad dropped Miss Flitrey's hand and shuffled over to the jury box.

Toby drew again. "Pete."

Pete couldn't believe it. "Me?"

"You," Leonard confirmed.

"You work, and you struggle," Pete went on, "and suddenly everything falls together for you."

He took the seat directly behind Wad.

"Roswell," Toby hollered.

Paul smiled, knowing where Roswell stood on this issue at hand. Roswell took his place.

"Jolene," Toby screamed.

Janet Bickerstaff jumped up and moved to her mark.

Toby drew out another slip of paper. "Trust," he announced.

To be honest, I hadn't even considered the possibility of my making the jury.

"I'll pass," I waved.

"You can't just shirk off your civic duty," Leonard said with disappointment. "Unless you've got some pressing matter to attend to, you need to be up here."

"I'm biased."

"Don't be gross," Sister Watson snipped. "A courtroom is no place for levity."

"I'm for the road," I clarified. "I can't think of anything dumber than this weather shelter Paul wants to build."

"He'll do fine," Sister Watson told Leonard, happy with my bias.

"He's honest enough," Paul quipped. "I'll give him that."

"Besides," I added, "why can't you do both?"

"This is a court of law," Leonard said officially. "Let's not make a mockery of it. The two ideas are incompatible, and we're here to prove that."

I thought about arguing some more, but instead I walked up and took a seat next to Pete in the makeshift jury box.

"That's everyone," Toby announced.

A few people moaned about not being picked.

"But we need six jurors," Leonard reminded him.

"I held my name out so that I could be one," Toby informed him. He then walked over and sat directly in front of me.

Leonard put his hands behind his back and paced in front of us. He tisked, pulled at his eyebrows, and then turned to face the audience. "These six people are putting themselves on the line for you," he said. "If you're happy with the outcome, thank them. If you're sickened, well, you know where they live."

Leonard stepped behind the counter and picked up the small ironbased snow globe that Roswell had gotten from his cousin's pawn shop in Virgil's Find. The plastic scene within the snow globe was of a mule bucking over a carton of apples. When you shook it, snow flurried and the mule's back legs swung wildly. Leonard had chosen the curio as his mallet. He banged it on the counter, watched the snow flutter for a moment, and then called the court into session. I looked around at where I was and what I had gotten myself into. I was in for another unforgettable afternoon in Thelma's Way.

"Sister Watson, you may present your case," Leonard told her.

She stood up and smoothed down her wig. "Your honor," she said.

149

Leonard smiled, happy about the sound of that.

"We need a road," she began. "For years this town has struggled with moving to and from Virgil's Find. I can't begin to tell you how many times I've twisted an ankle or scraped a knee on that worn-out and unimproved trail."

"How many?" Toby asked, wanting to be an informed juror.

"I can't remember," Sister Watson snapped.

Toby leaned over and whispered to Wad, "That doesn't look good."

"May I continue, your honor?" Sister Watson asked.

"The jury will strike what Toby just said," Leonard informed us.

Pete reached out and smacked Toby in the back of the head. Oddly enough, Toby acted as if he deserved it. He then took out his Ace bandage and wrapped it around his head in case Pete was asked to strike him again.

"A road would improve our quality of life," Sister Watson went on. "We could get things faster and easier. Not only that but it would provide us with some much-needed conveniences. Now, I'm not that young," she pointed out, "so a big part of what I'm fighting for is for the future generations. I did one of those exit polls at the entrance of the boardinghouse a few days back, and it seems to me that everyone's a tad uncomfortable with being so isolated anymore. Jerry's done a fine job of serving as the law, but—no offense to Jerry—we need some real authority here. And we're not going to get any until we establish ourselves with a road. We need to face the fact that Thelma's Way might not always be just how it is."

150

Roswell raised his hand.

"Yes," Leonard said.

"Can I say something?"

"Sure."

Roswell stood. "I think she's wrong." Roswell sat.

"Thank you," Leonard said. "Continue," he nodded towards Sister Watson.

"As I was saying, I have surveyed a great number of people, and most of them want this road," she reiterated.

Paul raised his hand. "Your honor, can we approach the bench?"

Leonard waved them over. Roswell, Toby, Pete, Janet, and Wad all wandered over as well so that they could hear what they were whispering about. It was unnecessary, really, seeing how I could hear their talking from where I sat.

"Mavis throwing out facts like that is unconstitutional and damaging," Paul whispered fierily. "If the jury knows that more people want a road, then the jury's going to go with that."

"He makes a good point," Leonard considered.

"You're the judge," Sister Watson said, obviously and oddly still somewhat taken with Leonard.

"The jury will discount everything Mavis Watson has said," Leonard ruled.

The jury made it back to their seats, and Sister Watson spoke.

"I rest my case."

"I don't blame you," Leonard observed. "I get tired of standing. Paul, you're up."

Paul stood and said calmly, "My case is this. I want to build a giant covering for the meadow. It will keep out rain, it will keep out snow, and it will have a small gold plaque that reads, 'Built for the community by Paul Leeper.' I don't want to die without leaving a little something to remember me by."

"You gotta admire his conviction," Roswell whispered to us.

"We don't want no cover," Frank Porter hollered out.

Everyone began to talk. Leonard slammed his snow globe. "One more outburst like that and I'll make Jerry stand by you," he scolded Frank. "Continue, Paul."

"The weather is a funny thing." Paul scratched his nose. "Who knows what heaven's going to toss at us in this unsteady time. You seen the Girth going all weird on us. Well, I think it makes sense to have some sort of protection. I personally am more frightened of what Mother Nature's going to toss down than some made-up spook that's been pestering us. Besides," Paul went on, "I've already begun to gather up some of the materials needed to build my shelter."

It was a powerful argument. No one in Thelma's Way liked to do unnecessary work. It seemed almost sinful to disregard the small effort that Paul had already exerted.

"But I wanna drive a car before I die," Teddy yelled.

Again Leonard whacked the globe. Pete leaned over and whispered to me, "I got an extra gun if things get ugly."

"Order!" Leonard demanded. "Do you have anything more to say?" he asked Paul.

"Not at the moment."

"The jury will remove themselves to Roswell's room for deliberation," Leonard instructed. "You are to talk to no one but yourselves about this. Is that clear?"

We all nodded and then got up. Once we were in Roswell's room, Jerry Scotch closed the door and stood guard outside.

"What do we do?" Roswell asked.

"Decide who made the best case," I said, sitting down on Feeble's old bed.

"They were both a little weak, if you ask me," Toby said, the Ace bandage on his head making him look like a wise swami.

"Let's take a vote," Janet suggested. "Who wants the road?"

Janet, Pete, Wad, and I raised our hands.

"Who wants the shelter?"

Roswell raised his. We all looked at Toby.

"I'm undecided," he said. "In a perfect world, we could have both."

"Well, this ain't no perfect world," Roswell spat. "I've got a spongy right eye and spider veins, but you don't see me complaining."

I did.

There was a tap on Roswell's window. We looked over to see Leonard rapping. Pete hoisted the window up.

"How's it going?" Leonard asked.

"We're deliberating," I said.

"Any idea on which way it will go?" he asked.

"Hard to say." Toby scratched his head. "What do you think should happen?"

"I'm for the road," Leonard restated. "But hey, you guys go with what you think."

Pete turned around and looked at us all. "Should we just go with the road?"

"Why not," Toby gave in.

"Not me," Roswell said defiantly. "I don't want no slick in-and-out to the town I love."

"You could get your ice cream home before it melted," I pointed out.

"Give us just a minute," Roswell said, pulling the blind on Leonard. "I think we should take one of them there secret ballots," he whispered to us.

"Do you have any paper?" Toby asked.

"There's a stack of old napkins in my top drawer," Roswell pointed.

Toby passed out napkins and we shared a pen. After everyone had written down what they wanted they handed their opinions to me. I read them aloud.

"Road."

"Street."

"Car thing."

"Pavement."

"Mavis."

"Ice cream," spelled with a K and a backwards R.

"Looks like we want the road," I said, standing. I walked over to the window and pulled the blind. Leonard was gone. I walked to the bedroom door and opened it. Jerry stood there with his arms still crossed.

"We made a decision," I told him.

He stepped aside and let us walk over to our chairs.

Paul and Sister Watson were whispering about what the outcome would be. We took our seats just as Leonard walked back in. He stood behind the counter and banged his globe.

"Jury, have you reached a verdict?"

I could tell the word *verdict* threw everyone off. "We have," I answered for them.

"What say ye?"

"We want the road."

The crowd went wild. Paul hung his head and then turned to shake Sister Watson's hand. He was definitely a different man than he had been a couple of years ago. I excused myself and walked out of the building. My job was done here.

Thelma's Way was getting a road.

27

DEFINITIONS

At five I picked a bunch of wildflowers and ran down the path to meet up with Grace on her return. She was nowhere to be seen when I got to the trailhead, so I hung out with Leo and CleeDee for a little while to wait. I filled the two of them in on everything they had been missing in Thelma's Way.

"There's gonna be a road?" Leo asked in amazement.

"Looks that way," I said.

"That'd be great. Then we could drag one of these houses in there for us." CleeDee clapped while frying up a big pan of bacon on a portable gas stove. Grease popped and crackled. A large splatter popped against her dry face, causing her to wince.

I suddenly realized that I should have voted against the road. I was so anti-Paul's weather shelter that I was temporarily blinded to what I was supporting. With a road and the possibility of financing, the entire Thelma's Way valley could soon be littered with little Leonard houses. Sure, the homes there now were not as well equipped and were somewhat aesthetically lacking, but they had character and represented the inhabitants better than fabricated boxes made by unknowns.

"How long are you guys going to stay here in this place?" I asked Leo.

"As long as Leonard will let us."

"Don't you miss Thelma's Way?"

"Luxury is awful distracting."

"What about you, CleeDee?"

"I'll go where Leo's job takes us."

"Leo has no job," I pointed out.

"I'm working on some things with Leonard," Leo told us.

"Really?"

"Big things," he went on. "Larger than wife."

His miswording didn't go unnoticed. CleeDee glared at him and then whipped him on the back of his head with a dish towel.

"Bacon, anyone?" she said, sitting down to the biggest plate of fried pork I had ever seen.

"She's eating for two," Leo explained. He reached for a piece of bacon and got a stare from his wife. He withdrew his hand. "So I guess Paul's pretty upset."

"He seems okay."

"That weather thing would have been neat."

"And impossible," I added.

"Nothing's impossible," CleeDee chewed. "Look at us."

"You guys have done well." I meant in a broad sense.

"It's like this, Trust," Leo said. "A man's supposed to cleave unto his wife and no other."

I was about to change the subject when I heard some-one coming down the trail. I jumped out of the mobile home and faced Grace and her mother.

"Trust, what are you doing here?" Grace asked.

I handed her my now-limp flowers.

"I'll walk on ahead," Patty said, taking her cue. She stepped away from us and down the trail.

"I wanted to say sorry." I tried to look meek. "Are you mad?"

"A little." Grace nodded, indicating that she wanted to walk. We shuffled slowly so as not to catch up to her mother.

"So, I go out of town, and you take a strange girl to the cemetery," Grace painfully recapped.

"Sort of."

"Sort of what?"

"Sort of dumb."

Grace smiled. "Trust."

"We were only talking," I explained. "She was explain-ing why she was here, and I couldn't just not listen."

"Heaven forbid."

"I'm glad you understand."

"Why is she here?"

"She wants to paint a picture for her dying dad."

"How can I compete with that?" Grace asked lightly.

"Slowly poison your father."

Grace stopped and looked at me.

"I'm joking, of course," I said, realizing I had gone too far.

She pushed back her hair, giving me a nice glimpse of

158

the right side of her beautiful neck. "When I first saw you, I knew that you were going to be something good for me," Grace said, as if remembering. "I also knew that it was going to be messy."

"Messy? Like cool?" I tried.

"Messy like falling in love while on a mission, beating up boyfriends, angering entire wards, bringing in ex-girlfriends, hanging out with gorgeous women in moonlit cemeteries."

"How'd you know about the moon?"

"We see the same sky," Grace laughed.

Nature was so conniving.

"So am I not worth the sticky parts?" I asked.

"Unfortunately, my heart thinks you are."

"And your mind?"

"It's pretty ticked off."

Grace let me hold her hand, and we began walking again. All things considered, she was being rather generous.

"So will you forgive me?" I asked.

"I suppose I have to," Grace said with more seriousness than I personally felt was necessary. "But this is strike two."

"What was strike one?"

"The twelve mistakes you made before this."

I was going to challenge her memory and make her list them. But I was afraid that in doing so she'd realize that there were considerably more than twelve.

"Paul's weather thing got shot down," I changed the conversation.

"That's good."

"The road's a go."

"If it happens, our town will never be the same."

"I really am sorry," I said, feeling that it needed to be added. "About Hope."

"I know."

"Never again," I promised.

"I'll be watching you," she smiled.

That made us even.

28

SAINTS

I was so thankful for Sunday. It was the end of a week and a chance to be recharged. Everyone headed over to the chapel dressed in their Sunday best, which just so happened, in most cases, to also be their Tuesday worst. Grace and I got there early and took a seat near the back. I then sat there in spiritual awe as folks continued to pour in. Last time I had attended church in Thelma's Way, we had topped out at no more than thirty people. Now, however, there were more Saints in attendance than most locals could count.

"What's this about?" I asked Grace.

We actually had to scoot down to make room for three of the Porter boys and Miss Flitrey and Wad. I couldn't believe it. I had worked my entire mission trying to get people to get out to church, and now it seemed as if the solution to that problem had been my leaving. I leaned forward and asked Teddy Yetch if it was always so crowded.

"For the last five or so months."

By the time church started, there wasn't an open seat. I saw Hope a couple of benches up and to the right. I slouched in my seat so that Teddy's head was blocking my view. Because of the crowd, a few people even sat up on the stand by President Heck and his counselors. Sister Heck played prelude music on the piano with fervor, softening it the moment her husband walked up to the pulpit. He signaled her and she stopped midnote.

"Welcome to sacrament meeting."

It looked as if every single once-lukewarm member was now here in church. I couldn't have been more blown away.

I stand corrected.

Todd Nodd was wearing a tie.

Initially Grace didn't seem to be as amazed by what we saw as I was. But when we began the opening hymn and everyone sang, I saw her feel her forehead as if checking to see if she were ill.

I don't know how he did it, but as I put my hymnbook away, I looked up and noticed Leonard squeezed in right next to me on the other side. It was the closest I had come to screaming in a long time.

"Where'd you come from?" I whispered, knowing that he had not squeezed past me.

"Too many people are afraid to crawl these days," he whispered back.

"Leonard," I sighed, realizing that he had come from below.

"I got a calling," he informed me after the sacrament.

I could only imagine what his "calling" was.

"You're looking at the new elders quorum president."

Despite Leonard's being older, he had never been made a high priest because he preferred the lessons the elders had.

"You're the elders quorum president?" I whispered in amazement.

"Didn't I just say that?"

"Congratulations, Leonard."

"President," he corrected.

The youth speaker was Greg Bickerstaff. His talk was on tithing. He told us how it was important and that the only reason his mother didn't pay it was because she said they never had enough money.

"Ma said she'd gladly pay if she found or won a huge pile of cash."

I looked over at Janet Bickerstaff. She was smiling—proud of what a good public speaker her son was.

After Greg, Toby played an intermediate hymn on the penny whistle. Toby was still wearing the Ace bandage wrapped around his head. His number wasn't too bad, but every time he caught his breath he would suck in through the blow hole and create a tremendously high-pitched wheeze that set poor Nippy Ward's hearing aid squealing.

"I never liked windy instruments," Leonard commented.

I wondered how he had any self-esteem.

I was really quite surprised when President Heck stood up after the hymn and announced that Winton and Jerry Scotch would be our speakers. I hoped that Winton had been struck by lightning or scared straight. That wasn't the case. He stood up at the pulpit not making a lick of sense and going on and on about who knows what.

"Weroiddiktj. Wisdspd difdjnneiowofn ddkal lllllaldku."

Everyone politely listened and nodded when they thought it was appropriate. Eventually he said, "Plisthub," and then just stood there.

Finally, Sister Watson figured it out and said *amen* loudly for all of us. Winton smiled and sat down.

Jerry got up and subtly let us know that he hadn't prepared an actual talk by saying, "I guess me and my uncle should have coordinated our talks. He said everything I was planning to. But since I'm up here, I might as well say something."

That was an idea worth debating.

"I sold seven corn dogs to one man the other day," he bragged. "I watched him eat them all. I don't know if any of you know, but I'm on a diet."

This was going to be good.

"I eat only meat," Jerry said. "It sounds funny, but I guess stuff that's not meat makes you fat. I had a little problem fitting this lifestyle in with the Word of Wisdom, but heck, it's not like I'm smoking. For breakfast I have a steak or sausage. For lunch I have a steak or something, and for dinner I'll eat some sort of meat. I know what some of you are thinking, and that's too kind, but I really could afford to drop a couple of pounds." Jerry scratched his head as if thinking of something else to say. He located something within his gray matter and smiled.

"I was reading Sister Watson's *Ensign* magazine," he

informed us. "There was a story about a woman on a cruise. She saved all her money and then went cruising. Since she spent all her money on the actual boat ride, she didn't have none left to pay for meals. So I suppose she hid in her closet or something—on that point I'm not quite clear."

"He sure can ramble," Leonard whispered.

"Anyhow, on the last day of her vacation she went up top and discovered that all the meals were free. So I guess she helped herself to a really big dinner. The meaning of the story is that we should get out and be seen. I've got a lot of Danish ancestors. That's always confused me."

"I hope he doesn't cut into our quorum time," Leonard complained.

"Sometimes I get scared," Jerry admitted. "Not scared like when Tindy showed me that gash. But heck, I'm in my forties and still single. You'd think someone like me could find one person. I'll tell you what shakes me up even more, though. The Last Days. Me and Pete did some addition on the cash register at my work, and our numbers show that we're looking at an end sometime in the next three to sixty years." Jerry paused as if trying to comprehend just how powerful and thought-provoking his last few words were. "Well," he continued, "I can't think of a stronger way to close. So with that I bid you amen."

President Heck stood up and patted Jerry on the shoulder. He then took the pulpit. "I am always amazed by what I hear here," he said. "I come to church thinking that I've heard it all. But then one of you opens your mouth and says what the Spirit's itching to have you say. It's like that

165

time Toby accidentally struck me with that diving board he found at the dump. I am suddenly dizzy with gratitude. You all are truly the best group of people I could ever hope to be caught broke with. I was talking to someone about some of the problems they were having, and it came to me that hurt is never going to stop. Heck, we are going to get scraped up and bruised our whole life through. What's important is that we let it heal and don't pick at it and make it worse."

President Heck said a few other things and then closed the meeting. I loved listening to him talk. He used a different English and at times a different reality, but he bore his soul so sincerely that I had a hard time seeing how anyone listening could help but feel the Spirit.

"Your dad's incredible," I whispered to Grace, putting my lips considerably closer to her ear than when I was whispering to Leonard.

"I already forgave you," she whispered back, thinking I was just trying to score some points.

Just for that, I sat extra close to her during Sunday School. Sister Knapworth taught the lesson. It was an inspiring lesson on tithing. She also gave us a tip that I found rather interesting. She told the class that when they write out their tithing checks, they should enter them in the check register as being for Heaven. Sister Knapworth was obviously unaware that there wasn't anyone there besides Grace and me who even knew what a check register was. Luckily, before people became too confused Sister Lando stood up and took the rest of the class time telling us all how God gave her headaches as a signal for her to make or not make certain choices. The only reason I was sad when the class was over was that Grace and I had to split up for Priesthood and Relief Society.

Still reeling from the pain of separation, I learned that thanks to the fact that President Heck had made all the men in his branch honorary high priests so no one would feel left out, Leonard and I were now the only elders.

"You're kidding."

"Serious as a soup stain on a prom dress," Leonard said cheerfully. "It's just you and me."

"We could join the high priests for their class," I suggested.

"You'd be happy throwing all order to the wind, wouldn't you, Trust?"

So I spent Priesthood meeting in a room with just Leonard and him refusing to talk to me like a single individual.

"Would everyone open their scriptures up to first Nephi chapter ten?"

I opened mine, wishing I were a woman and in Relief Society.

"Trust, would you read that for us?"

I did so. It's interesting how scriptures don't sound as moving when you read them with a chip on your shoulder.

"Who here has ever wondered if their faith were sufficient for our times?" Leonard asked.

I raised my hand.

"Anyone else?"

"Leonard, it's only me here," I pointed out for the tenth time.

"If angels can visit the choir," he said sternly, "then a few of them can certainly take some time to drop by our class."

"That's true," I joked. "I can see a couple of them sleeping over there," I said, referring to the slow-moving lesson.

Leonard looked around in excitement. "Keep talking, Trust, I think your voice is drawing them in."

I kept talking, but I don't think they were the words Leonard wanted me to say. He claimed he was hurt, closed the lesson, and then asked me if I thought he was shrinking. I told him yes and then went out to find Grace. She was still in class, but I opened the door and told Sister Watson, who was teaching, that there was an emergency and Grace was needed on the other side of the meadow near the river and below the high pines. Once outside, Grace pestered me to tell her what was going on.

I took her there and thoroughly explained the situation.

29

STAMPED

Monday was beautiful. The sky was as appealing as a clear conscience, the sun hanging overhead like a ball of wax, dripping its warm runoff over everything I saw. I helped Ed work out some of the kinks on his catapult. He was experimenting with which direction was best to fling things. Then I soaked up the environment, waiting for Grace to wander down from the hills. Before she emerged, the mail arrived, and with it were three boxes filled with Grace's and my wedding announcements. I hated to say it, but my mom was right. I should have worn a different shirt. Grace, of course, looked stunning.

As I was looking at them, Hope came into the boardinghouse. She momentarily seemed bothered by what I was doing.

"Grace is sure a lucky girl," she said sadly, her ideal face making me feel for her. "What I wouldn't give to find a guy like you. You really are a catch."

She was making such perfect sense. I couldn't just push her away.

"How's the painting coming?"

"All right, I guess." She looked sad.

"Is everything okay?"

"Daddy's slipping," she sniffed.

"I'm so sorry to hear that."

"I'm trying my best, but it takes me so long to mix my paints. I sprained my wrist pushing one of the children on the tire swing." Hope showed me her wrist. It looked better than all right to me.

Toby was just strolling by outside, so I hollered out to him. He couldn't hear me too well because of the bandage around his head. But after a strong whistle, he turned and I waved him inside.

"Hope's wrist is sprained," I pointed.

"Let's have a look-see." He grabbed her wrist and bent it wildly in every direction. Hope screamed appropriately.

"It's sprained, all right." Toby took the bandage off his noggin and fixed Hope up. If she hadn't been in such pain, I would have almost sworn that she was scowling at Toby and his less-than-sanitary bandage.

"That should take care of it," Toby confirmed. "Let me know if a bone starts to stick out, or if it swells bigger than a quart-sized melon."

Hope moaned as Toby walked away. "I'll never get my painting done now."

"Can't you mix with your left hand?" I asked.

"I suppose," Hope cried. "I just don't think it will be done in time for Daddy."

"Hold on a second," I said. "Let me see if I can help."

"Would you?" she asked with such hope that I almost forgot about every single thing in my entire life besides her.

"Wait here," I said, quickly pulling myself away and mentally splashing water on my mind by thinking of how Pete Kennedy looked two summers ago in a swimming suit.

Ed Washington was out in the meadow messing around with his catapult. He had been trying to work out every last bug. His creation had been well used. Instead of hauling their old furniture or clothing to the dump, people just put their stuff on the catapult and flung it into oblivion. It worked nicely because the direction it faced hurled most of the things towards the Heck home. More than once, I had heard President Heck talking happily about certain worn-out items the heavens had heaved at him. The only kink Ed couldn't seem to work out was the touchy trigger. At times, all you had to do was simply lay something on it and the weight would release it and send it flying. It had gone off on accident while Miss Flitrey was emptying trash from her pockets onto it. The pole snagged the elastic waistband of the skirt she was wearing and stretched it until it snapped back, leaving her with one gigantic, waist-long welt. Ed was working on the faulty trigger problem when I interrupted him.

"Hey, Ed, could you do me a favor?"

"Sure," he replied.

"How are your hands?"

He looked at them. "The rash has cleared."

"Perfect."

I sent him indoors to be with Hope. I was so proud of myself for doing what was right until I saw Hope walk out of the boardinghouse holding Ed's arm, and I realized that I was more than just a little bit jealous.

Hope was my pretend girlfriend.

I saw Sister Watson break from the tree line and come racing towards the boardinghouse. She had a purpose. Her wig was crooked, and her ears were steaming. I stood in front of her.

"What's . . ."

"No time, Trust." She pushed me and kept going. I followed.

"Leonard!" she screamed as she stepped up into the boardinghouse. "Leonard! He's never around when I need him," she ranted. "Roswell, you seen Leonard?"

"I ain't married to him," Roswell argued.

"Well, of course you're not married to him," she said in frustration. "I'm just wondering if you know where he is."

"Like I said, I don't know."

Leonard appeared from out of nowhere, darkening the door frame with his long head and thin body.

"What's all the noise?" he asked.

"I called the state," Sister Watson dove in. "I fished around for information like you said. I didn't tell them who I was but just that I was wondering what it would take to get a road put in where there wasn't one. You ready for this?" she asked.

Leonard had actually lost interest and was working a knot out of his shoulder. He noticed the dead air and told Sister Watson to go on.

"First they send a state employee out here to see how many people there are because there has to be enough for them to consider a road. And then some studies are done. They say it would cost about twenty or thirty thousand just to get the thing okayed."

"That's a lot of money," was all Leonard said.

"So the road's out?" I asked, feeling I needed to participate.

"The road's not out," Sister Watson insisted. "Progress can't be stopped. We need that Book of Mormon."

"Trust, didn't you say it was worth something big?" She turned to me.

"Could be."

"So we find it, and we're in business," she said with finality.

"You'll never find it," I pointed out. "Every inch of this place has been searched at least ten times over."

"It's got to be somewhere," she insisted.

"Sister—" I tried to reason.

"Brother Williams, there is no time for nay-saying."

I found some time for it in my head.

"I'm going to start looking right now." She turned on her big heels and headed out.

"Boy, some people get an idea in their head and they don't . . . where was I going with this?" Leonard asked me.

"I have no idea."

I noticed for the first time that Leonard's face was dotted with the beginnings of a beard.

"So you decided to grow a beard."

"It isn't coming in as fast as I'd like it to."

"Life's not easy."

"Tell me about it."

Leonard spotted the boxes of wedding announcements on the boardinghouse counter. He picked one up and looked at it.

"I guess you didn't want to dress up."

I was going to say something clever and cutting, but Leonard suddenly looked as if inspiration had slapped him on the chin.

"What is it?" I asked.

"Nothing," he said, trying to brush off what I had just seen. "Nothing. How many announcements did you and Grace order?" he asked.

"I don't know. A few thousand. Why?"

"No reason," Leonard said casually. "I'm just interested in you, Trust."

"Please be interested in a noninterfering way," I begged.

"You keep that humor coming," he laughed. "Enough massaging the fat, though. Let's go start looking for that book," he said, setting down the announcement and clapping his hands as if he were a parent trying to excite a young child.

"It's pointless," I said.

"That's the spirit."

I ignored Leonard as he had me, picked up an announcement, and went to see Grace.

As I walked through the meadow, I could already hear news of the new and improved Book of Mormon search being thrown around. The Thelma's Way meadow was one powerful conduit for spreading news. All a person had to do was toss some information into the air and stand back. Jeff Titter had once told Pete Kennedy that he thought he saw Wad down at the dump with a woman besides Miss Flitrey, and within twenty minutes, the entire valley knew. Thirty minutes later, Miss Flitrey was packed and looking for a place to stay until her husband got the help he needed. Luckily, the "woman" Wad had been spotted with turned out to be Digby after he had experimented with curling his own hair.

The meadow was a melting pot of information and activity. Everything involved, devolved, or revolved around it in some way. It had no official name, although Toby told me once when he was ill and of unusually unsound mind that it was once called Thorton's Patch and that Thorton Standly had been one of the original settlers of the area. He was a poor man who had foolishly followed Thelma and her misguided party the wrong way. According to legend, when everyone arrived here they just began throwing their things down, sick of traveling and tired of moving. Well, where their things had fallen their roots were planted. The Ford clan had dropped their belongings where the boardinghouse now stood. The Watson ancestors had collapsed where the old Watson home stood. Everyone insisted on sticking to where they first squatted. Thorton took the meadow. He spread his junk out over the entire area, a pan here, a shoe there—like a family spreading purses and jackets to claim an entire church pew all for themselves. He then sat in the middle of the meadow, insisting that no one crowd his space or touch his stuff. After a couple of days, he built a small lean-to and dug a latrine, thus making it known that he was there to stay. One night, however, the extremely nervy Thump Ford, Roswell's great-grandfather, ignored the invisible borders Thorton had established and selfishly parked his two wagons on Thorton's ground so as to free up some space in his own area.

Well, as the next day dawned, Thorton spotted the wagons and decided to claim them as his own. After all, they were in his space. Thump tried to drag them back, but Thorton's sturdy wife, Elisa Standly, taught Thump a few things about weight and gravity. So, with a bad back and permanent grass stains, Thump withdrew, leaving his wagons where they stood.

Unfortunately, that wasn't the end of it. Thump told Thelma about what Thorton had done, and Thelma instantly took Thump's side, simply because he was so much better bred than Thorton. Thorton called Thelma a brat, and Thelma called Thorton a burr. Thorton demanded a definition of burr, which Thelma gladly gave him, plus a few words more.

"*Burr*, as in thorn or irritant. As in the stupid thistle that infest this patch you've claimed as your home."

The argument was never settled due to Thelma's dying a short time later while trying to cross the Girth River. But the name Thorton's Patch stuck, even though Thorton and his wife eventually packed up and went elsewhere. It probably would have stayed named that if it had not been for Thump, who on his deathbed made his posterity promise to fulfill his dying wish—his wish being that they rename the patch so that Thorton's name would not live on. Well, Thump's posterity made the promise but couldn't think of a single thing to name it, so they went with "the meadow."

The meadow was now just an open space, lime green in summer and dirty white in winter. At any point in the year, trails crossed through it like shoelaces pulled through poorly placed loops. The only distinguishing characteristics that it bore were the two rotted wagons that had never been moved. They sat there as weathered and worn as a malt ball after a monsoon. There was a small hole in the center of the meadow that Toby swore was the remains of Thorton's latrine, but both Pete and Ed claimed that it was simply the spot where they had tried to dig for gold after a rainbow had supposedly stuck its end down there.

Despite its name, or lack thereof, I walked right through it and on to Grace.

President Heck was working on his rolling path.

"Trust," he called out happily. "Grab a trowel and bend."

"I'd love to," I answered back, thinking how I wouldn't let just anyone tell me that. "But I need to show Grace this first," I said, hoping he would ask to see the announcement I was carrying.

"Suit yourself." He whistled for a second as if that helped him think. "She's upstairs."

I walked inside and saw Patty Heck teaching Narlette how to make pie crust.

"Trust," she greeted me.

"Sister Heck," I threw back, still not completely

comfortable with calling her anything else. "The path outside is looking nice."

"Ricky's always been good with his hands," she complimented him. "He'd be the president if his brain was half as active as his wrists. But then, I guess God dishes out the gifts sparingly."

I smiled, thinking that this was probably the longest conversation I had ever had with my soon-to-be mother-in-law.

"Is Grace upstairs?" I asked.

"She is," Sister Heck answered.

"Mind if I . . . ?" I nodded towards the stairs.

"I mind only two things," she said casually, rolling out dough. "Hair in the dressing and a tight pair of shoes."

"What about Miss Flitrey?" Narlette asked, remembering something else her mother minded.

"I wouldn't mind that woman if she were the last person on earth," Sister Heck said with finality.

I walked up the stairs and found Grace sitting in the dormer window reading a book thicker than the last three books I had read.

"The announcements came," I announced, holding out the one I had brought.

Grace put her book down and took a look.

"Scary," was all she said.

"I know, I know. I should have worn something else."

Grace smiled. "You look perfect. It's just that seeing it really makes it look inevitable."

"Makes what look inevitable?"

"Marriage."

"That is the idea, isn't it?" I asked. "We didn't buy these just to see how the idea looked."

"I didn't mean that," Grace insisted. "They look great."

It was an unsatisfactory response.

"It's too late for great," I said. "Are you having second thoughts about all this?"

Her reply was much too slow for my personal comfort.

"No."

"Grace."

"I'm fine."

"Is it about Hope?"

"What about Hope?"

"Nothing about her," I said with passion. "It's just that on occasion women seem to read things into things that aren't readable."

"We do?" she asked.

"Not you," I backpedaled. "But some women. Like that one back in Southdale."

"Which one?"

"The one with hair and glasses," I made up.

"Oh, her." She seemed to understand.

"Grace, if you're having doubts about us, then we should talk."

"I'm not having doubts," she said firmly. "It's just that seeing it on those announcements really makes it hit home."

I looked at the announcement and back at Grace.

"We could retake the picture."

"There isn't time."

"Grace." I tried not to whine.

"I'm just kidding." She picked her book back up and ignored me.

I couldn't believe it. I had never known Grace to be so standoffish with me. Okay, there were those many times that she had run and hidden from me before we really knew each other, but that was it. I knew I wasn't a perfect person, but I was capable of change and willing to let her rearrange me. Plus, I didn't have any disgusting habits like spitting or scratching in places that were inappropriate.

Wasn't that enough?

I headed back to the boardinghouse to see if there was something there that could take my mind off everything. No one was there besides Roswell and the Knapworths, who were talking to one of their grandchildren on the phone. Sister Knapworth was holding the phone and speaking extra loud into the receiver, as if she needed her voice to carry all the way to Montana. I sat down on a hard chair by Roswell and tried to look as if I wasn't listening in.

Roswell nodded at me as he wiped the counter.

"You tell Grandma that you love her," Sister Knapworth hollered into the phone, her loud voice actually making Roswell jump.

"That woman can grate," he whispered to me.

"Tell them I love them too," Elder Knapworth insisted, tugging on his wife's sleeve.

"Grandpa loves you too," she screamed.

Roswell actually plugged his ears.

"What's that, honey?" she asked the phone.

"What'd they say?" Elder Knapworth asked, as if he sensed trouble.

Sister Knapworth put her hand over the receiver and yelled at her husband. "Marlo Ann is on the line now. She wants to know if they can send us anything."

"Tell them about those razors."

Sister Knapworth removed her hand and spoke into the phone again. "Grandpa needs razors." She listened for a moment. "Yes, they have razors here. But we can't seem to find the kind that he likes. You know, the double blade with the comfort strip. You can buy them at Stillman's down on Main," she instructed. "I'm sure you can get them at other grocery stores there, but Grandpa likes them from Stillman's."

"They're by the magazines," Elder Knapworth said.

"Father says they're near the magazines," Sister Knapworth shouted. She paused to listen and then said, "Are you going to be okay? All right then, we'll talk to you later. Love from Tennessee."

"Love from me," Elder Knapworth prompted her.

"Love from Daddy," she screamed. She then hung up and looked at Elder Knapworth.

"Is everything all right?" he asked.

"She just has a headache," Sister Knapworth told him. "I'm sure she'll be fine." She looked at me. "I saw those announcements of yours, Trust. What a good-looking pair you two make. And that shirt," she went on. "It takes a real man to pull that off."

"Thanks," I said weakly, looking around for the announcements. "Where are they?" I asked.

"I saw Leonard carrying them around," Roswell said. "I think he put them away for safe keeping."

"That Leonard is something else," Elder Knapworth said kindly.

I was just about to put my own spin on Leonard when the phone rang. Not wanting to hear Sister Knapworth scream anymore, I jumped up and got it. It was for Sister Watson. I stepped outside and hollered at Tindy, who was standing halfway across the meadow. She yelled at Wad, who was further down the way, and Wad instructed Digby to run off and fetch Mavis. A few seconds later, Sister Watson came tearing across the meadow holding her wig on her head. She reached the porch, and I pointed in towards the phone.

I had no idea who she was talking to, but it was a long conversation that made little sense on my end. When she hung up she looked more confused than usual.

"That's weird," she said, as if she were acting.

"What?" Roswell asked.

"Well, that was a guy from the state. He didn't believe that we were really here."

"What?" Roswell asked again.

"He's the one coming out this Saturday to evaluate our road potential," she explained. "But he said when he went to his supervisors, they insisted that there was actually no one here."

"What?" Roswell still didn't get it.

"That was Willis from Virgil's Find," she lied out of frustration. "He said that the bean delivery should be here tomorrow."

"Oh," Roswell said. "I'd better go clear some space." He walked off.

"So we're not really here," Sister Knapworth said to Sister Watson. "That'll make a person feel important."

"Is he still coming?" I asked.

"He seemed more certain about that than before," Sister Watson said reflectively. "Funny."

I was glad she thought so.

30

SPAMMON FROM HEAVEN

I don't remember many of my dreams. I never have. Occasionally there will be mornings when I wake up knowing that what I dreamed the night before had been pleasant or that it had been horrible. On a good day I may even remember a two-second snippet or a certain outfit that someone was wearing, but that's about it. As a child I was constantly being taught about all the great prophets and how they were repeatedly told things through visions and dreams. Back then I figured I simply knew it all and that there was no need for the heavens to show me more. As an adult I now knew that the real reason my memory held back was simply that I had never completely understood the short silent films in my mind. There was no way I could comprehend some epic vision that was packed with any more symbolism and depth than, say, the back of a cereal box. That's why I was so surprised to find my mind retaining the show my subconscious had played for me Monday night.

I had dreamed that Grace was standing by a canyon edge looking off into the distance. I wanted to run to her, but instead I picked up a phone that was placed conveniently in a tree by the canyon and called up Hope. I talked to her about myself, repeating every accomplishment I had ever achieved as a child while Grace took tiny steps closer to the edge. Just as Grace was about to step off the cliff, I hung up and then dialed my mother to see what she was doing. It was at that moment that a large boulder that looked like my old Sunbeam teacher but was actually Hope ran over to Grace and pushed her off. I didn't even hang up. I just kept on talking to my mom as if nothing had happened.

I woke up and lay there in the early morning dusk trying to figure out why I had been allowed to remember that particular dream. By the time the sun was up, I was wishing that God had left my head blank like he usually did. I sat up in bed and stretched. I sniffed at the air, recognizing a smell that wasn't usually there. I stood up and sniffed around. I looked out the window and saw a small crowd of people gathered around a small purple tent in the middle of the meadow. The tent I recognized as Paul's. He had pitched it in the meadow many times lately. His home was across the river, but the huge Girth was too hard to cross these days, so Paul would pitch his tent at night and then take it down the next morning. This morning, however, there looked to be a large circle of something surrounding his tent. Outside that ring were people standing and looking at the ground as if baffled.

I hurried and got dressed and then ran downstairs. The boardinghouse was empty. Everyone had gone out to look at what was going on.

I followed my nose to the meadow and up to Paul's tent. The ground was covered with some sort of white stuff. Paul stepped out of his tent and warned us all to stay far away.

"What is this stuff?" Sister Watson asked.

"I have no idea," Paul lied.

Toby Carver picked up a piece and stuck it in his mouth.

"Not bad."

Everyone except me bent over and began tasting what was lying on the ground. Paul tasted some as well and then stood in awe. He held his hands up.

"People," he shouted, "do you realize what this is?"

They had no idea.

"It's manna."

They still had no idea.

"From heaven," Paul elaborated. "Like in the Old Testament. This is heaven's way of saying that God still sides with me on the weather shelter. The one with the small gold plaque that says my name."

Paul was acting like his old self.

"The heavens know that this shelter will keep us safe from all that is to happen in these final days."

"Final days of what?" Frank Porter yelled.

"The world."

"Shoot," Toby said. "The world ain't going anywhere. It's too big. Not that I mind this manna, though."

"Look at the Girth," Paul pleaded. "Our river is swelling so much that it no longer stays within its banks. Can't you see that our time is running out?"

Teddy Yetch shuffled up from her home. Her old eyes were ringed from sleep. She pulled up next to me and asked what was going on.

"Paul's claiming there's manna on the ground."

Teddy bent down and picked up a piece. She tasted it and then stormed up to Paul. "That ain't manna," she chastised. "You stole my spicy snow sausage recipe."

"I have no idea what you're talking about."

"I know my own creations," Teddy yelped.

Everyone began gathering up handfuls of the one thing Teddy actually made well.

"It's Teddy's sausage," Toby confirmed.

"Would one small gold plaque really kill you guys?" Paul whined, looking hurt.

I'm sure he would have said more, but he was interrupted by the large billows of smoke erupting from his tent. Before anyone could adequately gasp, the smoke turned to flame and completely devoured Paul's tent, exposing a slightly charred portable grill. The fire followed a trail of lighter fluid, racing across the ground and directly underneath Pete Kennedy's legs. Flames then snaked across the meadow as if they knew where they were going and jumped up onto the boardinghouse porch. The fire twisted itself around the rails and shoved until it was inside and lighting the place like a Christmas village. It all

187

happened so fast that no one could react. The entire boardinghouse was on full-blown fire before we all began scrambling for water and ways to put it out.

I know it was selfish of me, but I just kept thinking how great it was that my goofy-looking announcements were going to be ruined.

We were able to get a sort of water chain going, but there were just too many weak links to make it effective. Toby would hand Ed a full bucket and then Ed would toss the water onto the next person in line. Miss Flitrey got the hose on the other side of the school working, but it wasn't long enough to reach the fire. Wanting to at least look optimistic, she stood spraying the hose in the general direction and watering the ground a good twenty feet in front of the fire. With a shortage of buckets but wanting to do their share, a few locals tried spitting.

It was pointless. The boardinghouse was toast. We all just stood there in stunned silence. Wood sizzled and crumbled as fire purged it of its soul. I heard a mournful tisking at my side. It was Leonard. His beard was coming in, and he was wearing suspenders made out of two old cloth belts. He fit in way too well here.

"It's a shame," he said.

I nodded in agreement.

"Roswell should have bought that insurance when I offered it," Leonard lamented.

I looked over at old Roswell. He had his thin hands in his pockets and was staring at the aftermath as if it were a confusing piece of art that he would never understand. I noticed Paul standing right behind him. I had never seen

Paul look so genuinely miserable. It had been his stunt that caused this. It would only be a matter of moments before everyone remembered that and turned to tar him.

"I can't believe it," Toby whispered. "I just can't believe it." He felt around for his Ace bandage and then remembered that Hope was wearing it on her wrist. I suppose he thought it might bring someone some comfort in a time like this.

"Everything was in there," Roswell said, stunned.

"It'll be okay," Teddy tried to comfort him. "You still got your wagon."

Roswell looked over at his almost-ready ice cream wagon. The right side of it was dark from the smoke that had filled the air.

"But my ice cream was inside," Roswell said angrily, as if he were talking about his children.

Sister Watson was the first to remember that this was all Paul's fault. She turned, locked eyes with him, and then like a brittle volcano began to harp.

"This is all your fault."

"I didn't mean . . ."

"That boardinghouse was as important to this town as any rock or tree could ever be," she interrupted.

"I only . . ."

"You had your chance to push for that shelter, and you were turned down. Why couldn't you have left well enough at home?"

"If you'd let me speak," Paul said, trying to act in control.

"She's right, Paul," Pete agreed.

"She's more than right," Frank hollered. "She's dead on."

"I think you're all jumping to conclusions," Paul tried.

"I think you're right," Ed admitted.

"Let's just . . ."

"Let's just nothing," Frank argued. "You burned down the place I got my first kiss in. Under the stairs, behind the boiler, next to the mops."

"That's where Feeble taught me how to play harmonica," Jeff Titter reminded us.

"It's where Bishop Watson proposed to me," Sister Watson spoke. "Right after I chipped my tooth on that high stair."

"It was my home," Roswell cried.

Paul was in trouble.

In times past whenever Paul was about to be lynched by the town, he had simply run off towards the Girth, jumped on a raft, and paddled across. This time, however, the river was just too deep and too wide. I suppose that's why we all couldn't believe it when he did just that. Paul pushed through Teddy Yetch, bowled over Tindy Mac-Dermont, and ran straight for the river. There were no rafts anymore due to the fact that the river had overflowed the shores and washed all of them away. So Paul ran past the catapult and dived straight into the water.

Toby and I gave chase, but neither one of us jumped in after him. There was no way I was going to take another ride down Hallow Falls. I had done it on my mission and had no desire to do it again. The moving water growled at us as we stood on the ground, searching for any sign of Paul.

"Is that him?" Toby pointed across the water to what

looked to be a moving branch or person on the other side and well down the way.

"Could be."

"So he's all right?"

"If that's him," I answered. "I can't tell for sure."

Whatever it was we saw slipped behind a rock and out of view.

"What'll we do?" Toby asked.

"I have no idea."

It was not shaping up to be a very good day in Thelma's Way.

31

YOU REMIND ME OF . . .

◈

Life was so much more bearable if he could sleep through the day and then roam at night. Today, however, the smell of smoke had pulled him from slumber. He quietly worked his way towards the meadow.

The fire was gone by the time he arrived. So was the big house that had once sat right in the middle of the field. He imagined the size of the flames that must have consumed the place. In his mind he saw the red tongues of fire licking the place down to nothing. The thought of red made the tiny gears in his large head whiz and click. He pulled out the crumpled picture and stared until it hurt.

He worked his way back to the deep spot where he hid and tried to fall back to sleep.

32

PATIENCE IS A BIG STINKING PAIN AND ANYONE WHO TELLS YOU OTHERWISE IS SIMPLY REPEATING WHAT HIS MOTHER DRILLED INTO HIM

Cindy was growing sick of this. There was not a single fiber in her body that could tolerate much more of what was happening.

What was happening?

Nothing.

Sure, something had burned, and someone had maybe

drowned, and blah, blah, blah. It all had so painfully little to do with her. She couldn't take being Hope much longer. It was torture not being able simply to wring Trust by the neck until he pledged his perfect love for her. This waiting and playing coy was for the stupid birds. And Grace! Come on, how was it that the man of her dreams could even be interested in *her*?

Cindy was sick. She tugged on the Ace bandage that what's-his-name had wrapped on her wrist. It was dirty and smelled of sweat. She unwrapped it and tossed it in a heap on the floor.

"This place is a sloppy hole of dysfunction."

Cindy cracked her knuckles and bit her lip. It was time to step things up a notch. She was not content to wait around any longer. Trust would be hers by next week, or he would be no one's.

Cindy picked up her book, *Passion's Pupil*, and read the last two paragraphs:

> *Grade school teacher Marguerite Bookworth smelled the scent of her man, Michael, as he walked past her in the hallway of their apartment building. His hair seemed to cry out to her, "Touch me." His ringless finger reminded her of his two former wives who had both died tragic deaths exactly six months apart—both deaths involving small appliance fires. True love had truly eluded him until now. But times were changing, for she was the pill that would make him whole, the drug that would taint his blood with the taste of Marguerite. But first she would*

need to cleanse his palate of Mandy, the beautiful artist in apartment 2-B who was currently after him.

Marguerite's plan was simple. She would enlist the help of the building's slow-witted superintendent to coax Michael down to her empty school at night. There, Marguerite would be waiting. When Michael arrived, she would cling to him until the superintendent got Mandy to come by and catch them together. Mandy would never trust Michael again, and with Mandy out of the picture, Michael would be all hers.

Cindy sighed and held the page to her chest. Then she smiled a wicked smile. She dog-eared the corner for later use.

33

BULKING UP

I suppose you could say that Thelma's Way was experiencing technical difficulties of the worst kind. We had lost our center, and everyone was in a funk. The destruction of the boardinghouse had been a real blow, and with Paul gone, nobody had anyone to take it out on. Most people felt confident, however, that they would eventually get a chance to yell at him. No one believed for a second that Paul was dead. They all felt within their vengeful hearts that he would be back.

With no boardinghouse, Roswell was forced to move in with Toby, and I somehow ended up in the large tree house that Slippy Rockwell had built. Slippy was a hermit who had passed away a few years back. He had been a big man best known for his ability to whistle through his ears—unfortunately, I had not had the good fortune of hearing him do so for myself. Before Slippy died he had built a huge and elaborate tree house in a couple of the trees back behind Lush Point. He had grown paranoid in his old age and wished to construct an abode that bears and ne'er-do-wells couldn't easily bother. The tree house had remained mostly empty since his death. Sybil Porter had tried to live there, but she kept getting motion sickness whenever the wind swayed the trees. Sister Lando had tried to turn the tree house into an herb store, but she quickly found that her older clientele didn't really enjoy scaling the twenty-foot ladder to procure herbs for their arthritis and other ailments. Sister Heck had tried to run a sewing store there, but again, those interested just weren't interested enough to climb for it.

It wasn't a bad place to live. I wished it came with running water and other facilities, but I had learned to live without those when I had first arrived here—I could adjust again. Despite my new home, I did miss the boarding-house. The meadow looked so bare without it. The burnt ruins were as painful to look at as anything I had ever seen in my life. Wad had given Digby a leave of absence from his hair education to let him help Ed and Pete clear the ashes and remains away. They, along with a number of other folks, had kept at it the last couple of days with great fervor. It wouldn't be long before all that was left of the town's soul was an empty spot of nothing.

To make things worse, the Girth continued to swell. It had grown so big that it was now seeping under the Knapworths' far wall. It had also saturated the lower part of the cemetery enough to cause a number of caskets to pop up and float off downstream, including Feeble's full one and Roswell's empty one. I thought that everyone would have been sick about this, but the general reaction was simply: Why worry, since those affected are dead and all.

The town was falling apart at the seams.

Sister Watson was trying to make folks feel better by talking about how we could build a new boardinghouse as soon as we got a road. She claimed she was busy searching the same nooks and crannies that had been searched a million times before in hopes of finding the Book of Mormon. The state people were supposed to be out to check on us sometime on Saturday. I was only slightly interested in having them visit our town until a conversation I had with Leonard Friday morning by the catapult. He had said, "So are you excited for Saturday?"

I went with, "Sure."

He followed up with, "I hope you're not nervous."

To which I replied, "Why would I be nervous?"

Then in a tone far from confident, he said, "It is your reception."

"What?" I asked.

"Your reception."

"What does my reception have to do with Saturday?" I laughed, blinded to the evil that lay ahead of me.

"I like to help people," Leonard informed me.

The evil was peeking out.

"Mavis seemed so concerned about there being ample people here when the state came and all. So, what's done is done. Let's just run with it."

"Run with what?" I asked.

Leonard laughed for a moment and then put his hands on his knees as if whatever he had inside his head was just too funny to let out. Unfortunately, he finally managed to do so.

"Remember those wedding announcements you had?"

"The ones that got burned?"

"One and the same."

I nodded.

"Well, I got good news and bad news," he explained. "The good news is that they're all right."

"How?"

"I took them out of the boardinghouse before she burned."

"That's great," I said without enthusiasm.

"So where are they?"

"Remember that 'helping others' spiel I gave you a few minutes ago?"

"Leonard."

"I mailed them out bulk rate to a few of the poorer neighborhoods in Virgil's Find. Don't worry, though, I pulled out a couple of handfuls and sent them to some of the important people in Southdale."

"What?"

"I hate to repeat myself, Trust."

"Why did you do that?"

"I just wanted to see if we couldn't get a nice-sized crowd here on Saturday."

"What do my announcements have to do with Saturday?"

"Oh," Leonard waved. "About that, I crossed most of the printed information out and wrote in that we were having a reception this Saturday and that there would be food."

"That is the absolute . . ."

"Save the praise for later. We've got a lot to do."

"Leonard, there is no way that anyone who receives a wedding announcement from someone they don't know with crossed-out dates and handwritten instructions is going to come."

"Two words," Leonard said. "And then I don't want to hear any more of your negative talk. Door prizes."

"I don't believe it."

"God does work in mysterious ways."

"Leonard, this isn't good."

"Trust, you've got your gloom glasses on again. All you have to do is pretend like you're newly married for an afternoon and, *voilá*, we've got ourselves a road."

"I don't want to pretend."

"It'll be fun."

"I'm serious, Leonard."

"It's too late for that," he frowned. "We've got guests coming. I've already tipped off Mavis, and let me just say, she's thrilled."

"Oh good."

"That's the spirit. Teddy's working on some food, and Mavis is going to spruce up this meadow a bit. It's going to be spectacular and classy," Leonard insisted. "Apparently Party Shack in Virgil's Find has crepe paper on sale."

"Can't someone else besides Grace and me pretend to be married?"

"Those were your pictures on the announcements,"

Leonard chided. "Do you think these people won't know? Come on, Trust, I need you to keep up on this one."

"Grace is not going to go for this," I said, hoping to place some of the complaining on her shoulders.

"Women love receptions."

"She won't."

"I'll tell you what, Trust. I'll talk to her. No offense, but I think I'm a little fancier with the English language than a certain someone I know."

Leonard paused for a moment.

"I'm talking about you," he clarified.

"I gathered that."

"Good. Now that that's settled, we're in business."

"This is ridiculous," I argued.

"We're doing it for Mavis. Besides, it will give us all something to think about besides the boardinghouse tragedy. A good time will be had by all."

I should have shot myself right then and there.

34

A LITTLE BIT OF HOPE

◈

The reception was on. By the end of Friday all the arrangements had been made and everyone was gearing up for our fake get-together. After listening to the weather reports, Sister Watson began stringing crepe paper up Friday afternoon. She wrapped it around the catapult and any trees close enough to participate. Wad and Leonard dragged out tables, and Toby mowed down the grass where the reception line was supposed to be.

Grace had been leery at first about the idea of pretending we were married, but she warmed up to it when she realized that there was no possible way to get out of it. She also saw how it might help people unwind from everything else that had been going on. Patty Heck actually became enthused and she began stitching a dress for Grace as fast as possible. Teddy Yetch called for ingredients, and folks hauled in bags of flour and sugar or anything they had in abundance to her house. From there she began whipping up and concocting what would be our hors d'oeuvres for tomorrow. President Heck was so nervous about what he was going to say to those coming through the line that he set aside his cement work and began working on how to greet those who would be falsely congratulating him.

Leonard had taken up a collection to fund the door prizes. I felt he was overly shocked by how little money people actually contributed. He bought a couple of gifts at the dollar store in Virgil's Find.

All the preparations reminded me of the hubbub before the sesquicentennial pageant the town had put on during my mission. If this reception turned out to be anything like the pageant, we were in a lot of trouble.

Friday night after I climbed up into my home and tried to fall asleep, I was suddenly disturbed by a small tap against the one glass window that Slippy had built into his place. I ignored it, thinking it had been just the wind or a stray bug hitting the invisible blockade. A few seconds later the tap became a larger *whap*. I looked up but saw nothing. I told myself that it must have been a branch scraping or a disoriented bird bumbling into it. A few moments later, a fist-sized rock came hurtling through the window, sending broken glass all over. I jumped up and looked out, expecting for some reason to see Leonard. I was wrong. It was Ed.

"What do you want?" I yelled down.

"There's been an emergency," he said nervously.

"Is everyone all right?"

"Sure," he said, baffled. "But I need you to come."

"Hold on."

I got dressed again and climbed down. A blanket of stars pinned down the dark night. A partial moon was hanging low in the unusually clear sky and looking like the toenail clipping of a large toe.

"So what is it, Ed?" I asked as we walked towards somewhere.

"I don't know for sure," he admitted. "But you're wanted at the school."

"Miss Flitrey?"

"No, I'm Ed," he said, baffled.

"I know that," I smiled. "Is it Miss Flitrey who wants me?"

"Last I heard she was happy being married to Wad."

"I'm sure she is," I said, slightly frustrated. "But does she need me to help her with something at the school?"

"No," was all Ed said, picking up the pace and walking a good two strides in front of me. It was obvious he didn't want to get any more confused by my questioning.

When we got to the school, it was pitch black. The meadow was empty. Not a soul was to be seen.

"Wait here," Ed insisted.

"For what?"

"Just wait." He turned and walked away.

The schoolhouse wasn't pretty. It was old and leaned to one side. The best proof of its bad balance was to stand in the front doorway and see how it didn't exactly frame you at right angles. Miss Flitrey complained all the time about how Thelma's Way needed a new school. But the fact of the matter was Thelma's Way needed a lot of new things.

It was about as unpolished and outdated as a town could be. The school would probably be last on the list for improvements. The people here weren't actually against education, but most of them figured they had done all right without it and so could their kids.

I stood outside the dark school listening to the low wind and wondering what I was doing. I was just about to go back to my tree house when I heard something move inside the school. I pressed my face up against one of the windows and looked in. I couldn't see much because of the dark, but I could barely make out a hunched-over silhouette sitting in the third row of desks. I walked around to the door and pulled it open.

"Is anyone in there?"

A soft crying was the only reply. I thought about flipping on the lights, but I didn't want to frighten whoever was there.

"Hello?" I said, stepping in and closer to whoever it was.

"Are you okay?" I asked.

The crying stopped, and the shadow sat up and wiped her eyes. I say *her* eyes because the shadow was a she, and the she was Hope.

"What are you doing here?" I asked.

Hope brushed her eyes and spoke. "I'm sorry," she said, "I didn't know anyone would be here."

"Normally there's not at this time of night."

"I'm sorry, Trust," she said, standing as if to leave.

"It's okay," I tried to calm her. "Are you all right?"

"No," she sobbed, falling into my arms.

What could I do? I held her as she cried. It was harmless. I felt nothing more than if I were a young Scout embracing an elderly shut-in while trying to earn my hugging merit badge.

I suppose I shouldn't add lying to my list of sins.

All right, it was nice, in a really I-shouldn't-be-doing-this sort of way. Hope clung to me as if I were the only thing worth clutching in the entire world. She cried as I tried not to smell her perfume or feel her in my arms. After a couple of minutes, she sighed the kind of sigh that says things words could never convey.

I brushed her hair with my hands and tried to push her back. She wouldn't budge.

"I'm sorry, Trust," she whispered. "I just feel so vulnerable right now."

She was a big help.

"My father," she gasped. "He passed away tonight." She sobbed bravely into my right shoulder.

"I am so sorry," I said with feeling.

"He never got to see my painting," she moaned. "Trust, I don't know how I can go on. Hold me," she insisted.

I wanted to point out that I already was, but it seemed a little insensitive.

"Hope . . ." I tried to say.

"There is no hope anymore," she cried.

"There's . . ."

"No hope," she interrupted again.

My last two attempts at speaking had not gone over that well, so I remained silent. Eventually she spoke.

"Thank you, Trust," she whispered. She looked up at

me and into my eyes. "I don't know what I would do without you."

I thought for a moment that God had thrown down a bolt of lightning to lay waste to me and my hugging arms. In reality it was Grace flipping the lights on. Light flooded the room, exposing Hope in my arms.

Where was lightning when you needed it?

"Trust?" Grace whispered.

"It's not what you think," I said in a panic.

Grace turned and ran off.

I looked down at Hope. If I hadn't known the tremendous pain she was suffering, I would almost have sworn she was smiling.

"Don't leave me, Trust," she said, clinging to me.

I pushed her away and went sprinting for Grace.

Grace was gone. I stopped in the middle of the meadow, realizing that there was no way I would find her in this dark night. I called her name, but there was no answer. I looked over at Ed's catapult and considered flinging myself out of this mess. I stood hopeless for awhile, then returned to my tree house, where I cleaned up the broken glass and then lay down, not getting a wink of sleep.

35

FED UP

◇

Cindy had had it. No more nice. No more smiles and nods. No more hellos and how-are-yous? If the plot from *Passion's Pupil* hadn't worked, then what would? She was through with it. It was time to pack it in. Never in her life had she met a man more pigheaded and dumb than Trust. He had left her crying and in need to chase after a silly mountain girl.

Forget it.

It was clear now that Cindy could never completely take hold of Trust's heart. How could she have been so committed to someone so flighty? The time and effort she had put forth had been for naught. She would return to Homerville beaten and empty-handed.

Grace and her goofy red hair.

Trust and his broad shoulders.

"Ahhh!" Cindy screamed as she stormed through the woods towards Sister Watson's house.

"If I don't get out of this place immediately, I'm going

to die," she said aloud. "How could I have lost when the contestants are so inferior to me?"

It was the losing that hurt the most. So she didn't have Trust. What really burned her was that Grace did. How could Cindy ever look herself in the mirror again if she gave up? How could she be the complete woman she knew she was if she let Grace take her prize? Cindy thought of Jasmine Lovely, the heroine of *Peeking for Love*. Jasmine had lost everything, including her Nobel prize and lucrative singing contracts, in her quest for love. Jasmine didn't give up. Cindy couldn't either. She couldn't quit yet.

A rustling to her right stopped her in her tracks.

"Who's there?" she demanded.

There was nothing but wind.

36

TAILED

◇

He had been staring at her house, wondering if she were asleep, when a man emerged from the trees and began tossing pebbles at her window. Moments later a light flashed on and the window was pushed open. Words were exchanged, but he had not caught them all.

The man walked away.

He waited. A short while later, a feminine shadow stepped out from the house and began walking towards the meadow. Having nothing better to do, he followed. He stayed far behind, worried that she might hear him.

She didn't.

He watched her walk over to the school, only to run away from it seconds later. He saw her boyfriend bolt out and lose her. He smiled, pulling himself back into the trees and deep into the forest. When his tiny mind simmered enough to let him think, he headed out to see if he could spot her making her way home.

He never found her.

He did, however, meet up with someone he had only recently become interested in. It was the dark-haired girl with the electric eyes. He watched her walk right by him, and then he crept slowly behind her. The thick scrub beside the trail bristled as he stepped in it. She turned around and looked in his direction.

"Who's there?" she demanded.

He frowned. He really didn't like being talked to like that.

"Who's there?" she said again.

He bit his lip and considered his options.

37

FAKING IT

Saturday morning I was a mess. Lack of sleep left me cranky and troubled. Plus, it felt like I had small flecks of glass covering every inch of my body. I tried to pretend that what had happened last night was just a bad dream, but I had never been very good at make-believe. I knew the first thing I needed to do was to find Grace and begin groveling. She was mad, but I hoped she might forgive me. I mean, I really hadn't done anything wrong. Right?

It was a long shot.

I replayed what had happened over and over in my mind, trying to imagine exactly how it must have appeared to Grace when she flicked on that light. In my mind I saw a caring young man supporting a hurting daughter of God. I'm sure, however, that Grace saw it somewhat differently. I wondered why Ed had dragged me to the schoolhouse and what Miss Flitrey had wanted anyway. Thanks to Hope, I had never found out what I really was supposed to be doing there.

Walking through the forest towards the Heck home, I was stopped by the sight of Leonard leaning against a tree as if he were waiting for me.

"Morning," he said.

"Yeah."

"You seem a little tense," he observed.

"I didn't sleep much."

"Everything okay?"

"Not really."

"Sister Watson's got all the details done," he tried to sound enthusiastic for my sake. "We just need the people now."

"I'm not sure Grace and I can fake it for you," I said as we walked. "I'm not sure we're even on speaking terms, much less sham-marriage terms."

"Well, I'm sure you'll work it out."

"I wish I were as confident."

"Listen, Trust," Leonard said with strength, stopping me on the trail. "We need that road. I got a house down the way that I want to live in. Do you think it's easy having your home four miles away?"

"Where have you been living?" I said, once again curious and realizing that I still didn't know where he had been laying his head at night.

"That's information for me only," he said seriously.

"Sorry."

"Don't worry about it," he said forgivingly. "What's important is for you to play your part today. This celebration is going to boost everyone's spirits. I can't have you doing this halfway."

"This wasn't my idea," I pointed out.

"That's all the more reason for you to stick with it."

"Grace is pretty mad at me, Leonard."

"Say something sweet to her. Women like that."

"It's not that easy."

"I know." Leonard scratched his stubble-covered chin. "I'm not even sure she'll talk to me."

"Let me take care of it then," he volunteered. "I've done a lot of talking in my lifetime. I'm sure I could find a few words to throw at her."

I shouldn't even have entertained the thought, but it had some appeal. Leonard could test the waters and find out just how mad she was. It was crazy, but like a coward I agreed to let him do it.

"Will you tell her I'm sorry?" I asked.

"If it comes up."

"Leonard, that's the whole reason you need to talk to her."

"I know, I know." He waved me away. "I just don't want to go in there sounding all rehearsed and stilted. Women can spot insincerity easier than a sale blouse in the right color."

I was sincerely worried.

"Don't get all jumpy. I'll meet you down by the boardinghouse in a few minutes," he said, patting me on the shoulder and heading out towards the Heck home. "I'll patch things up tighter than a youth belt on an adult boar."

"The boardinghouse is gone," I reminded him.

"Then I'll meet you at the catapult."

We parted ways. I crossed through the woods and out into the meadow near Wad's shack. Sister Watson had incorporated his shack into part of the reception decorations. I think she had been hoping to make the old outhouse shell look like some sort of gazebo. Thanks to the decorations, I could tell that our colors were peach and mint. Wad was instructing Digby as he gave Frank Porter a facial.

"Morning, Wad, Digby, Frank."

"Morning, Trust," they all threw back.

I walked over to the crepe paper-covered catapult and sat down on the base of the thing. I noted how much closer the Girth seemed to be. It was as if the river were growing daily. I saw Roswell leading his ice cream wagon around the meadow looking for prereception sales. I heard him try to bully Lupert Carver into buying something. When Lupert refused, Roswell took out a cone and started licking it in front of him, acting as if it were the greatest thing he had ever eaten. Sister Watson had been adamant about not letting Roswell peddle his treats while the reception was going on, but Roswell had ignored her. He saw this whole thing as an excellent opportunity to make some big sales.

Sister Watson came out of the woods and over to me. She looked as if she had something besides her wig on her mind.

"Trust, have you seen Hope?" she asked.

"No," I answered quickly.

"I need the truth here," she insisted.

"I haven't seen her."

"She didn't come home last night," Sister Watson said with concern. "I don't want to mother her to death, but I can't just turn a blind eye to what she's doing."

"What's she doing?"

"How should I know?" she snapped. "She didn't come home last night."

"I'd love to help," I lied. "But I haven't seen her since late last evening."

"How late?"

"I don't know. Eleven, twelve," I guessed.

"And just where did you see her at such a late hour?"

"The school."

"What were you doing there?" she demanded.

"Nothing," I insisted. "She was upset and crying about her father dying."

"Mighty sensitive girl," Sister Watson said. "Seems unhealthy, though, to be crying about something that happened seven years ago."

"Seven years ago?" I asked. "He died yesterday."

"Trust, you're making it hard for me to believe a word you're saying. Hope's father died seven years ago in a freak train and plane wreck. He was hauling myrrh to poor children across the Bering Strait."

"Mir?" I questioned.

"As in Frankenstein."

I think she meant frankincense, but I didn't pursue that line of questioning any further. "That's impossible. Hope's father died just yesterday."

"Well, I guess we've got one more reason to find her."

"I have no reason to find her," I said. "Besides, she

probably left town since her father passed away and there's no longer a need for her to paint for him."

"Paint what?" Sister Watson asked in confusion. "She was here to study flight patterns of the Flute Goose."

"I think we're talking about two different people."

"I'm not," she insisted. "I'm talking about Hope, and this conversation is not helping me find her." Sister Watson looked at her wrist as if there were a watch there. "I really need to get moving. Guests will be arriving in a few hours. You'd better clean yourself up," she instructed me.

Sister Watson turned and walked away, dragging a piece of peach-colored crepe paper on the bottom of her shoe. She stopped after a few steps and tried to shake it off. I had never seen an older woman convulse so. Just before her left leg detached from its socket, the paper fell off, and she continued on her way. When I turned to look in a different direction, there was Leonard.

"It's all taken care of," he said proudly. "Grace would be honored to be your fake wife for the afternoon."

"She would?"

"She told me to tell you that she thinks it's okay."

"Is she mad?"

"Let's just say she doesn't smile easy at the moment."

"You told her about my being innocent and sorry?"

"Oh, I went on and on about how sorry you are," he waved.

"So she's okay with it all?"

"She'll be here," Leonard said. "Speaking of food, I wonder how Teddy's coming with the party favors."

Before I could ask him what the heck he was talking

about, he was gone. I went over to Sister Watson's place and used her shower. I then got dressed up in the old tux that Toby had worn once on his wedding day and was now letting me borrow. It didn't fit at all but was in fairly good shape. Toby had kept it pressed between his mattresses for the last twenty years. He had thought that like a corsage stuck in the pages of a thick book, a tux too needed to be preserved. The sleeves and legs were too short and the tails were longer than I would have preferred, but it would do for a faux reception.

By the time I was all ready, the locals were beginning to filter into the meadow in anticipation of the reception. Most everyone began to lay claim to tables, wanting to make sure they had a seat before all the out-of-towners arrived. I saw Ed pacing around the sign-in table. He had been unhappy ever since he had been given the responsibility of manning the guest book. It wasn't so much that he couldn't handle the obvious aspects of the assignment as it was that he was also in charge of giving out the door prizes, and clearly there was no actual door. He got into a heated argument with Leonard over how he felt that they should rename them *Meadow Mementos* instead of door prizes.

Tindy MacDermont was sitting near the tables with a huge harp in front of her. She had found it at a swap meet a couple of weeks ago. She didn't know how to play it, so she just sat there strumming it back and forth. Pete was right next to her playing his trombone, and Jeff Titter had a Jew's harp in his big mouth. They were creating really interesting music together. Pete and Jeff were playing two entirely different songs, and Tindy kept yelling at them because they were messing up her strumming.

Teddy Yetch was fussing around with all the food, laying out tiny sandwiches in spirals and layers. I sidled up to her and complimented her on the effort.

"I read in *Woman's World* that ham is best rolled and turkey is better chunked," she explained.

I spotted President Heck off in the distance talking to himself. I was certain he was going over what he would say to everyone and working on his toast. Seeing him made me realize just how nervous I actually was. I wasn't worried about the reception itself. I was more concerned with the reception Grace would give me. We still had not talked since the incident last night. I knew that Leonard had attempted to explain my side, but I could only imagine what he had actually said.

I walked around trying to look calm and waiting for Grace to appear. About half an hour before three, she emerged from the forest and joined our gathering. Let me just say, she had never looked better. The wedding dress that her mother had whipped up was more flattering than a room full of gung-ho underlings. Most of her red hair was pulled up on top of her head, but a good number of strands hung down loose. I would like to say that she waltzed beautifully into the meadow and took her place by my side. But she was by no means waltzing. It was obvious that she still wasn't happy with me. She walked right past me without saying a word, stopping on her mark where the line was supposed to be. I sheepishly stepped up next to her.

"Don't talk to me," she said before I could get a word in.

"Grace."

"I'm serious, Trust. I'm only doing this for Sister Watson and her dumb road. I wouldn't even be doing it for that if my mother hadn't spent all morning lecturing me on how important it is."

"Did you tell your parents about last night?"

"No," she glared at me.

"You have to let me explain," I pleaded.

"I'm sure you have a perfectly good explanation for being with Hope in a dark deserted building in the middle of the night."

"It's not a great explanation," I tried. "But I have one."

"I don't want to hear it."

Grace turned to look at Sister Watson, who had stepped up to her and was pulling a small thread off her dress.

"Now, folks will be arriving any moment," she said. "So everyone should get in line, and you two need to start pretending like you're married."

Grace scowled.

Sister Watson drew back. "Now, Grace, you look like Edna Wilchester after forty years with Wyman. That won't do. We're going for the newlywed married look," she instructed her.

"This will have to do," Grace said firmly.

"Do you think people will show up?" I asked Sister Watson nicely.

"I hope so," she answered. "By now Leo and CleeDee should have checked the announcements of a number of people. They promised to send Lupert on ahead to notify us. Places," she hollered. "And remember—Grace and Trust are married."

I tried to scoot closer to Grace, but she just moved away.

"Grace," I begged out of the side of my mouth. "Nothing happened between Hope and me."

"That's too bad," she said, smiling a fake smile for the part, "because that was probably all the affection you're going to get for quite some time."

"We're supposed to be married," I pointed out.

"We'll be divorced by sundown."

Lupert Carver came tearing across the meadow and up to Sister Watson. He caught his breath and said, "They're coming."

"Look sharp," Sister Watson hollered.

That was a tall order for this town.

I glanced up towards the trail and saw the initial trickle of wedding guests. A bald man with a hairy woman walked up to the table, signed in, and then asked Ed where their door prize was. Ed handed them a plastic back scratcher, and they came over and went through the line. They shook everyone's hands as if they actually knew us.

Our line consisted of Grace and me, Patty Heck, Ricky Heck, and Narlette in white overall shorts. Digby was there with highlighted hair, and Leonard stood positioned in tight sky-blue slacks and a fake tux T-shirt. Sybil Porter was chosen to be a member of our line simply because Sister Watson felt the girl needed every opportunity she could find to wear a dress.

The bald man shook my hand and then winked at me

as if he knew something I didn't know. By the time he had made it through the line, others were already on the scene.

Sister Watson squeezed up between Grace and me and whispered, "Remember—one of these people could be the state guy here to see about our road."

People kept coming. Everyone would go through the line and then sit around munching on food.

"This isn't too bad," I whispered to Grace.

"I think it's awful."

"I said I'm sorry," I pleaded.

"That's not good enough." She smiled as an older lady with long ears came through the line.

"You know I would never cheat on you," I tried to explain.

"I do?" she asked sarcastically. "What was that last night?"

"Her father died."

"That's not all that's dead."

"You have to believe me."

"I believed you last time."

"See," I tried to joke. "So it should be easy."

"It's not funny, Trust."

A stout man breathing loudly came through the line and shook Grace's hand with more feeling than I felt was appropriate.

"She's a pretty one," he told me. "I'd hold on tight, or someone might steal her away." He then made a creepy motion.

I thought maybe Grace would be so bothered by him

that she might cling to me. Instead she said, "I'm already looking for something better."

The man smiled as if he might be that something better. Grace turned to shake the hand of the next person. I was in trouble. If Grace was mad enough to be flirting with a heavy-breathing stranger, then I had real problems. I was trying to think up something healing to say when suddenly Doran Jorgensen and Lucy Fall were standing right in front of me. The last time I had seen either of them had been in Southdale. Doran was an ex-companion that had made Grace's and my relationship fairly interesting a while back. I couldn't believe he was here now with Lucy.

"Doran?" I asked in amazement.

He answered by hugging me tightly. Then he gave Grace a squeeze. Lucy did the same.

"What are you guys doing here?" I asked.

"We got your announcement," Doran said happily. "Flew out here as fast as we could. I can't believe you two went off and got married early. I understand, though. There's wisdom in short engagements." Doran winked at Lucy.

Grace and I would have explained ourselves, but there were people listening in line.

"Yeah," was all I said.

"Well, we got our own good news," Doran said, bursting. "Show him, Lucy."

Lucy lifted her hand to display a huge diamond ring.

"We were so jealous of you two that we eloped to the temple. We got hitched yesterday. We're on our honeymoon too."

I felt like covering my eyes just in case he exploded.

"You're kidding," I said in amazement.

Lucy blushed for both of them.

I looked closely at her as she smiled up at her husband. She was certainly not the girl I had dated all those years ago. She was just as beautiful, but the Lucy I knew would never have even entertained the idea of honeymooning here. She would have insisted on a month-long vacation to Greece or a three-week Caribbean cruise and shopping spree. But then again, the Lucy I knew was long gone, replaced by a confident, kind individual that wanted to do what was right. She and Doran had been dating for a while, and even though it wasn't ever mentioned outright, we all figured that they would end up together. I guess we had figured right.

"So how long are you two going to stay here?" I asked.

"We weren't sure we could stay long at all," Doran explained. "This ring set us back a bit, and the plane tickets here weren't cheap. But luckily we ran into Leo and CleeDee living in Leonard's mobile home at the start of the trail. Nice to know Leonard's here," Doran added.

"Real comforting," I agreed, looking over at Leonard as he shook people's hands and slipped them pamphlets explaining some of the products he sold.

"Anyhow," Doran went on, "Leo said we could stay at his place on Lush Point for as long as we needed. He said he hadn't had a chance to clean up his place before he left and that a couple of his dogs were feeling ill, but the place is ours if we want it. I tell you, Trust and Grace, the heavens are blessing this union already."

A relatively sweet-looking lady started pushing Doran because he and Lucy were holding up the line.

"We'll talk more later," I said as he was shoved away.

"Actually," Doran said, "we were going to run off to Leo's place and, uh, get . . . situated."

Doran kissed Lucy, Lucy kissed Doran, and they both left.

"Can you believe they're here?" I asked Grace after shaking the woman's hand. Grace didn't answer.

"You can't be mad at me forever," I pointed out.

"I only have to be mad at you until you're gone."

"You're joking, right?"

Again, Grace was silent.

A pear-shaped woman with an orange-shaped mouth shook our hands and then looked us over.

"You look a little nervous, dear," she said to Grace. "I understand. Why, I was scared to death on my wedding night—"

Mercifully, Sister Watson stood up on one of the lawn chairs and cupped her hands to holler at the crowd.

"If I could have your attention," she yelled. "We'd like to take a break with the line for a little musical entertainment. Some of you may not know that Thelma's Way has its own singing sensation."

I was among the unknowing.

"They're here to tickle our ears and celebrate the union of this happy couple," Sister Watson pointed at Grace and me.

We looked anything but happy.

"Anyhow," she went on, "here is Thelma's Way's very own barbershop quartet, One Note."

Toby, Wad, and Roswell walked into the center of the crowd. They linked arms and began to sing. I couldn't understand why they thought they were a barbershop quartet, seeing as how there were only three of them. If forced to speculate, I would have guessed they must have thought that Wad's being a barber was close enough. How they got their group's name, however, was perfectly obvious. They all knew only one low deep note, making their music sound like one continual belch. After each number I felt like saying, "Excuse you." On their third number they added some choreography. Roswell would swing Toby on his elbow while Wad would cross his knees and wink in our direction. Then they would line up and try to go up and down in sync.

Unfortunately, Roswell's old knees quickly ruined any fluid movements they got going. So they just stuck with a lot of hand waving and hat tipping. During their fourth number quite a few people got up to leave. Sister Watson, feeling their pain, kicked Toby in the back of the leg to get him to turn around and look at her. When he did, she slid a finger across her throat to signal them to hurry up and end their act. They wrapped things up, and Toby told the gathering that if anyone was interested in autographs, the group would be over by the catapult right after they got a little something to eat and Roswell put ointment on his knees.

I think the crowd was star struck—or speechless.

"Before we have a toast," Sister Watson announced,

"Pete Kennedy and Ed Washington have a special cheer they would like to do for the newlyweds." She motioned for them to come up.

"Well, Grace is like a sister to us," Pete said kindly. "And, well, Trust—he's become a brother. So we'd like to give a special holler to celebrate our brother and sister getting married."

I tried not to cringe too openly.

"Give me a C," Ed began.

The whole crowd yelled, "C."

"Give me an E," Pete followed.

They gave us their best E.

"Give me an L."

They had lost a few, but a majority was still participating.

"Give me an I," Pete screamed.

Only about half said anything. I think everyone was thrown off by the misspelling of what we all assumed would be *celebrate*.

"Give me a B," Ed whooped.

Only a few of our locals, who had not yet noticed the misspelling, yelled back.

"Give me an A." Pete put his hands together as if motioning the crowd to clap.

"Give me a T," Ed said with uncertainty, obviously thrown off by the nonparticipating crowd.

"Give me another E!" Pete tried to make the ending strong.

No one said anything. The crowd was silent. A skinny

man with a ball cap three tables back coughed. Pete and Ed slinked off in cheer defeat.

"I think they were trying to spell *celebrate*," I said to Grace, as if she might possibly not have known that.

"I think their mistake was very appropriate."

Before I could act hurt, Sister Watson was talking again. "Thank you, Pete and Ed," she said. "Now I understand why you were looking around for a dictionary earlier. Anyhow, it is now time for the toast," Sister Watson informed us all.

President and Sister Heck stepped up by her, and she figuratively handed President Heck the spotlight.

"Grace, Trust," he waved us over.

I stuck out my hand for Grace to take it, but she kept her hands folded and walked over all by herself. I followed closely behind, trying to make it look as if we actually liked each other.

President Heck signaled for us to take a seat. Grace sat first, and I sat as close to her as I could without making her madder.

"This is a happy day," President Heck began. "I know I'm particularly thrilled, seeing as how I've never had a son before."

Patty Heck elbowed him. "What about Digby?" she whispered through clenched teeth.

"Aside from Digby," he said defensively. "I appreciate you all coming out. I know that it means a lot to Trust and Grace."

I looked around at everyone I didn't know and wondered how I would ever thank them all.

President Heck went on and on, talking about us and the importance of the decision we had made, while Grace and I sat side by side trying to appear happy.

"I really am sorry." I smiled.

"Knock it off, Trust." She smiled back.

"We have to talk about this." I gazed at her affectionately.

"There's nothing to say," she cooed.

"That's it, then?" I said with love in my voice.

"Am I just supposed to forgive you?" She batted her eyelashes.

"I didn't do anything wrong," I whispered.

"It was strike three, Trust."

President Heck finished his toast, and Sister Lando and Nippy Ward wheeled out a big cake that said "Happy Hitchin" on it. Janet Bickerstaff handed me a knife and the crowd watched in anticipation. I cut a slice and tried to feed it to Grace. She nibbled a corner, and I followed tradition and pushed it into her face. I was hoping the playful banter might ease the tension. It didn't. I cut a piece for her to give to me. After making it clear that she wasn't going to pick it up, I did, and pushed it into my own face. I think it was then that the crowd really began to sense the problems in our relationship. Sister Watson made her way up to us and hissed at us to smile.

It was hopeless. I had never felt worse. I would have pleaded with Grace a little more, but all the locals were suddenly whispering about something. I looked to see what the fuss was about and spotted Paul walking our way. He had not been seen since he had burned down the boarding-house. He walked right up to us and stopped.

"What do you want?" Sister Watson stepped up to him.

"I have a right to be here," he insisted.

"You burned that right," Roswell growled.

"I came back because I've got big news," he announced.

"We thought you were dead," Toby said, uninterested in his announcement.

"I could have been," Paul said. "The current was too strong to swim across."

"You went down the falls?" I asked, knowing that it was dangerous but having lived through it myself.

"That's the big news," Paul said. "There ain't no falls no more."

"What do you mean?" President Heck asked.

"They're gone," he insisted. "There's nothing but a bunch of water. I floated to a stop someplace well past the falls. It took me a couple days to make my way back. But I'm sure as sugar there's no falls."

"That's the stupidest thing I've heard since Pete claimed he saw that fairy," Sister Watson said with vigor.

"It's true," Pete defended. "She was pink and floating."

"I don't care about no fairies," Paul said. "But there is no falls anymore."

"I've never heard a bigger or dumber lie," Sister Watson forced herself to say.

"It's true," said a man sitting at a nearby table and eating cake. He had been eavesdropping and now wanted to join the conversation.

"Who are you?" Sister Watson asked, bothered.

"I'm from the state road department."

"You're here about the road?" she asked, showing him a little more respect.

"Well, sort of," he hemmed. "I was initially going to come out here for the road, but then when I talked to my supervisor, he informed me that there were no people in this area."

"He's wrong," Teddy threw in.

"I guess so," the man said. "That's why we've got a real problem."

"Don't tell me we don't get a road," Sister Watson said sadly. "Just 'cause you didn't think we were here doesn't mean we don't need one."

"Actually, the problem is bigger than that." He tried to sound friendly. "The state has dammed up the lower-forty dike. In a short while your town will be a big lake."

"What?" everyone hollered.

"This area's slated to be a lake bottom."

"You can't do that," Roswell shouted.

"Why didn't you tell us sooner?" Sister Watson demanded.

"I was going to," he explained. "But I wanted to have a piece of cake first."

"Not that sooner," Sister Watson ranted. "Sooner as in before you dammed up anything."

"Like I said, we didn't know you were here."

"See, I told you the falls were gone," Paul gloated.

"What about Triply Cove below the falls?" President Heck asked. "What happened to all those folks?"

"They were moved out long ago. In fact, our contact

there was supposed to make sure that everyone here knew this was happening."

"I can't believe this," Toby said sadly. "How could you have overlooked us?"

"These things happen."

"Well, you'll just have to undam it," Roswell insisted.

"That could be tricky," he tisked. "Besides, the state will pay you good money for your land and relocate you somewhere else."

"How much money?" Roswell asked.

I turned to ask Grace if she could believe all of this, but she was gone. She had fulfilled her duty and was done. I looked for any traces of her but saw none. Most of the gathering was still talking and eating and coming and going. The line broke up, and the man from the state helped himself to a second piece of cake while answering questions.

We were in the final days of Thelma's Way.

38

SUNDAY SICK

The next morning we were all in shock. Everyone just shuffled around the meadow, cleaning up from the reception and trying to think of something other than the fact that our town was drowning. President Heck announced that we would have a late worship service so that everyone could have some time to mourn.

The man from the state had been quite clear on the point that it couldn't be stopped. He insisted that everyone simply take the money they would be offered and move on. He claimed that the state was doing us a favor, that no one would pay more for this forgotten land, and that they were giving everyone a chance to move somewhere normal. He tried to convince Sister Watson this was a good thing by explaining that she could move someplace where there were lots of paved roads.

She wasn't convinced. In fact, she was so angry she chased him out of town.

Teddy Yetch chained herself to the cemetery gates in

protest. She vowed never to leave. But as the first hour stretched on, she became uncomfortable and went back to her house, where she promised she would stay until she needed to go out.

Paul was cashing in on our town's being unable to focus on more than one thing at a time. With everyone up in arms about becoming a lake, no one seemed to fuss about his having burned down the boardinghouse. Seeing the silver lining in this calamity, Paul jumped on the bandwagon and began speaking louder than anyone about what a great injustice this was. He and Sister Watson were organizing an emergency fireside meeting for this evening, the purpose of which was to discuss and commiserate about all the horrible things happening to our town.

Leo and CleeDee had sent word from the mobile home that they felt sorry for us and they were praying for our plight. I figured they had forgotten that they actually lived here. Leonard was livid as well. He couldn't believe how the laws of the land kept batting him around. First his hang-ups in Southdale, and now the free land he was going to be given was going to be made a lake bottom. Just when things seemed as confusing as they possibly could get, Thelma's Way got a visitor.

My father.

He strode into town in midafternoon. I didn't see him coming as much as I heard him coming. Everyone was clapping and cheering as if welcoming home a long-lost hero. I didn't know how to feel. I was standing by the wagons picking up pieces of crepe paper when he walked up to me.

"Dad," I said emotionlessly.

"Trust."

The whole town was completely shocked.

"He's your . . ." Sister Watson gasped.

"You're his . . ." Paul pointed at me.

"How is it possible?" Pete asked.

Miss Flitrey pulled Pete aside to explain a few things about life.

Toby looked us both up and down and then whistled. "I can't believe we hadn't figured it out before. I ain't never seen such twin noses."

"But you never told us you were Trust's father," Sister Watson said in disbelief.

"I should have," my dad said. "But I didn't want you to treat me any different from anyone else."

"Heck," Jerry said, "we would have still been nice to you."

My father smiled. "What happened to the boarding-house?"

"Paul," was all Sister Watson said.

"The important thing is that you're back." Paul shifted the conversation to where it had been before he came up.

Everyone patted my father on the shoulders and back. I couldn't believe how much my people seemed to love him. I wondered how they would feel if they knew his real reason for liking them.

After a couple of minutes of greeting, my father spoke. "Can I talk to Trust for a moment?" he asked the audience.

Everyone nodded, staying exactly where they were. We moved away towards the cemetery.

"Mom told me you found out," he said when we were alone. "She forgot to mention it until last night. I took the first flight out."

"Why'd you come here?" I asked, still not knowing how to feel.

"To explain."

"How about the first time you came? What was your motive then?"

"I bet you have a pretty good idea," he answered.

"To get the Book of Mormon," I said with disgust.

"Yes."

"I can't believe it."

"I may have come here for that, but I left here not caring one ounce about it anymore."

"I find that hard to believe."

"I love this place, son. I love that you served here, and I love these people."

"You love this place?" I asked in disbelief.

"I didn't at first," he explained. "At first I couldn't imagine how you had made it more than two weeks here. But then these people started to grow on me. Right before the accident, I was packed and ready to get out. I was afraid of how I was feeling. After the accident, I knew I was hooked."

"Then why didn't you tell me you had been here?"

"I was going to," he defended himself. "You have to understand. I had never experienced anything like when I had stayed here. My whole life has changed thanks to these people and this dirt." Dad picked up a handful of earth and let it fall to the ground.

"I was also embarrassed about what had brought me here in the first place," he added. "I didn't even know the name of the town, even though you had served here two years. And yet I gave it my full attention as soon as I knew there was something I wanted. I'm sorry, Trust."

"I still don't believe it," I said, not yet ready to give up my feelings of betrayal.

"I don't know what else to say," he said sincerely.

It's not as if I didn't want everything he was claiming to be true, because I did. I wanted him to feel as attached to Thelma's Way as I did. I just didn't want to be made a fool. My father had gone a long time not caring about anything besides business and gain. Now he was expecting me to believe that he had experienced the same sort of growth spurt during his two months here that I had experienced in two long years.

"How does Mom feel about all of this?" I asked.

"She's all right," he answered. "She still has a hard time understanding the importance you and I place on Thelma's Way."

"That makes sense," I said. "I'm not sure I always understand it."

"How is Grace? I didn't see her." He looked around.

"Well," I sighed, "we're not exactly speaking at the moment."

"What happened?"

"It's a long story."

"Don't blow it with her," he said kindly. "She means more to our family than I think you realize. Abel and Margaret would never speak to you again."

"I'm not trying to blow it," I insisted. "I just have a way of making things more confusing than they need to be."

"I'd like to see her."

"Throw in a couple of good words for me," I joked.

"Is she at home?" he asked.

"I assume so."

My father put his hand on my shoulder and looked me in the eyes. Apparently he couldn't find any more words to use because he turned and walked off. I watched the back of him as he hiked up over the small hill right in front of us.

"I think you should believe him," a voice said from above.

I thought for a moment that the heavens were asking me to be charitable. As it turns out, however, it was only Leonard sitting up in a tree right above me. He shifted on his branch, and small flecks of bark floated down into my eyes.

"You were listening?" I rubbed my eyes.

"Don't cry," Leonard pleaded. "I just couldn't help hearing," he said, swinging to a lower branch and sliding down the trunk. He planted himself on the ground, raising his arms like a dismounting gymnast.

"I'm not crying," I corrected him.

"No need to worry. I won't tell a soul," he comforted me. "Hey, did you know Pete was bawling like a baby when he found out about the town going under? Don't tell him I told you, though."

"Leonard, what do you want?"

"I don't want anything," he insisted. "I was just trying

238

to find a few minutes alone, and you and your father inter-rupted me."

"We didn't know you were up there."

"I guess thoroughness is simply another outdated virtue."

I had no idea what he was talking about.

"By the way, what do you think of that Watson woman?" he asked me.

"Sister Watson? She's fine," I said, wondering why he was bringing her up.

"I don't know if I'd go that far," Leonard said thought-fully. "But this morning while I was helping Ed pull deco-rations off his catapult, I think she tried to hold my hand."

"Really?"

"Well, she was real cool about it," he explained. "She had some trash and asked me if I'd hold it for her."

"That is cool," I joked.

"Let's just say when she placed the garbage in my palm, her hand lingered."

"Sounds like love."

"She is a few years older than me," he said, as if I might not have noticed.

"If by 'a few' you mean twenty."

"No. I think that's a bunch. By the way, have you seen Hope?"

"Nope."

"Mavis is worried about her not showing up."

"I think she's gone."

"Don't be morbid," Leonard chastised me.

"I just mean that she went back to Georgia."

Toby walked up to us and just began talking. "I wonder if you two might know where I can find that girl with the sprained wrist."

"We were just talking about her," I told him.

"Small world," he said in amazement. "Well, it seems that Sybil Porter twisted her ankle in a fox hole and is in need of my bandage. Hope's wrist should be feeling better by now."

"We don't know where she is," Leonard explained.

"I hope my bandage is okay," Toby said, concerned. "This town would face a medical crisis like it's never known if that wrap is lost."

Leonard and I stared at Toby until he went away. I then stared at Leonard until he did the same. I had way too much on my mind. The last thing I wanted was to speak to anyone at the moment. Unless, of course, that anyone had red hair, green eyes, and my future dangling by a string.

39

FAIR WARMING

The fire crackled like plastic in a deep fryer. I watched Toby throw another log on and then sit down next to Lupert. The entire town was gathered around the gigantic fire that Pete and I had built in the middle of the meadow. Shadows danced on every face as the flames, thirsty for oxygen, stretched out their tongues and gulped. We all had been sitting in silence as everyone continued to come down from the hills and gather round. Toby kept the fire going as each family and individual found a place to park their posteriors. The Knapworths were the only happy-looking couple. They sat on their spread-out blanket looking like this was simply a romantic evening by the fire. Right after dark Sister Watson stood. She walked around the flames once and then spoke.

"We haven't always agreed," she began. "There have been many times when I have not seen eye to eye with all of you over at least a dozen things. There's been debates about Paul," she nodded towards him. He nodded back.

"There's been arguments over pageants and education." Miss Flitrey nodded her head. "There's been disagreements concerning roads and rivers. But I dare say that we've never stood more together than now. Now, when someone wants to simply wash our town away."

There was a low murmuring.

"I don't want to live somewhere else," she shouted. "I don't want to grow older in some town with no roots. I don't want Toby to settle in Virgil's Find and the Porters to try Collin's Blight. I don't want to die and be buried in some foreign soil. I want my last breath to be full of Thelma's air."

I watched everyone as Sister Watson spoke. It was obvious that she was dead on. There wasn't a single fire-lit face that didn't appear to agree wholeheartedly with her. The only people I knew who weren't there were President Heck and Grace. President Heck had needed to finish his chair path. He wanted the cement to be long dry by the time the water rose high enough to cover it. And Grace? Well, she had not been seen since she had walked away from the reception yesterday. I had tried in vain to find her, but she had hidden herself too well. I explained to President Heck and his wife about what had happened, and they promised to talk to her about the misunderstanding as soon as she came around. Then they lectured me about the evils of dark school rooms.

My father was also missing from this gathering. He had been sick when he found out what was happening to Thelma's Way. He was so disturbed, in fact, I almost thought he was being sincere. He had skipped out on tonight because he wanted to help President Heck with his path. Right now the two of them were probably putting the finishing touches on the last long shoot that President Heck had laid from his house to the far edge of the meadow.

Oh, Doran and Lucy were missing from our gathering as well. But no one had seen them since they had left the reception, and no one expected to see them soon.

"I want to be perfectly honest with you all." Sister Watson was still talking. "Things do not look good. The state claims to have every right to do what they are doing. They said that we would bring more good to Tennessee if we were covered up."

"They can't just flood us," Pete argued.

"They are trying to," she answered.

"Is it too late to build Paul's shelter?" Toby asked.

"I'll field this one," Paul said, standing. "That shelter would have been a nice addition to this meadow. But I'm afraid that even it, with the small gold plaque thanking me for my dedication, would not be enough to stop the rising water."

"This is wrong," Janet Bickerstaff hollered.

"It is," Sister Watson agreed. "Fortunately for you, Janet, your house is close enough to Virgil's Find and on the other side of Dimple Ridge. The lake won't even touch you."

"Oh," Janet said. "Well then, good luck, you guys." She got up with her son, Greg, and headed for home.

"There are others who won't be touched either," Sister Watson explained, "but the majority of us are done for."

"How long until it's filled?" Frank asked.

"A couple of months," she answered.

We all were silent for a long while. No one said anything except Ed, who asked if it were possible to build a big airtight bubble over our town.

"Let me field that one." Leonard stood. "Ed, I've lived in a bubble, and believe me, it isn't easy." Leonard sat down.

"Thank you, Leonard, for sharing with us," Sister Watson said, gushing.

The light summer wind blew gently, pushing the dark around. I couldn't imagine Thelma's Way ever not being here. It was the one constant in a completely changing world. Sure, it wasn't polished and always civil, but it was home to these people and a place unlike any I had ever known.

"You know, we could pray," Digby suggested. It was hard to take him completely seriously due to his new fluffy layered hairdo, but the idea was one we all should have entertained some time ago.

"I've been praying in private," Teddy Yetch informed us, wanting to make sure we all knew how spiritual she was.

"Me too," about twelve others said.

"But that's different," Digby said.

"He's got a point," Toby threw out.

"That he does," Paul agreed.

"Well, it's not like I'm against praying," Sister Watson defended herself. "I never said that we shouldn't. I'm just not sure that we should get our hopes up."

"Then let's pray," Toby said.

"Around the fire?" Sister Watson asked. "It seems so pagan."

"Around the fire," Leonard insisted.

"Who should say it?" Todd Nodd asked.

"Hold on a minute," Sister Watson said. "The important thing isn't who should say it, it's who should ask someone to say it. I know when Bishop Watson was alive, he always was the one to call on people to pray at our house. It was proper. Now here on the meadow it should be no different."

"Bishop Watson's dead," Pete pointed out.

"I didn't mean him," she said. "I was thinking maybe Leonard would like to call on someone."

"No offense," Frank argued. "But Leonard isn't even from here."

"None taken," Leonard motioned.

"Roswell's the oldest," Jeff Titter pointed out. "Let him call on someone."

"I ain't that much older than Briant," Roswell said, as if hurt. "Besides, I hate picking things."

I was going to argue that point, but Toby stood and started praying. At first no one knew what he was doing. After a few moments we all folded our arms and let him go on with it.

"Please bless that this whole mess is something you can straighten out. Keep our highlands dry, and our lowlands green. I know we don't always do things the way you probably would, but in all honesty we really have no idea how exactly you want it."

I did the unpardonable and peeked while he was praying. I know it was dark, and I know it was an emotional time, but I could have sworn that the entire circle of locals was glowing. Not glowing like the time Teddy fed them that phosphorescent stew, but glowing as if the heavens had switched us on.

"And if you decide to cover this place with water, don't let us forget what we once had. Amen."

No sooner had Toby closed the prayer than a heavenly angel dressed in white walked amongst us and stopped in front of the fire. After my initial shock, I realized that the heavenly angel was actually a messy-looking man carrying what looked to be a white robe.

Everyone just stared at him.

"I know you," Sister Watson said. "You're Bean's boy, Daryll, from down below the falls."

The stranger seemed to understand.

"Well, what are you doing here?" she asked. "Your town is gone."

Before anyone could respond, Pete hollered, "Those are my shoes." He pointed to the shoes the man was wearing.

"And that's my shirt," Briant spat.

"Don't tell me you're the one that's been terrorizing our place," Sister Watson said in amazement.

Daryll stepped back a few feet, suddenly scared of what everyone was saying. It was as the shadows changed on the robe he was carrying that I noticed it was not a robe. It was the wedding dress Grace had been wearing yesterday. I stepped through the crowd and up to him.

"Where'd you get that?" I demanded.

He stepped back.

"That's Grace's wedding dress," I explained.

Daryll held it out, dropped it, and then ran like no one I had ever seen run before.

"Do you think he has Grace?" Leonard asked.

"I have no idea," I said, worried. "Has anyone seen her since the reception?"

Everyone shook their heads.

"This doesn't look good, Trust." Sister Watson was concerned. "Someone better go get Ricky. Trust, you and Pete try and follow Daryll."

"I got guns," Pete informed us unnecessarily.

"Let me go too," Digby asked.

"And me." Frank raised his hand. "I got a couple of flashlights."

"I don't care who comes with me," I said. "Let's just go."

We all took off in the direction that Daryll had run.

I couldn't remember ever being more scared.

40

BOARDED UP

◇

We were the most pathetic posse I had ever known. Two hundred yards into our chase, Ed started complaining about his feet hurting. He dropped out just past the meadow's edge. A few minutes later Pete remembered that he had left something cooking in his oven and took off to take care of it. Frank Porter scraped his leg on a low branch and asked Wad to help him get back to the meadow. Then he insisted we give him back his flashlights because last time he lent one to somebody, it came back missing a battery. So he bailed, leaving Jeff Titter now as the only person with a flashlight. Digby tried to stick with us, but then reality set in, and he began to question the whole meaning of the chase. Maybe Daryll had found the wedding dress. Maybe Grace was hiding out on her own accord.

Maybe I should have been running alone.

Jerry Scotch kept up as we tried desperately to guess which direction Daryll had gone. But I could tell his heart wasn't really in it, due to the fact that every time we stopped to speculate which direction we should go, Jerry would always point back towards the meadow. Eventually I told him to go his way and I would go mine. That left me running alone with Jeff Titter.

Jeff and I had never really spent much time together. He was a tall man with thin shoulders and wide knees. I was told he had blond hair, although to me it looked two shades darker than muck brown. He wasn't a talker and had an unusual laugh. If he found something to be funny, he would let out one explosive giggle and then quickly suck it back in and pinch his lips. He was married to a woman named Farence and had three kids, all of them named Jeff. I felt most sorry for his daughter. A part of his livelihood was to care for the Thelma's Way chapel. The Church paid him a small amount of money to keep things in order. He did a lousy job. Not only that, but he usually did his lousy job on Sundays, while attending church. He would switch from pew to pew during sacrament meeting, wiping down the benches and straightening hymnbooks. If he saw you going in to use the bathroom, he would ask you to wash out the sink. There had been many a Sunday School lesson interrupted by the sound of the vacuum being run in the hall.

Somewhere just left of nowhere, Jeff began to whine about his lungs burning. I ignored him until he fell on all fours and began heaving.

"Go on without me," he huffed.

"I have no idea where I am," I said, knowing that if I went on alone, I'd never find my way back—or forward, for

249

that matter. "We're probably nowhere near where he went, anyhow. Besides, you have the only flashlight."

"I think it's pointless, Trust," he huffed. "We'll never find him in this dark."

"I think you're right," I almost cried.

So, feeling helpless, we waited for Jeff to get his breath back and then turned and started retracing our steps.

"Do you know where we are?" I asked him.

"I think so."

"Are we anywhere near the small cabin Grace used to hide out in?"

"We ain't too far."

Jeff turned slightly and then led me where I wanted to go. I figured it wouldn't hurt to check out the home to see if by some chance Grace was there. We hiked for a good while before coming to the hidden place where Grace used to retreat. We pushed open the door and walked inside. The place was pitch black, and Jeff's tiny light did little to illuminate the inside. There was a lamp on the table, which I lit. It turned the night to day. Jeff switched off his flashlight.

"Why'd we come here?" he asked.

"I was hoping that Grace might be around."

"She's not," he pointed out.

"I can see that."

"It's late," Jeff informed me. "The little woman will be wondering about me."

"Let me just think for a minute," I said, disheartened.

"Suit yourself," he said, walking out and leaving me alone.

The entire cabin reminded me of Grace. It was the place where she had hidden out for a good part of my mission. It didn't actually belong to her, but no one knew who it belonged to because it had been abandoned for so long. Grace had fixed it up and made personal touches to it that now made me miss her more than ever. I sat down on a small chair and willed myself to think.

Where could she be?

I leaned back in the chair, and one of the old back legs folded, sending me to the ground and up against the wall. My shoulder pushed one of the long wallboards in, making the bottom end flair out. I stood up. I kicked at it to force it back in, and it snapped backwards as if it were supposed to slide in a different direction. I got down on my hands and knees and tried to jimmy it into place. Instead of sliding in, it slid out, exposing an opening in the wall.

The opening looked empty except for an old rag. I pulled on the cloth and it slid out. It was wrapped around something.

It couldn't be.

I unwrapped it as fast as I could, my fingers unable to respond quick enough to the commands my brain was giving them. Once untucked, the rag fell off.

I gasped louder and longer than I had ever gasped before.

It was the missing Book of Mormon.

My first thought was, Who could have put it here? My second, Grace. I couldn't believe it. This book had been more sought after than anything in the entire town's history. I opened the cover and read the inscription that Parley P. Pratt had written so many years ago.

I looked over my shoulder to make sure Jeff wasn't witnessing what was going on and then wrapped it back up. I put it under my arm and walked out, acting as if I didn't have anything. Jeff didn't notice.

"What now?" he asked.

"I guess we go back to the meadow."

"I'm sure Grace will be all right," Jeff said. "I remember way back when her father dropped her on her head down by the Girth River. She was only a kid, and everyone thought she was going to die."

I looked at Jeff, wondering if he was going to go on.

"She didn't," he finished.

Half an hour later and with a good distance still to go, Jeff's flashlight went dead.

"I should have borrowed one of Frank's newer batteries," he said.

It was slow going, but we finally felt our way back to the meadow. When we got there, no one was around. I had no idea what to do about finding Grace.

I had even less of an idea about what to do with what was under my arm.

41

HOPE FLINGS ETERNAL

Jeff left me to go home to his family. I felt completely alone standing there in the meadow in the dark by myself. My stomach was treating the rest of my body like a germ it wanted to dispose of. I was so sick and worried about Grace. I prayed my twenty-three-hundredth, thirty-second prayer, begging that she would be all right. I looked at the empty meadow and realized that I was mad about the boardinghouse being gone. If it had still been here, it would have been filled with people waiting around to find out what had happened. With it gone, however, no one had anywhere to hang around. Folks had tried to make the Watson home the new watering hole, but it was on the edge of the meadow and too small. Besides, Sister Watson only allowed people with shoes to come into her house. That one rule eliminated a good portion of Thelma's Way.

I was just about to make my way back to the Heck

home when I thought I saw a shadow moving closer from across the way. I tried to get my eyes to focus, but it was dark and the night was misty. I held my arm tight against my body, securely holding the Book of Mormon. By the time I saw who it was, it was too late to run.

"Hi, Trust."

"Hope," I said, surprised to see her but in no mood to talk.

"What are you doing here?" she asked.

"Looking for Grace," I answered.

"Grace is gone," she said as if she actually knew.

"What?"

"She's gone, Trust. She wanted me to tell you that it could never work. She was going to just leave and not say anything, but I talked her into letting me tell you."

"So she's not been kidnapped?"

"I suppose she's in Virgil's Find or halfway to Knoxville by now."

"You're kidding, right?"

"I'm sorry, Trust. I wish it didn't have to be this way."

"I don't believe you."

Even in the dark night Hope looked hurt. So hurt that I began to feel bad about what I had just said.

"I just can't believe it."

"I know exactly how you must feel," Hope said, brushing my shoulder. "Remember Fernando?"

"Who?"

"Fernando, the boy I was engaged to."

"I thought you said his name was Rolio." I said.

"Oh, yes," she hemmed. "His name was Rolio, but we

called him Fernando because he loved the sport of bull fighting so much."

"He liked bull fighting?" I asked in confusion. "I thought he was into animal rights."

"He was." She sounded caught. "But, well, you must never tell anyone that I told you about the bulls," Hope pleaded. "It was his one weakness. If it got out, many important animal laws would be in jeopardy."

"Why?"

"I don't want to talk about me," Hope changed the subject. "Enough about my past love and all that . . ."

"Bull?" I offered.

"Trust, do you want to talk about something important or not?"

"I don't really want to talk at all," I said. "I've got to go find Grace."

"You're going after her?" she asked in confusion.

"Of course."

"But she told me to tell you it's over, Trust. Hopeless."

I hated the way my name sounded on her lips.

"I don't care if Grace left the country and got a restraining order," I said. "I would still go after her."

"You can't."

"Why not?"

"She's out of the picture."

"What?"

"You're free, Trust," Hope said, sounding desperate. "You and I can see each other now."

I realized for the first time that nature was finally helping me out. The dark was keeping my senses firmly in check. Hope had no spell on me when all I saw of her was a shallow outline.

"Hope," I said. "No offense, you're a great girl, but I could never settle for anything less than Grace."

There was an incredibly heavy silence.

"Less than Grace?" she sniffed. "Are you implying that I am less than that redheaded hillbilly?"

"Excuse me?" I said in amazement.

"I offer you me, and you take the table scraps."

"You don't understand . . ."

"No, I don't," she insisted, tapping my chest and causing me to step backwards. "How someone could possibly pass up me for anyone else is unbelievable. Don't you read, Trust? Don't you know how the story ends? I get what I want, and you get the girl, the most beautiful and sought-after creature in all the land."

"You're crazy."

It was unexpected in every way, but Hope produced a thick, hard book from behind her back and swung at my face. I didn't even have a chance to flinch. I saw new stars in the sky and felt the Book of Mormon tumble out from beneath my arm and onto the ground. Before I could pick myself up, I was hit again on the back. I rolled and pulled myself up.

"Hope . . ." I tried to reason.

"You were meant for me, Trust. Unfortunately, you're just too thickheaded to ever know it. Well, let's see if Grace likes you once you're all marked up."

She swung again, and I stopped her with my hands.

"Oh, so big and strong," she mocked. "I bet Grace

256

would love to see you now. I'll tell you what," she spat, "I'll tell her how valiant you were when I see her later tonight."

"I thought you said she was gone."

"Guess what, Trust," she laughed. "I lied."

I know what my mother and father had always told me. And yes, I had had lessons on etiquette and respecting women. But I disregarded everything I had ever been taught and lunged at Hope. I pulled her to the ground and tried to hold her down. She rolled out of my arms and jumped up.

"My contact," she screamed. "My contact popped out, you fool."

"I don't care about your contact. Where is Grace?"

She ignored my question. "You are most likely the biggest idiot I have ever had the displeasure of knowing. Someday you'll look back on this night and cry over what you passed up."

I stepped quickly towards her. She could see that I wasn't in a good mood.

"Happy pathetic existence," she hollered, turning and running towards the other end of the meadow. She probably would have kept right on going if it hadn't been for her bad eyesight and the dark night causing her to run right into Ed's catapult. I didn't know that it had been ready to fire. I suspected that was the case, however, when I heard it release. The popping of the spring was followed by a gigantic *wizz*. I then saw and heard a screaming Hope fly past the little bit of moon and out towards the forest. It was the most horrible and amazing sight I had ever seen. I prayed frantically that she would land someplace softer than her heart. Sick about all that was transpiring, I ran back and tried to find the Book of Mormon I had dropped on the ground. The dark night seemed to camouflage it well. I finally felt it. I picked it up and ran to the one place I thought it might be safe to hide it. I locked it inside, put back the key, and then ran as fast as I could to Sister Watson's house to get help.

Sister Watson didn't know what to do, so we jogged as fast as she could all the way to the Heck home. We figured President Heck would have some idea where we could begin to look for his daughter and what to do about Hope.

When we got to the house, Patty Heck was rubbing her husband's back as he sat on the dirt. On the ground next to him was Hope lying in Ed's lap and looking all but expired. Next to them was Winton, who, like Hope, was out cold. Mixed in amongst all of them were Toby and Leonard, one looking amazed, the other bewildered. President Heck's rolling chair was scattered around in about a hundred pieces.

"What happened?" I asked.

"We don't know," Leonard admitted. "Ricky was pretty shook up about Grace being taken. So Toby and I told him that it might help him relax if he scooted about a bit. Winton saw him doing it and begged for a chance. Well, no sooner did Winton start to roll than Hope comes sailing through the air, landing right on top of him. Let me tell you, Trust, it was a spectacular collision."

"Are they all right?" Sister Watson said, holding a hand to her mouth.

"We think so," Toby said, taking all medical questions. "We sent Trust's father to get help."

"So what happened to President Heck?" I asked, looking at him as his wife held him and realizing that he had not been included in the story so far.

"He's just shook up over losing the chair," Patty explained.

"I can't believe this," Sister Watson sighed.

"What about Grace?" Sister Heck asked. "Did you find her?"

"No, but I think she's all right," I responded. "Hope said she knows where she is. Can she talk?" I pointed to Hope.

"No," Ed replied as she lay in his lap. "She's way out."

I had never seen Ed look happier.

"We need to keep looking for Grace," I said. "I need to get a few people with a better sense of direction than I have to go out and help me look."

"Let me get my light," President Heck said.

"I'm in," Leonard chimed.

"Me too." Toby stood tall. "We'll find her."

He was right.

All right, he was wrong; she found us. Well, she and Daryll found us. Before President Heck even came back outside, both Daryll and Grace emerged from the forest. I thought at first that I was just seeing things, but if that were the case, I never knew a vision could feel so good. I held Grace until her father came out and wanted a turn of his own. He stopped when Patty Heck demanded to know what had happened.

"I was walking away from the reception yesterday when Hope stopped me," Grace began to explain. "She said she needed help identifying a tree. I was in no mood to help, but she seemed so desperate."

"What kind of tree was it?" Ed asked.

"There was no tree, Ed," Grace said kindly. "She led me over to Martin's Cavern and pushed me down Martin's Pit before I knew what was happening. She told me to change out of the wedding dress and into these clothes because she thought I had made a mockery of the whole institution. She was screaming and acting so crazy, I didn't know what else to do."

"Marriage is a sacred union," President Heck threw in.

"I guess she tossed the dress out in the weeds," Grace went on. "Luckily, on this occasion—disturbingly, on any other—Daryll had been following us." Grace looked up at Daryll and smiled. "He took the dress and brought it to you guys so you could help."

"We ran him off," Toby informed her.

"That's what he said," Grace nodded. "He was only trying to help. After you scared him away, he came back to the pit and pulled me out."

"You did good, Daryll," Sister Watson commended him.

Grace did a nice job of filling us in, but she verbally left out one very important point—a point that I feel needs mentioning. Grace was extremely happy to see me. I guess while she had been in the pit, Hope had told her all about how she had tricked me into being seen with her and how she was going to make me hers. I would have let Grace go on and on about how glad she was that it was over, but I silenced her by pulling her towards me and kissing her instead.

It's not really that great kissing your fiancée in front of her mother, so I broke it up. Toby and I carried Hope, and Leonard and Ricky carried Winton down to Sister Watson's house. A short while later my father showed up with help from Virgil's Find. Winton and Hope were whisked away.

I slept very well that night.

42

'FESSING UP

Cindy ("Hope" had even lied about her name) and Winton were going to be fine. I say *going to be* because they were both looking at a little recovery time. Cindy was worse off than Winton. She had a broken this and a fractured that, but her injuries were nothing from which she couldn't eventually fully recover. She was incredibly lucky even to be alive. If she had not landed on Winton, who knows what might have happened. Unfortunately, all the injuries and bumps had not changed her insides one stitch.

She was just as rotten as ever. I tried to have a brief conversation with her as soon as she came around, but she kept ripping on me for not being interested and passing her by.

I couldn't imagine ever pulling over.

Her family had flown up from Georgia and were staying with her at the hospital. I had never seen people that I felt more sorry for.

Winton was allowed to come home, but he was restricted

to bed. He had a broken arm and a bruised back, but he was going to be all right. Jerry had hoped that the accident might loosen his tongue up, but it didn't. In fact, if I didn't know any better I would have sworn that Winton was now jabbering with an Australian accent. Sister Watson invited him to use one of her spare rooms so he wouldn't have to stay in Jerry's place deep in the woods. Well, while Mavis was getting the room ready, Paul, who had helped carry Winton back, discovered that he could understand his jumbled speech. Paul claimed it was his gift of tongues that made it possible. We let him think that, happy that Winton had someone to communicate with.

President Heck instructed his wife to put together a funeral for Thelma's Way. He figured that folks needed a chance to mourn.

"If it were a person, we'd sit around and say nice things about her," he explained. "Well, I dare say that this town will be more missed than a good chunk of people would."

So as our Relief Society president, Sister Heck began making preparations for Thelma's Way's funeral service.

I had not had a chance to talk to Grace about the Book of Mormon or the fact that she had lied to me all this time. I had been tempted to tell my father that I had it, or President Heck, but I figured it would be best to talk with Grace about it first. I figured I would sit down with her Monday afternoon and get some answers. But my plans were altered due to the fact that Monday afternoon the entire town gathered in the meadow to hear Sister Watson deliver a discourse on the evils of lying. She was so upset and disheartened about all the damage that Hope's lies had caused that she felt she needed to speak out.

It was a powerful sermon. So powerful, in fact, that as soon as it was over, everyone began feeling as if they needed to confess something immediately. Well, President Heck was gone for the day trying to find a new chair. So, folks assumed that I would make the next best choice, seeing as how I had been the branch president before he was. I told them quite plainly that I was not the person to talk to, but all day long people kept coming up to me and getting things off their chests.

"Trust, you got a moment?" Ed said as I was standing on the ever-rising edge of the Girth River.

"What is it, Ed?"

"Well, remember when I told you that there was an emergency at the school that one night?"

"Yes."

"That was a lie."

"I appreciate your telling me that."

"Also, I threw a rock at Grace's window that night and told her to go down to the school. Hope made me do it."

"It's all right, Ed."

"Whew, that feels good," he smiled. "Oh, and Toby needs to speak at you."

Ed walked off looking carefree and happy, while Toby strode up looking heavy and concerned.

"I just need a moment of your time, if that's all right," Toby said.

"That's fine, but you realize that I'm not the person to talk to," I explained.

"Don't put yourself down," Toby said. "Do you remember when Paul cooked up that sausage stuff?"

"The manna?"

"Yeah, yeah." Toby looked crestfallen. "Well, I knew he was going to do that. In fact, I had been the one that brought out the lighter fluid and gave it to him."

"But you voted for the road."

"According to Paul, that trial was tainted. Besides, that weather thing just kept fascinating me."

"Well, what's done is done."

"That's not the worst part," Toby went on. "When I brought him the lighter fluid I squirted a whole bunch on the ground. Actually, I spelled out my name, thinking that it would kill the weeds in the form *Toby Carver*. That's the reason the fire ran over to the boardinghouse. It's my fault."

"Does Paul know?"

"Yep. He said that it was still his doing."

"Then let's leave it at that."

"You mean it?"

"Sure."

"Thanks, Trust," he said. "By the way, I think Teddy Yetch is behind that tree waiting to talk with you."

"Yes, Teddy," I hollered.

She shuffled up, her old bones making her stride short and labored.

"You know that I'm not the person to talk to," I pointed out.

"Don't be silly," she insisted. "Listen up. For the last thirty years I've been living a lie," she disclosed. "I hate cooking. I can't stand to pick up another whisk or spoon except maybe to eat with."

"But I thought you loved . . ."

"Loved?" she spat. "Loved to spend all day making things over a hot stove? Why do you think I always make such disgusting dishes? I kept hoping someone would tell me to knock it off."

"You made those things that way on purpose?"

She looked at me with her kind wrinkled eyes. "What, are you daft? Do you think I'd really want to create things like tainted meat loaf and soggy liver spread?"

"I thought you liked it."

"Have you ever seen me take a bite?"

"Well, no."

"I'm done, Trust. I'm old enough to let others do the cooking."

"Sounds fair to me."

"Really?"

"Sure."

Teddy let out a deep *whew*.

"Thanks."

As soon as Teddy walked off, I did the same, hoping to find a spot where not quite so many people would want to confess. Just past the chapel Leonard *psssted* at me.

"Over here," he waved.

I moved back behind the church. Leonard was wearing a pair of long johns with loose shorts over them. He had the makings of a small beard, and his hair looked unkempt. He was evolving. I asked him what he wanted.

"Mavis's speech on lying has really got me thinking."

"About what?"

"About being honest. Trust, I don't want to shatter your image of me," he said humbly, "but I think you should know that I'm really poor."

"I never thought you weren't."

"Don't try to be kind, Trust. Treating the symptoms and ignoring the problem will only prolong the pain."

"Really, I thought you were poor."

"Funny."

"You haven't had a job for almost a year," I pointed out.

"Maybe I'm a shrewd investor," he said defensively.

"You spent your early retirement on Star Wars memorabilia."

"Hey, that stuff's going to be worth a fortune in a couple hundred years."

"I'll make sure someone sprinkles the earnings on your grave."

"Would you, Trust?" Leonard said with hope.

"Leonard, what's the point of this confession?" I asked.

"It's just that all these business ventures of mine haven't really paid off."

"Coming thousands of miles across the country for free land you had never seen sort of gave that secret away."

"Darn't, Trust, would you let me come clean about something?" he said adamantly.

"All right. How do you feel about Mavis Watson?" I asked.

"Of all the nerve."

"Well . . ."

"She makes a mean shepherd's pie," he said sheepishly.

The confession was crystal clear.

"Do you feel better?" I asked.

"You know, I think I do," he admitted. "I got some things to think about."

Leonard disappeared. I came out from behind the church to find Grace looking for me.

"Just the person I was looking for." She smiled.

"Don't tell me you have something you want to get off your chest."

"I think I'm in love," she joked.

"That'll pass."

"How about you, then," Grace said slyly. "Is there anything you want to tell me?"

I decided that now was as good a time as any to let Grace know what I knew.

"Actually, there is."

"Really?"

I took her hand and led her over to the cemetery and up to the Watson Mausoleum. From where we were standing, we could see that the entire back half of the cemetery was in ruins due to the water that had saturated it and caused the caskets to pop up and float away.

I picked up the pet rock that was resting next to the mausoleum and retrieved the key that Sister Watson kept there in case anyone wanted to visit her late husband. No one ever did. The entire town had been quite open about how creepy it was to bury someone above ground. Lupert Carver had been dared to go in there once but chickened out at the last moment because he remembered that it was a concrete shelter filled with rotting Watson ancestors.

Even Sister Watson never went inside. She excused herself by saying that she would wait to look at her husband after she was dead. She did visit it once a week, but all she would do is crack open the door, stick just her arm in, and spray a couple of squirts of Lysol so that her deceased husband might have some nice-smelling air to breathe.

"We're going in there?" Grace asked.

"I figured it out," I played. "I know where the Book of Mormon is."

"What?"

I watched her eyes closely. She gave everything away without even knowing it.

"I figured it out," I said again.

"Trust, what are you talking about?"

"This has got to be the only place no one has looked," I explained. "It has to be in here."

"Who would have put it in there?" she asked.

"I don't know," I said. "Anyone could have. I mean, the key is there for us all. And everyone knows that no one ever goes in."

"Or comes out. It's not in there," Grace said.

"How do you know?"

"I just don't think it is."

I turned the key and pulled the heavy concrete door open. A smell like that of a long-neglected dirty clothes hamper and pine-scented Lysol billowed out.

"That's pleasant." Grace waved the air in front of her nose.

Daylight pushed in the doorway and lit the six large shelves, five with coffins on them.

"The empty one's for Mavis," I pointed out.

"Trust, this is ridiculous."

"Don't you see the logic in my idea?" I asked. "There is no other place that the book could be. Every home and inch of Thelma's Way has been scoured and searched. I can't imagine anyone throwing it in the Girth or burning it, since we all know it has value. And we know no one has sold it because every single person here is just as cash poor as always."

I stepped inside, acting as if I had not been there the night before. I looked around while Grace stuck her head in, trying to make out what I was doing. I did a weak job of pretending to search and then looked at the dark space between Bishop Watson's coffin and the wall where I had put the book the night before.

"What's this?" I said, reaching my hand back and grabbing at air.

It was gone.

"It's not here," I exclaimed.

"See, Trust, I told you. Let's get out of here."

"No, but it was here," I explained. "I found it up at your cabin while searching for you the other night."

"What?" she asked, startled.

"I found it at your place."

"You did?"

I nodded. "Why didn't you tell me you had it?"

Grace stepped inside and closed the door almost all the way shut, making it almost pitch black.

"Don't talk so loud," she *shhhed* me.

"Why'd you take it?" I asked.

"I didn't, really," she explained. "I walked down from the woods right as the big debate was turning into a food fight. I saw Toby get a hold of the book, and then Frank rammed him in the back. The book flew into the air and landed right at my feet. I looked around, and no one seemed to notice it had landed there. I picked it up and stuck it under my dress. I had it on me when you were talking to me right after."

"You're kidding."

I think she shook her head, but I couldn't tell because of the dark.

"I was going to give it back after everything settled down, but then I realized that it would just make everyone crazy. Or the town would sell it for money that they would simply squander in one way or another. So I hid it in the wall."

"Amazing."

"So where is it now?" Grace asked.

"I have no idea," I answered. "I stuck it back here right after Hope went for a ride on Ed's catapult. I didn't think anyone would find it."

"Well, it's got to be here some . . ."

The mausoleum door shut tight, and we could hear the key turn.

"Hey!" we screamed.

We thumped on the heavy door, but it was no use. There was no way anyone could hear us.

"What do we do?" Grace asked, sounding far less concerned than I felt.

"I have no idea."

"Can't we break the door down or something?"

"You felt that door," I said. "Even if all these bodies came to life and helped us push, we could never get through it."

"We're stuck?"

"Let's hope someone out there is smart enough to figure out where we are."

We were in trouble.

43

DECEIVE UNTO OTHERS

The Watson family mausoleum was not a pleasant place to be trapped. Let's just say that just because bodies are dead doesn't mean they're through making noise. Grace and I felt around the entire room looking for a spare key or something that might help us get out. There was nothing, just five coffins and one really unlucky couple. It was actually fairly clean, considering what it was. Eventually, we lay down on the empty shelf and tried to act positive.

"We could die," she said sadly.

"At least I'm in good company."

"You had better scoot over a couple of inches more just in case we live," she said, being far more virtuous than I was.

"You know, if we're going to die anyway . . ." I teased.

"So you think we're doomed?"

"No. Maybe the person who took the Book of Mormon will come and put it back," I said, trying to be optimistic. "Or Sister Watson will come for her weekly spraying. We just have to wait."

"I don't think it looks too good," Grace whispered.

"That's true," I replied. "If I'm going to die by your side, I'd at least like to be able to see you."

Grace shifted on the cold hard shelf and a couple of seconds later I felt her kiss me on the forehead.

"Thanks, Mom," I joked, referring to the area she had chosen to kiss.

"I was going for the lips, but it's just too dark."

"I'd be happy to let you try again."

"Why don't we wait until we're both a little more dizzy from starvation?"

"You temptress."

"I'm sorry about Hope," she said. "I should have believed you."

How perfect. It took the possibility of never seeing the light of day again to have Grace say she was sorry.

"We've been through a lot," was all I said.

"Would you ever have thought when you wandered into this place almost three years ago that it would end up this way?"

"Never."

"You know, I love the way you put up with my town," Grace said, brushing my neck. I think she had been aiming for my cheek.

"I'm all about giving," I joked.

She was quiet for a few moments. I listened to the

sound of her breath next to me and mourned the fact that we might never get a chance to live the life we had seen coming. The life where I was her husband and she was my wife. She shifted again, and I could feel her breath on my face. It was a welcome relief from the musty stillness.

"Trust, kiss me," she said in hushed tones.

"With everyone watching?"

Her aim was right on this time. Right before I thought my soul had left my body and started to mingle with those around us, she pulled away and wondered aloud about the time.

"It's got to be pretty late," I said, catching my breath. "Go to sleep, and I'll wake you right before I expire."

"That's not funny," she replied.

"Tell me about it."

I expired quicker than she did. It seemed to be only a few seconds before I had fallen asleep on the cold slab. I awoke to the sound of someone messing with the lock on the door. I nudged Grace's shoulder and whispered for her to be quiet. We still didn't know if we had been locked in here on purpose. The door opened, and faint moonlight slid inside and covered the floor. I could see our footprints in the dust and wondered if whoever was coming in would be as observant.

Someone entered.

Because we were tucked in on the bottom shelf, we remained in the dark. It wasn't really easy to see, but due to the silhouette of her wig, I could tell our visitor was Mavis Watson. Grace was about to crawl out and say something, but I quieted her by squeezing her shoulder.

Mavis came all the way in and stuck the crypt key in her pocket. She left the door open so that light could rest upon all those resting in peace. She rubbed her hand up against her late husband's coffin and let out a small laugh.

"It's been a long time," she said softly. "But I suppose you know how much I dislike crowded places with dead people. I made that perfectly clear on our honeymoon."

I could feel Grace hunch her shoulders.

"Well," Mavis said with strength, "I couldn't put off talking to you any longer. Seems I've got some things to air out. Remember how you used to say that I should find another if you passed away? It seems like I may have done that. You'd like him. He's not from around these parts, but he thinks like a Wayian. Leonard's his name. Leonard Vastly. It doesn't have the punch of Watson, but I like it."

I wasn't too terribly surprised by Sister Watson's confession. Most folks had noticed the way she straightened her wig and adjusted her gait when she was in Leonard's presence. It was her next disclosure that caused my jaw to drop.

"I'm sure you would want me to be happy," she continued. "I'll never forget you." She became teary. "But I suppose it's wise that I'm moving on. In a short while this place will be nothing but water. You always did enjoy a swim." She laughed again and then let out a long sigh. "I must say I'm having second thoughts about what I've done, though. I hope you'll forgive me. I know how much this place means to you. But I suppose if it was left up to everyone here, they would never make the decision. So, I made it for them. I guess this isn't news to you, seeing as how you're in heaven and looking down. Yes, yes, I knew they were going to dam it up and flood our town. Someday they'll realize that I've made it better for them. I wanted to get that road in before the water. Our land would have been worth a lot more," she whispered. "But at least I think my road idea got them a little prepared for the idea of progress. Now maybe it won't be so hard for them to consider moving on to another place. I've worked out a swell deal with the state. Everyone will get a nice amount, and yours truly will end up with that fancy red brick house near the drug store in Virgil's Find. I guess it's better this way," she sniffed. "I couldn't stand to see our town really change. Did you know that over half the women here now have their ears pierced? Makes me wonder where we're going. I do feel bad about leading folks on. It ain't no great secret that I love these people, but you already know that."

I couldn't stay silent any longer.

"You knew they were going to dam it up?" I said, standing up.

I had never heard Sister Watson really swear before. She also jumped at least two feet.

"Trust?"

"You lied to all of us."

Grace stood up by me.

"Just what are you two doing in here?" she demanded.

"We were locked in," I said with equal fervor. "What do you mean, you knew they were going to do this?"

"What have you done?" Grace asked.

"They were going to flood it anyway," she defended. "I just got us all a better deal."

"I think you need to explain yourself."

So Sister Watson leaned up against her husband's coffin and filled us in. It was my sixth and greatest confession of the day. Many months ago Randle from down at Triply Cove had come up and met with her. He had told her how the state was going to dam up the lower forty and how he and his people had already sold out for pitiful amounts. Sister Watson promised to pass on the news and contact the state herself. Instead, she had a dream in which she received inspiration to let the state go ahead with the dam. With things locked in motion, the state would have to pay the residents of Thelma's Way more than they had shelled out for those below the former falls. The reception that Leonard had blindly pulled together had been the perfect icing on the deception. The state couldn't believe that they had not been notified of so many people. In turn— and in embarrassment—they were now willing to give more substantial settlements.

"I've made things better," she defended her actions.

"You could have stopped this."

"I had no choice."

"That's not true," Grace said. "This town deserves to exist. Or at least to decide whether it deserves not to."

"What's done is done," Mavis said, sounding slightly remorseful. "I could see no other answer. Do you think I like this better than anyone else? The responsibility and the secret have been driving me mad. Besides, I could lose my new love."

"Leonard?" I asked.

She sighed.

"I don't know that he'll take to living in Virgil's Find. He might head out to some other part of the world. He's an adventurous soul."

"I can't believe you betrayed us all."

"You make it sound so dirty," she moaned.

"It is," Grace jumped in.

"So you didn't actually contact any lawyers, did you?" I asked.

"No."

"And you set the state up by not responding after Randle told you about all of this?"

"Maybe."

"So what was that speech you gave this afternoon about lying?" I laughed.

"It actually was yesterday afternoon. In an hour it will be morning. And," she added, "sometimes you have to make sacrifices for the greater good."

"When I tell Leonard what you've done, he won't give you the time of day."

"You wouldn't do anything so cruel," she said in disgust.

"You're washing away our whole town."

"You don't understand," she cried. "They were going to do it anyway. I just helped everyone get a better deal. I couldn't have stopped them."

"She's kind of got a point," Grace conceded.

"Well, it's not too late to do something," I threw out.

"We can't do anything without money." Sister Watson was crying. "And the Book of Mormon's gone. Not that it was worth anything."

"What do you mean? Were you the one that took it from in here?"

"So it was in here?" she said. "Leo said Roger found it somewhere. He was carrying it last night when he ran past him and CleeDee at the trailhead. Leo stopped him for a moment to find out what was going on and saw the book. But that doesn't matter anyhow," she sighed. "Roger said it really wasn't what everyone thought it was, and that it probably wasn't worth more than fifty dollars. I think he donated it to a thrift store there in Virgil's Find."

"Really?" I asked with anger.

"Funny that it's so worthless. All those people putting all that time into locating it. Your father included."

"Funny," I seethed. My father had sold this town almost as short as Mavis had.

"Do you know if my dad is still around?" I asked.

"I know he's not," she answered. "He left town—told Leonard he had some business to take care of."

I looked over at Grace. It was obvious from her eyes that she knew the truth as well as I did.

"What should we do?" she asked, putting her arm around me.

"I've got some calls to make," I said, stepping out of the crypt and running all the way to Virgil's Find.

44

GOOD-BYE

◇

I called a number of state agencies and lawyers, looking for someone who could put a stop to what was happening. Everyone I talked with gave me the same response.

"Sorry, but I don't see much you can do."

I went to every bank in Virgil's Find, hoping to find someone who would give me a large enough loan to entice some lawyer to take our case. No luck. Every bank saw me as way too big a risk. Around noon I called home. My mother insisted that she hadn't heard from my father in a while. She then questioned me about the marked-up wedding announcement she had just received in the mail.

"You're not married, are you?"

"No."

"Well, I find this in poor taste."

"Leonard sent the announcements out."

"Oh," she said with relief. "People would expect this from him. He has the most interesting sense of humor."

"Mom, do you have any money I could borrow?" I asked.

"Are you in trouble?"

"No, but Thelma's Way is."

"Son, you know how tight things are."

"They are?"

"I'm not sure. Your father handles all the money."

I was tired of talking.

"Mom, if Dad calls or shows up, will you tell him I need to speak with him?"

"Of course."

"Don't forget," I begged. "Last time it took you days to give him my message."

"Trust, watch how you speak to your mother," she chided. "But that reminds me. Sister Cravitz told me a while back that you might want to watch out for her niece. She said she was heading your way. Cindy is her name. Apparently, she's not the nicest person. I know we shouldn't judge, but remember when I gave Sister Barns the benefit of the doubt. I knew her hair was colored."

"Mom."

"Yes, Son?"

"If you had told me about Cindy earlier I could have avoided a lot of misery."

"I can't always be there to dry your tears and wipe your nose."

We hung up, and I hiked back. The clouds moved in and began to push one another around. Rain looked inevitable. When I got to the meadow, the Knapworths were packed and preparing to hike out of town for good.

"You can't go," I pleaded as rain began to fall.

"Trust, honey, the town is disappearing," Sister Knapworth said in comforting tones. "Our place is half flooded already."

"Aren't you at least staying for the funeral?" I asked.

"I just hate good-byes," she said. "See you."

They walked off hand in hand while I glumly made my way over to the chapel. The funeral for Thelma's Way would be starting soon. People were filing into the building and taking their places. It was obvious that no one here owned any suitable-for-funeral umbrellas. I saw pink and purple ones, a few with cartoon characters, and one with a dog face and ears sewn onto it. Most everyone was wearing black. Digby had covered his whole body with plumber's tape. Nippy Ward was sporting a trash bag with arm holes, and Ed was wearing his mother's black bathrobe.

I had never noticed Ed's dandruff problem before.

Sister Heck and some of the other Relief Society sisters had decorated the place with old bed sheets, draping them over everything except the benches. There was a closed casket lying on a table near the front. I assumed it was there simply for effect. It looked oddly familiar, however. Teddy Yetch had put together a couple of big floral arrangements in two of her larger pots. Unfortunately, Thelma's Way didn't have much to offer in the way of flowers right now, so the vases were crammed with weeds and long twigs. Right inside the front door was an easel with a large piece of poster board propped up on it. The poster board was covered with pictures of Thelma's Way that the local children had drawn. Most of them had colored a rough sketch of the meadow with a knife stabbed into it. Greg Bickerstaff had shown some originality by making his meadow get hanged. No matter how they drew it, Thelma's Way was dying.

I slipped in and took a seat near the back of the chapel next to Grace and Leonard. Sister Heck had been so busy putting this thing together that she had asked Narlette to play the piano so that she could fuss up until the last minute. Narlette wasn't bad, but the only song she knew was "Music Box Dancer." It sort of made the whole funeral feel way too peppy.

President Heck stood up and welcomed everyone.

"We are gathered here to not only mourn the loss but to celebrate the life of Thelma's Way. This is a time of great sadness and great joy. For we are blessed to know that our town isn't really gone."

"I love Mormon funerals," Janet Bickerstaff whispered to Teddy. "They're always so uplifting."

"First off, we will hear a few words from Roswell," President Heck announced.

Roswell stood and walked to the front. He rubbed his old hands across the empty coffin and wept. After a few minutes of him crying, President Heck walked up and whispered something in his ear. Roswell turned and faced us all.

"You don't understand," he snapped. "Most of you haven't been here as long as I have. That's what makes you ignorant. I'm not crying because I'm some sissy boy who lost his frog down a culvert. I'm crying cause I'll probably end up in some fancy house in Virgil's Find. A house with curtains and finished ceilings. I don't want that. I made do this long—why should I be forced to see what I've been missing all my life? It will only make me mad that I didn't move out sooner. So, you see, my memory of Thelma's Way will be ruined. Amen."

He sat down.

"Thank you, Roswell." President Heck wiped at his eyes. "We will now be honored to see a special slide presentation by Paul."

Paul wheeled out a serving cart from the kitchen with a slide projector on it. He then unwound a long cord and handed it to Toby, who passed it down his pew so that the far person could plug it in. Once it was plugged in, Ed hit the lights and Paul pressed *play* on a small tape recorder. Poorly recorded flute music filled the room as Paul flashed pictures up on the wall. There was one of the meadow during what looked to be a Christmas celebration. Another showed Ed riding his old motorcycle with long ropes tied on the end of it. The third picture was of President Heck eating a big piece of watermelon. I actually found myself becoming emotional.

"Are you crying?" Grace whispered.

"No," I sniffed.

It was obvious that Paul had no more than three actual slides, because he just kept showing those three over and over until the song mercifully stopped. The lights were flicked on, the cord retracted, and the cart wheeled away, all without incident. Unless, of course, you consider the twelve people who were sitting in the row where the cord was ripped back getting wire welts an "incident."

"Thank you, Paul," President Heck said. "Now comes the tough part. How do you eulogize a town like Thelma's Way?"

I was curious how a person eulogizes any town.

"I hope my future son-in-law doesn't mind me using him as an example," President Heck said.

I nodded, signaling that I didn't.

"When Trust first came here, he was miserable. I remember his face when old Feeble had one of his visions. He pointed right at poor Trust and promised him things would change." President Heck picked up a Kleenex and blew. He then looked around for someplace to put the used tissue. Seeing no good place, he stuck it into his front pocket. "Well, things changed for Feeble soon after that. He died. It took a bit longer for Trust to fulfill his part of the prophecy, but he did. The boy that's marrying my daughter is a far cry today from the kid that entered this valley a few years ago. And you know what switched him around?"

Lupert raised his hand.

"Yes, Lupert?"

"My dad said that it's okay to fish on Sunday if you're hungry."

President Heck smiled at him as if he had answered perfectly. "Thelma's Way changed him," he answered himself. He took another tissue and blew. "I know that we will all survive. Heck, we might even discover there are things about someplace else that we like better than here. But we will never know what could have been if this place had been allowed to live."

Everyone nodded. President Heck blew—his pockets were getting fuller. Rain beat against the roof as we all thought about what might have been if only our town hadn't been taken at such a young age.

"I remember what Feeble used to say about this place," President Heck continued. "He said that God led Thelma here so that we all might enjoy the blessings of her bad decision. Well, I've enjoyed my share and then some." He blew. "I don't know what I'll do without the meadow or the Girth River. Can't imagine Christmas without seeing snow up on Lush Point or us all getting together in the boardinghouse to pick apart Teddy's food. Even this old church building will be sorely missed." He honked twice. "But as sad as all that is," he sniffed, "it would be even sadder if any of us ever forgot what we once had here. Will you remember?" he shouted.

"I will," Toby stood.

"Me too," Teddy hollered.

One by one, everyone stood up and made it known that whatever happened, no matter where they were, or how many other things they forgot, they would always remember Thelma's Way.

"She was like a town to me," Roswell wailed.

"I never got a chance to say I'm sorry," Pete stood and said soberly. I tried to imagine what he thought he had to be sorry for.

After everyone had their say, President Heck closed his remarks. It was just in the nick of time—tissues were beginning to spill out of his pockets. He then had Toby say a closing prayer. It was obvious that Toby was operating on "autoprayer."

"And please bless that our town will get better."

After the benediction, Sister Heck opened the coffin, and we all shuffled by it and looked inside. I don't know what I was expecting to see, but what I saw was simply a couple handfuls of Thelma's Way dirt. We then left the chapel and sat out in the hall eating small pieces of really thick cheesecake and looking out the door at the rain.

"It was a beautiful service," Mavis said.

"That was my coffin," Roswell bragged. "Paul spotted it when he was washed down river. He dragged it back for me. I figured the least I could do was give it to Thelma's Way."

"Mighty charitable," Leonard commended him.

"I'll miss this place," Frank admitted.

"I can't imagine living anywhere else," Teddy said with tears in her eyes.

"Me neither," Briant moaned.

"Let's try to look on the bright side," Sister Watson said, looking at me.

I had decided not to tell folks her secret unless it was absolutely necessary. I knew that somewhere in her bald head she felt she had simply exercised tough love.

Even though we were inside, Pete pulled out one of his guns and pointed it into the air to try to make things feel better.

It misfired.

Halfway through my second piece of cheesecake I noticed that the small cabin where I had once lived, and the Knapworths had just left, seemed to be moving. I could see it out the front door, and it was definitely sliding away.

"Do you guys see that?" I pointed.

Everyone looked out.

"Yeah," Pete lamented. "Just what we need, more rain."

"Not the rain." I stood. "The house—it's drifting away."

We all pushed outside just as the land beneath the small cabin crumbled and fell into the Girth River— cracking and screeching as it broke apart. The entire cabin slowly sank beneath the water like some ghost that was having a difficult time making an exit. In a few minutes it was almost completely gone. The top of its pitched roof was all we could see as it was pulled downstream. I looked around. We were all standing there openmouthed and painfully aware that what we had just seen was only the beginning.

"This is all my fault," Ed said, wiping rain from his face. "I attract bad luck like fly paper. I'm cursed."

"Don't say that, Ed," Paul insisted. "If any of this is any-one's fault, it's mine. If I hadn't of burned down the board-inghouse, we'd have a place to rally."

"It's my fault," Toby cried. "I prayed for a wet summer."

"It's my fault," I spoke up, wet and angry. I squeezed Grace's hand and went on. "My father lied to you all. That Book of Mormon was worth enough to maybe get us out of this."

"Roger wouldn't do that," Ricky Heck insisted.

"He did," I said, sickened. "Now he's taken it and left us anything but high and dry."

"I suppose he needed it more than us," President Heck said sincerely.

"I sure hope it helps him," Toby threw in.

I couldn't believe this town. Everything that every decent person in the world professed to desire was played out here daily. These people had found the answer. They had created a haven where the world had a hard time reaching. They were like the city of Zion, only less educated. They had the one-mind thing down, but it was the one heart that was a giant understatement. Sure, they weren't lifted up, but they were humble and cared for each other more than people in any other place I had ever known. My father had done the entire town wrong, and people were ready to wish him the best.

"Besides," Roswell said, water dripping off his nose, "that book probably wouldn't have been worth enough to save us."

"Roswell's right," a voice from behind us said.

Everyone turned around in shock—partly because someone was claiming that Roswell was right and partly because that someone was my father. I couldn't believe that my dad had come back. I think I was happy about it.

"Roger," Ricky hailed.

My dad walked in to the middle of the group. He glanced around, getting a good look at all of us. The rain continued to fall, but we all just ignored it, focusing instead on what my father was going to say. "I thought I could sell the Book of Mormon and make enough to help us out. I told Leo it wasn't worth much because I didn't want to get his hopes up. That wasn't true. It's worth quite a bit. But even if we got its highest price by auctioning it off, it wouldn't be fast enough or bring in enough to completely fix this mess."

Everyone was quiet while the rain had its say.

"I guess it's really over, then," Toby said.

"Actually, it's not," my father said, smiling. "It seems I have a good friend from college who now works for the Tennessee government—a good friend that owed me a favor. He's already getting together the papers to stop the water. I also just hired the best lawyers Knoxville has to offer to start fighting for us."

The way he said *us* almost made me cry.

"You mean we might be all right?" Ricky asked.

"I mean Thelma's Way isn't going to get any wetter than it is now."

That wasn't completely true, seeing as how it was still raining, but people threw up hats and canes, and a few even pulled off their shoes and tossed them into the air in celebration. The cheer was one of complete happiness. Sure, there was a little complaining as the objects tossed up began to come down on us, but Thelma's Way was going to survive.

My father hugged Ricky Heck and Toby Carver. He then worked his way over to me. Everyone went silent.

"Trust."

"Dad."

"I'm sorry that I ever lived in such a way that you could think I was capable of taking that Book of Mormon," he apologized. "After Cindy collided with Jerry's uncle, I ran down here on the way to get help in Virgil's Find. When I got to the meadow, I saw you searching for something. I was going to holler out, but you found what you were looking for, and I could tell it was the Book of Mormon. I saw you put it in the crypt. I waited until you ran off, and then I retrieved it, thinking that I might be able to put it to some good. Will you forgive me?"

"Of course." I hugged him.

Pete let out a sort of goofy *ahhhh*.

"Where did you find it, anyway?" my father asked.

"I had it," Grace answered. She was wet but far from watered down. "It was hidden up in my cabin."

The soggy crowd whispered.

"I didn't want it to change us," she added.

"I can understand that." My father smiled at her.

"Where is it now?" I asked.

My father motioned as if he were going to pull it out of the bag he was carrying. Before he could do so, however, Ricky Heck stepped up to him and pushed his hand away.

"I'm sure you left it someplace safe in Virgil's Find," he winked, hoping my father would catch on. "I mean, you wouldn't have brought it back here to confuse everyone."

"Of course not," my dad played along.

"Enough about that anyway," Ricky insisted. "This is a time for celebration."

"Amen," Sister Watson said with genuine emotion.

Always looking for a reason to kiss Grace long and hard, I took her in my arms and kissed her like a man who knew he would be getting married soon. She kissed me back like a woman who wanted to give me a taste of things to come. August eleventh seemed mighty far away.

"I wish we had the boardinghouse to celebrate in," Pete voiced for all of us.

"We could go to our place," Patty Heck said with excitement. "Ricky's got his path done, and I don't mind wet feet."

It was an invitation nobody could refuse.

Thelma's Way was breathing again.

45

TO WEATHER FOREVER

The sky tilted to let the falling stars run parallel with the landscape. I stepped further out onto the porch and breathed in deeply. I stood there alone, knowing that the only other soul around was inside and married to me.

How lucky could one man be?

We were staying at a small bed and breakfast in the deep woods outside Virgil's Find. I had stepped out onto our private balcony to get some night air and contemplate everything that had brought me to this point in my life.

When my father said he had hired good lawyers, he had not been telling tales. The water never rose any higher. In fact, it receded just a bit. In the end we had lost a big chunk of riverbank and half the cemetery, but everything else was intact. The state kept the lower part dammed up, leaving a huge lake at the end of our river. Hallow Falls would never be seen again. The state named the new lake

Lake Lawrence, but the locals affectionately called it Mistake Lake. Our lawyers also made Tennessee pay to build a bridge across the Girth for us, so that people could safely cross it. They were constructing a nice solid bridge that would make the other side of the river more accessible than it had ever been. An additional plus to the bridge was that in order to assemble it, they had to bring huge trucks and machines down the trail and into our town. The process had taken out a few trees and widened parts of the path, but our simple trail remained largely intact. Seeing them get through, however, convinced Leonard that it was entirely possible to pull his mobile home into the meadow. So he bribed a couple of the bridge builders with some of his multilevel overstock, and they pulled his place into the valley. The trip gave Leonard's home a number of scrapes and scars; plus, it took out the home's back left corner. But the damage simply made it look more like it belonged here. With Roswell's permission and Leonard's promise to give Roswell a room, Leonard placed it right where the boardinghouse had once been. It took about two seconds for everyone to accept it as the new center of town. It looked like Leonard was here to stay—a fact that made Mavis Watson extremely happy. The two were officially courting. I had always thought Leonard was slightly goofy in life. Well, he was even more so in love. Goofy, that is.

We found that it had been Ed who had accidentally locked Grace and me in the Watson vault. He had been walking through the cemetery on his way to get his axe back from Todd Nodd when he saw the cracked door and thought he would do Sister Watson a favor by locking it up for her. I suppose if we had died, I would have been very bothered by his favor. But since we lived, I let it go. Ed had been retrieving the axe so he could disassemble the catapult. He figured it was just too dangerous to have lying around. It was one of the most logical conclusions I had ever seen him make. His schooling was obviously paying off.

Digby had learned all he could from Wad. So he set up a competing barber shack just a couple feet over from Wad's. To show there were no hard feelings, however, Miss Flitrey graciously had half her hair done by Digby and the other half by Wad. She looked like a completely different person, depending on which side of her you were looking at.

Pete opened up a gun shop in the same tree house I had once stayed in. It was a great idea, actually. It seemed that gun lovers didn't mind climbing up into forts to do business. He signaled the opening of his place every day by firing off a few rounds. And he notified everyone of its closing by playing Taps on his trombone at five each afternoon.

The Knapworths never came back. President Heck had called the mission home and told them that our town was not going to be flooded, but the mission president still didn't return them. He said they needed to be someplace less intimate and beautiful.

Daryll Bean had become a permanent member of our society. He moved in with Frank Porter and all his boys. He was a little slow, which made him seem like family already. Sybil Porter had even begun to show an interest in him. I caught her cursing behind the new boardinghouse about how she shouldn't have these feelings for her brother. I then explained to Sybil that just because Daryll was living with them didn't make him an actual brother.

It was the first time Sybil had ever smiled at me.

Our town received a nice surprise a short while back when Paul Leeper came strolling in from Virgil's Find holding Cindy's hand. Cindy had been forced to stay in the hospital a long time due to some weird reading they kept getting from her head x-rays. Well, while Cindy was recovering, Winton told Paul all the stories he knew about her when she had lived near him in Georgia. Paul was intrigued. It isn't often that a person discovers a woman with equal embellishing powers. So, every day Paul would pass by her room on his way to the mall or some other place in Virgil's Find. After the twentieth time of passing by, he worked up the nerve to walk in and compliment her on how well she could fabricate. Cindy returned the compliment, having heard stories of Paul's powers of deception as well. The two of them told stories about themselves until both were hopelessly in love. Sure, Paul was a little older than Cindy, but she felt their relationship mirrored that of the one in *Aged Heat*, the novel she was currently reading.

Jerry Scotch was writing a traffic cop who had pulled him over while he was driving Winton back to Georgia. Jerry had borrowed a car from one of his co-workers at the Corndog Tent. Well, he had no license and no insurance and had been caught driving backwards on the median. The female cop gave him a break, letting him go if he promised never to drive through her state again. Well, to

Jerry that was like whispering sweet nothings in his ear. He had written her every day for the last three weeks. When I asked him if he had ever gotten a response, he told me that mail took longer to get here than it did to go there. He then asked me what a restraining order was.

Since Teddy's confession about hating to cook had not been confidential, I took it upon myself to tell everyone how she really felt. The town rallied by sending around a sign-up sheet to feed her for the entire next year. By the time I actually saw the calendar, it was completely filled except for two days in February and the third Saturday in May.

President Heck found a new chair to use on his path. He spent many afternoons holding the hose and rolling around the house to water the potted plants or feed his chickens. He said it was the perfect place to think about all the things God needed him to contemplate. I'm certain that one of the things he thought a lot about was the fact that he had received word that the Church would make our branch a ward again soon. It was obvious that he would be going from president to bishop any day now.

CleeDee had her baby just a few days ago. It was a huge girl with more hair than half the grown men in Thelma's Way. They named her GunnySue after CleeDee's great-grandmother. If it had been a boy, it would have been Toebert, the name of CleeDee's grandfather. I actually thought Gunny was kind of a cute nickname, but when I called her just that CleeDee quickly corrected me.

"GunnySue. We don't call you 'Tru.'"

I had actually forgotten that the newly married Doran

and Lucy had even come to Thelma's Way until a couple weeks after the fake reception when they came down from the hills and reminded us of it. No one had seen anything of them during that whole time.

They had then headed back to Southdale to continue with their jobs, schooling, and future projects.

Grace and I would soon be doing the same, but for the moment we were enjoying just being happily married. To say that our wedding went off with no hitch, though, would be like listing your favorite Christmas songs and not including "Carol of the Bells." There were the usual problems, but on top of those, there was Leonard trying to make sales outside the temple and my mother crying through the entire ceremony. I was touched, until she confessed that the only reason she was bawling was that another woman there was wearing a dress just like hers.

"I'm joking, Trust," she had smiled. "I'm just so happy for you."

Grace had looked marvelous, of course. I would have sworn that there had been angels in attendance while the ceremony was taking place. But any angels would have been crazy to think that they could muster up anything more than a weak glow in the presence of someone like Grace.

We had held a reception in Southdale and another in Thelma's Way. The one in Southdale went off smoothly, which is more than I can say for the one we had in Thelma's Way. If you think my mother cried at our reception in Southdale, you should have seen her at our reception in Thelma's Way. I wondered if the surroundings had anything to do with it. I'd go into depth about our reception there, but it pretty much ran exactly like the fake one we had put on previously. The only major differences were that Grace was happy to stand by my side and that at the reception's end nobody stood up and told us we would all be covered in water in a short while. I guess there was one other major difference. This time we had really been married.

Thelma's Way had done its job. It had brought two people together who might never have met any other way. I couldn't wait to produce future generations so that I could tell them all about it.

I looked out over the mountains. I could see a shadow growing in the far distance, making a patch of dark sky darker. It was most likely coming from Mistake Lake. You see, the lake had an unusual effect on Thelma's Way. Every night at around ten, great clouds of mist would rise up off it and settle over our town. The mist made the ground greener and gardens thicker. It kept clothes on wash lines wet and windows spotted. But more than anything, it seemed to cover up Thelma's Way each night, holding us down until we could wake and live again. It was like a pleasant veil, hiding the great secret that Thelma's Way really was.

Sure, our town wasn't on many maps. It wasn't about to be voted an All-American city or chosen to be the number-one place to live and raise children. No one vacations in Thelma's Way. In fact, I can safely say that in the history of time I bet there has never been a single travel agent who has ever uttered the words, "Might I suggest a six-day stay in Thelma's Way, Tennessee?"

People didn't know what they were missing.

But Thelma's Way was one of the few dreams that God was allowing me to remember. It had filled me up, out, and in. It had been the connecting point to Grace and the outlet for countless wonders. The leash my Heavenly Father had given me was longer than anything I would ever have trusted myself with. He had let me wander over his creations, scraping my knees and skinning my hands on the textures and surfaces of his miracles. I could never repay him for the experience.

I was reminded of that one scripture somewhere that said that one thing. I couldn't really remember a single exact word of it, but I was confident it expressed precisely how I felt.

I thought about the sought-after and fought-after first edition Book of Mormon. No one speculated or asked about it any longer. At first Paul had talked about how it could still finance a weather shelter, and Mavis tried suggesting a road again. But in truth, no one really wanted those kinds of changes anymore. We liked Thelma's Way just how it was—endearingly flawed. I think most folks assumed that my father had simply sold the Book of Mormon to defer some of the lawyer bills. He hadn't. My dad had given it to President Heck and told him to put it someplace where it wouldn't cause any trouble and couldn't get lost. It was an important part of Thelma's Way history that needed to be put away until people forgot about it. President Heck never told me exactly where he had ended up hiding it. I did notice, however, the last time I was in his house his couch no longer wobbled.

I heard the balcony door open behind me. I turned and there was Grace. I looked at her and smiled. Love was a funny thing. At eight, it was a new bike and a chocolate milk shake. At twelve, it was a video arcade and a pocket full of quarters. At sixteen, it was a label for something I was certain I was lacking. At twenty, it was a blonde named Lucy who wore a lot of sweaters and shiny black shoes. Now, at twenty-four, I finally understood. Love was deeper, better, and larger than even Thelma's Way could contain. Love was a woman with red hair and green eyes. Grace.

"Had enough?" she asked.

"Never," I answered honestly.